DINE WITH ME

A Table for Two Novel

____

LAYLA REYNE

Dine With Me

Cover Design: We Got You Covered

Cover Photography: Wander Aguiar Photography

Editing: Edits by Kristi, Angela James

Second Edition

March 2025

E-Book ISBN: 978-1-962010-15-3

Paperback ISBN: 978-1-962010-33-7

Content Warning: This book deals with topics some readers may find difficult, including descriptions and evaluation of treatment (and non-treatment) of a life-threatening illness.

About this Book

The best dish you never expected…

Ingredients:
One surly, tattooed chef on the brink of losing it all,
including his sense of taste.
One sexy, bespectacled doctor who jumps at the chance to
dine with his foodie idol.
A cross-country culinary adventure, from picnics to dive
bars to fine dining and home-cooked meals.

Directions:
Combine ingredients in one plane, in one hotel room, in
each other's company for ten days over Christmas and
New Year's.
Add shared struggles, simmering attraction, inconvenient
feelings, and a splash of angst.
Do not remove from oven until fully baked or else there
will be no saving it.

Let stand for a lifetime of love and dining together.

Enjoy this emotional age-gap M/M romance novel with plenty of snacks and a box of tissues.

To every chef, kitchen, and staff that has opened your doors to me, shared your time and talent, poured your heart onto the plate, and made me feel at home in yours.

Prologue

DINE WITH ME
THE CULINARY EXPERIENCE OF A LIFETIME

Tour the country and experience the best meals in America with a Michelin-starred chef as your guide. Two weeks, eight incredible meals, coast-to-coast destinations. A once in a lifetime opportunity for food and travel enthusiasts. Singles or couples welcome. Please respond via the reply email for additional details.

Chapter One

CALIFORNIA

Miller Sykes expected his luck to run out.

Climbing as fast and as high as he had in the culinary world, it was bound to happen. Icarus and all that shit. He'd known the bottom would fall out. He'd only hoped it would be fifteen or twenty years from now. A single quick hit that would send him gliding toward the water on the golden parachute he'd cobble together by then.

Hope was for fools.

And he sure as shit didn't have his parachute ready. Much less any gold.

Six months of one hit after another, the last coming two weeks ago on his fortieth birthday, and he'd been a fiery meteor hitting the water at warp speed, sinking below its murky surface like a dead weight.

Dead weight.

Heh.

"Chef?"

The Aussie accent startled Miller back to the room, to

the worried gaze of his sous-chef, and to the rest of his staff giving him similar confused looks. Only Sloan, his best friend and soon-to-be ex-wife, wore a different expression —the are-you-about-to-lose-it one she'd given him a lot lately.

Not today. He'd sulk in a corner, nurse a Negroni, and lament his mile-long what-might-have-been list later. Today he'd hold it together for one last staff meal, for one last service.

He cleared his throat, ignored the stab of pain there, and stepped to the end of the weathered farm table. It was the one piece of furniture he liked here. Not shiny and lacquered like the tables and stations in the main dining room, just well-used and well-loved. A place for friends and family to gather around and share a good meal. At odds with the main dining room's upscale decor, it had been relegated to the private dining room, which was rarely reserved and mostly used for staff meals like the one today.

"Last service," he started, and the activity around the table quieted. "I want to thank you all for your profession-alism, good humor, and hard work. It's been my absolute pleasure to work with each of you these past few years. You made coming to work a joy." When so much of the rest had become joyless—dealing with investors, critics, and the hotel they were situated in. His staff had been a singular bright spot. "If I could serve you all staff meal every day, I would."

"Hear, hear!" went up from the servers and cooks at the table.

"Unfortunately, us hanging out and eating comfort food"—like the pulled pork he'd smoked himself and brought in, with all the fixings—"doesn't keep the lights on." Customers did, and while there'd been an initial rush of interest, the crowds had long since waned. Too many choices here in Napa Valley, too much similarity in the fine dining scene, too many proverbial cooks in the kitchen. Dollars—and heartbeats—were just too short to keep operating. "You all know best how tough this business is. We're journeymen. I'm sad to see *this* journey end, but I hope you'll remember it as a good stop on yours."

"The best!" one of the line cooks said, and the sentiment was echoed around the table.

Miller savored the small victory. He'd managed to shield his staff from the worst of the restaurant's troubles, but not enough to prevent its eventual closure. He inhaled deep, pushed down the rising regrets, and wrapped it up. "I know most of you have your next positions already sorted, but if you need anything, please reach out. You have my number, you have Sloan's." He nodded toward where she stood by the corner bar. "We're happy to help any way we can."

"Do you know where you'll be, Chef?" a server asked.

His eyes flickered to Sloan, who'd averted her gaze, staring out the window. She'd given him that non-look a lot lately too. "Keeping my options open," he told the server. "You'll all be the first to know. Now eat, before the food gets cold."

Everyone dug in, stuffing their faces and chattering among themselves. Miller loaded up a plate and carried it to where Sloan was mixing a drink behind the bar. All her favorites on the plate, she shoved a Negroni into his hand and fell on the food like she hadn't eaten in weeks.

Miller laughed. "So, it's a good day, then?" he asked, voice lowered.

"Relatively." She popped a honey-buttered hushpuppy into her mouth. "For at least the next few hours."

"How long's the morning sickness supposed to last?"

"A while still. I'm only two months along." She paused long enough to gather her ginger curls into a bun, then attacked the barbecue sandwich. "And whoever said it was just in the morning lied. More like twenty out of twenty-four hours."

He jostled her shoulder. "Four non-puking hours."

"Shut it," she groused around a bite. "I'm fairly certain none of this will be nearly as tasty revisited. Let me enjoy it for now."

She reached for his Negroni and Miller slapped her hand away, ignoring her exaggerated pout. "Ty will never forgive me." Behind the bar, he placed a hand on her still-flat belly and gave it a rub. "That's my future godkid in there."

Covering his hand, she held it there gently while conversely sharpening her voice. "So, you've decided on a future now? Does that mean—"

He withdrew his hand and turned away from her assessing gaze. "Please don't go all lawyer on me. It's unfair."

Nails digging into his chin, she forced his face back around. "What's unfair is you letting yourself die."

He wrenched out of her hold and circled around to the other side of the bar. "You just said how good all this food tastes." He swept his hand over their plate, then gestured at the table. "I can't imagine a life where I can't taste any of it, which is a very real possibility if I get treatment. I'm not willing to risk it. What the fuck would I do with myself? The kitchen is all I've ever known. Who would I even be?"

"You'd be my best friend," she said, voice further quieted by the edge of sadness. "And the cannoli's godfather."

He ignored the tear in his chest, the guilt that settled in the hollow there, and chuckled at the reference to his future godchild's Italian conception. "So, what, I'm supposed to spend every day babysitting the herd of ginger terrors you and Ty produce?"

She shrugged with a grin. "Could be worse."

"You're just terrified of the day care bills."

"You know me so well." She patted his cheek distractedly, then her lips turned up in a smile, her eyes over his shoulder. "Incoming."

Miller turned to find his sous-chef approaching, hand out.

"Chef," Sarah said. "It really has been an honor learning from you."

"All mine, Sarah," Miller said, shaking her hand. "You're going to make an incredible head chef, wherever you land." She'd been the best sous he'd ever worked with. Coming to the kitchen after a previous non-culinary career, she'd found her passion in food. Laid-back and happy, and with a stellar work ethic, she was a superstar waiting to break out.

"Because of what you taught me," she said. "When you have your empire of restaurants and need someone to run one, call me. I'll be on the next plane."

Miller laughed through the heaviness in his chest and lied through his teeth. "Count on it."

She was back to her seat before Sloan called him on his bullshit. "You won't keep that promise."

"That's not what she needs to hear." Miller picked out a forkful of pork from the sandwich and forced it down. It had been two weeks since he'd gotten over the stomach bug that had driven him to the hospital, where he'd learned the pain in his throat wasn't just from retching. "It's a safety net. She knows she has it, even though she won't need it."

"You're a good teacher."

"Doesn't help me much, does it?"

"I don't know, it might," she said with a smirk.

That look of hers always worried him, would worry anyone who knew the trouble Sloan Thatcher could so easily get up to. "What have you got up your sleeve?"

"I think I've found you the perfect companion for the tour."

Miller's middling appetite vanished, as it did every time she proposed another companion. "A baby chef?" he asked, reflecting on his teacher comment and her response.

"No, but an eager, intelligent, young foodie, according to his parents."

"His parents? He's a fucking kid?"

"It's a gift, of sorts. And he's not a kid." She wiped her

hands off on a napkin and came around the bar to stand next to him. "He'll have plenty of questions. You can answer them."

Miller rolled his eyes and got a smack to his ass for the sass.

"Shut it," Sloan said. "You love talking about this shit."

He did, no sense denying that, but the "foodies" who'd answered their ad so far fell into one of two categories: golden-age retirees or thirtysomething women, wed and unwed, looking to bed or bag a famous chef. The ad they'd posted didn't state his name or gender, only that a Michelin-starred chef offered a guided culinary tour, but assumptions had been made, which were not unfounded given the industry's piss-poor job at recruiting and retaining women chefs. Add to that the trade magazines and local newspapers making more of a deal of his restaurant closing than warranted and connecting the dots wasn't hard. Which was why Sloan had been screening the candidates.

He'd prefer to make the trip alone—and he would make this trip, come hell or high water—but reality was, funds were tight and he wanted a nest egg to leave his family. He could use someone else's deep pockets, and people were willing to pay big bucks for this sort of epicurean adventure. So be it. But retirees with long lists of dietary restrictions or apron-chasers were not who he wanted to spend two weeks with, enjoying—or not—his favorite meals one last time.

"What makes you think this prospect is different?" he asked.

"You're not making this easy on me," she deflected.

"Maybe *someone* should do a better job screening candidates."

She snagged the last hushpuppy, munched through it, and swallowed. "Between junior partner grunt work, planning a double wedding, and barfing my guts out, you're lucky I'm helping at all."

Fuck. She had him dead to rights there. The last thing he wanted to do right now was fuss with travel details, which he'd never been particularly good at to begin with. Sloan was doing him a huge favor, considering. Before he could apologize for his shitty attitude, however, she carried on.

"Just meet him," she said. "Give him a chance."

Him, at least. A meet was the least he could do for Sloan and all the work she'd put into this. Maybe *he* was the one. "Fine. When and where?"

Her smile was victorious. "Goose & Gander. Tomorrow night."

"Surprise!"

The boom of noise rocked Clancy back a step, right into the medical office doors, his elbow banging the metal handle. He cursed and clutched his throbbing ulnar while struggling to take in the scene before him.

Clapping, shouts, party horns. Maracas? He'd thought the waiting room behind the frosted glass looked more packed than usual, but he'd had no idea the crowd was for him. Not just a crowd, a party. Blue and gold streamers were draped from the ceiling, a gold foil CONGRATS banner was strung across the front of the reception desk, glasses of champagne were lined up on top of the counter, and a giant WELCOME TO THE PRACTICE banner was tacked on the far wall above the door that led to the patient rooms and doctors' offices. And standing in front of the cheering crowd were Clancy's parents. His dad and stepdad beamed while his mom, standing between them, half smiled, half smirked. Miranda was no doubt behind this surprise shindig.

"Boo-boo, darling?" she said teasingly. "Did it rob you of words? That'd be a first."

He dropped his arm and shook it out at his side. "What is this?"

"Please tell me we did not put you through all that schooling for nothing. I think it's rather obvious."

"Go easy, dear," his stepdad, Robert, said. "I think we managed to surprise him good this time."

Clancy couldn't help but laugh at his mother's answering victory dance. He got it, appreciated it, but... "I meant *why*?"

"Have you met your mother?" His dad stepped forward and drew Clancy into a hug.

"This was your idea, Alan," Miranda said behind them.

Clancy drew back, eyeing his dad with a raised brow. His mom had always been the party planner of the two, leveraging decades of it at home into a successful personal concierge business. "Your idea?"

"You didn't think we'd let this day pass without celebrating, did you? Finishing your residency and joining the practice are major milestones."

"Dad." This wasn't like when he'd finished medical school or passed the last of his boards. He'd effectively been working the past five years. Now he was just going to be doing it in a private office instead of at the hospital. He ignored the twinge of sadness that thought caused and accepted the glass of champagne his mother held out to him.

"Don't 'Dad' Alan," she said. "And don't 'Mom' me. You worked your tail off to get here. You deserve a toast, and a party," she added with a wink.

"To Clancy." Glasses clinked all over the waiting room, everyone getting in on the merriment. He spent the next half hour making the party rounds, exchanging hugs and handshakes with the nurses, staff, and other doctors in his dad's practice, each warmly congratulating and welcoming him to the group. Of his parents, his dad circled back to him first. "Got something to show you," Alan said. "Think we can sneak away?"

They looked over their shoulders to where Miranda was holding court, telling some story that had the circle of people around her cackling. "I think she's distracted," Clancy said. "Let's do it."

He followed his dad through the door to the larger area of the leased space—exam rooms, a surgical suite, a consultation lounge, and the doctors' private offices. They stopped in front of an office a few down from Alan's at the end of the hall.

On the door, a brass nameplate read, Dr. Clancy

Rhodes, MD—Plastic Surgeon. His dad threw an arm around his shoulders, hugging him tight. "I can't wait to work with you, son. It's a dream come true."

Clancy nodded, at a loss for words, eyes fixated on the shiny nameplate. Where his life was headed—and where it wasn't—suddenly became very real. That twinge of earlier sadness returned, tangling with excitement, appreciation, and a healthy dose of fear. He didn't want to disappoint his father; he looked forward to working with him too. Who wouldn't want to work with their best friend? Even if the work wasn't exactly what he wanted to do, Clancy was good at it. He could make a difference in patients' lives here too. "Mine too," he managed.

"I have an idea for your first project."

Clancy blinked away the doubt clouds. "Patients already?"

"Oh, we're overflowing with those, always. Having you on board will be a huge relief, but this is something else."

Clancy followed him into the—*his*—office. The furniture matched the slick decor of the practice space—befitting its Hollywood location and clientele—and the view out the floor-to-ceiling windows was stunning. Yet, it felt cold and sterile, more so even than the hospital. His dad's office had never felt that way, decorated as it was with pictures, plaques, and paintings. Clancy was considering a yellow accent wall when a folder appeared under his nose.

"I think this will align with your interests," his dad said.

Clancy took the folder and flipped it open. The tightness in his chest eased a little at seeing the logos of two prominent cancer foundations atop the sheets inside.

"They're doing a benefit here in LA in the early spring and requested someone from the plastic surgery community be on the steering committee. I thought it dovetailed nicely with your oncology interest and with the reconstructive work you talked about for your practice here."

"It's perfect." He closed the folder and pulled his dad into a hug. "I'd love to do this, thank you."

"Something else we know you'll love."

Clancy startled at his mother's voice behind them. Of course she'd found them. And if he'd thought she'd been wearing a mischievous smirk earlier, it was nothing compared to the evil-genius grin she wore now.

Robert handed him an envelope. "A present, from all of us."

"Before you start here in the new year," his dad said, "we wanted you to have a real vacation."

Vacation? Clancy didn't recognize the word. He hadn't had one of those in twelve years. He withdrew a sheet of paper from inside the envelope and unfolded it. It was an online ad from *Eater*, a food blog he regularly visited, though he hadn't seen this ad yet. He would have remembered it. A chef-guided tour of America's best meals. His heart fluttered, his stomach rumbled. "What is this?"

"Did you forget how to read, darling?" Miranda said.

"I read it." He glanced up at his smiling parents. "It sounds awesome."

"Which is why when I saw it," his dad said, "I called your mom."

"And I contacted the organizer," Miranda finished.

The flutter and rumble turned into a galloping stampede of excitement, bubbling all through Clancy's body. "Wait, so I'm going on this?" He shook the sheet of paper. Was he bouncing on his toes? "For real?"

"For real," Robert said, smiling.

"Who's the chef?"

"Our lips are sealed."

Except Miranda's. Clancy doubted she knew the meaning of the expression. "You'll meet him tomorrow. In Napa."

"Him? Napa?"

"Miranda!" Robert and Alan groaned together.

She waved them off. "I'm doing all the travel arrangements. Make a good impression so my efforts don't go to waste."

Clancy glanced again at the ad. *Eight incredible meals, coast-to-coast destinations.* "Can I guess the restaurants?"

The collective "No!" didn't stop him.

Last service yesterday had gone better than expected. Ditching the restaurant's normal upscale menu in favor of dishes selected by the staff, the pressure to be perfect, to serve "Michelin-level" fare, had been removed. Miller couldn't think of a better way to go out.

Go out.

Laughing at his ironic choice of words, Miller drew Sloan's sharp glower from where she sat at the bar. The twinkling lights overhead burst like tiny explosions in her wide blue eyes.

He waved her off and went back to sipping his Negroni, waiting for the beef chicharrones on the plate in front of him to stop crackling. He wasn't in a hurry, and he was actually hungry for a change. This was his third Negroni, his second order of fried beef skins, and his ninth —tenth—plate of bar bites. Chicharrones, corn croquettes, roasted bone marrow, duck fat fries, the list went on. Goose & Gander had one of the best bar menus in town, fitting as it was one of the best gastropubs in Napa Valley. Casual dining/pub on the ground level, proper tavern with stone walls, an oversized fireplace, and a huge wooden bar in the basement.

And an annual stop on wine country's holiday pub crawl, thus the multicolor lights strung overhead and the numerous patrons wearing Santa hats and puffy white beards. G & G drew a steady crowd, even on weeknights, even outside the holidays. With clean-out underway at his old restaurant, Miller could waste hours sitting at a pub table in someone else's, drinking and eating in the shadows while waiting for their tour prospect to arrive.

Ugh.

Sloan cut her eyes to him again, and Miller realized he'd made that sound out loud too. Oops.

He tilted his glass at her, grinning, and she turned back to the bartender with a huff. He returned his attention to the food in front of him, taking small bites and savoring his food—the crispy beef skin crackling and melting on his tongue, the texture light and crunchy, the pop of flavor salty and rich. He only looked up again when Sloan's manicured nails snatched the last chicharron off his plate.

"You need to perk up before our guest arrives." She popped the beef skin in her mouth and climbed onto the stool beside him. "The first reservation is in a week. You're out of time to dick around."

"Maybe this whole thing—"

"Is not a bad idea," she said, reading his mind. She snagged a chicken wing off the plate a server slid in front of them. "We've discussed this, ad nauseum. If you want some savings left to leave to your niblings, then you need a financial backer." Her eyes skirted over his shoulder and widened with interest. "And you're out of time for this argument. He's here."

Miller rotated his head and lost his breath.

Stunning.

There was no other word to describe the young man shoving his way through the group of cellar rats in Santa hats at the far end of the bar. Well, except maybe also *tired.* His black-rimmed glasses were drifting down his nose, his mop of brown hair was tousled, and his broad shoulders, snug in a corduroy blazer, were slightly slumped. But the weariness in his tall, trim frame didn't detract from the overall package.

Stunning.

"Gorgeous, isn't he?" Sloan whispered beside him. "If I didn't have Tyler waiting at home."

"Is he even old enough to drive?" Miller tore his gaze from the bespectacled stranger and tossed back the rest of his drink.

"Thirty."

Only Sloan's hand over his mouth at the last possible second saved her white silk blouse from a shower of gin, vermouth, and Campari. Once he swallowed, Miller gasped out a "Bullshit" behind her hand.

"I didn't believe it either." She lowered her hand and wiped it off on a napkin. "So I had one of the firm's PIs check. Thirty, swear it."

Glancing over his shoulder again, Miller tried to find thirty years in the younger man and managed twenty-two, twenty-three at best. As the man's eyes roved toward their corner, Miller turned back to Sloan. "Better go do your job, dear." His voice dripped with saccharine sarcasm.

As did her reply. "Hold down the dark corner, honey." She polished off another wing, tossed the bone on the plate, smacked his cheek with a sticky kiss, and moved to climb off her stool.

Before her second heel hit the floor, a slender hand appeared across their table and Miller looked up to find the stranger standing there.

"Ms. Thatcher, it's a pleasure to meet you," he said.

Sloan shook his hand. "Clancy Rhodes, I presume?"

"That's me. I'm sorry I'm late. I had a last-minute meeting with some benefit organizers and got held up." He cut off his ramble and shifted his big green eyes and outstretched hand to Miller. "Chef, it's an honor."

"You know Miller?" Sloan asked.

Miller checked his grip, afraid he'd crush Clancy's long, slim fingers in his bear claw, but the other man's handshake was confident and firm. His eyes lingered on

Miller's tattooed forearm, bared beneath his rolled-up dress sleeves, before he withdrew his hand and cleared his throat. His gaze darted back up and he adjusted his glasses.

"Miller Sykes," he said. "Self-taught wonder-kid of the cooking world. James Beard Rising Star Chef. Staged at the top restaurants in New York, then relocated to the Bay Area. You earned two Michelin stars for the restaurant where you were chef de cuisine before leaving to open your own place three years ago." He interrupted his Wiki-page recitation—with all the correct pronunciations, Miller noted—to take a deep breath and return his attention to Sloan. "When my parents showed me the ad, then said I was meeting the chef in Napa, I did the calculations. Chefs, stars, and the timing. I'd wheedled it down to a handful. Miller was on the list."

Possibly also a stalker. Or an apron-chaser. Neither good.

And yet Sloan seemed more intrigued than ever. "Your mom said you're a huge foodie."

"Isn't anyone who wants to go on a trip like this?" An eager, guileless smile stretched across his pale, lightly freckled face.

Miller discounted his stalker theory—this kid was pure fanboy—but there was something in his innocence, in his youth, that called to more than Miller's ego.

"The destinations haven't been disclosed yet," Sloan said. "If you're a foodie, you may have already visited some."

"If they're not in LA, I probably haven't been there.

Aside from visiting family in Chicago, this'll be my first real vacation in twelve years."

"What's kept you so busy?" Miller finally spoke up.

Clancy's gaze snapped to his, pronounced brow furrowing behind his glasses. Miller got that reaction a lot. Despite ten years in New York, followed by ten in the Bay Area, he hadn't lost his North Carolina accent, probably owing to weekly calls with his parents and sisters who still lived there.

Once he shook off the surprise, Clancy held up a hand and started counting off on his fingers. "Three years of undergrad, four years of med school, five years of residency."

A doctor, of course. Miller was sure that had absolutely *nothing* to do with Sloan's hard sell yesterday. Miller was about to object—this was worse than the retirees or the apron-chasers, even if the kid was cute and a foodie—but Sloan cut him off, asking Clancy, "What's your specialty?"

"Plastic surgery." His smile dimmed for the slightest second before he forced it back in place. "But I hope to continue some of the work from my residency in reconstruction for oncology patients."

Fucking hell, Sloan.

Her head whipped to the side as Clancy's eyes grew wide, and Miller realized he'd said that bit out loud too. He was too angry to care. His wife's motivation with this one was clear as day—someone to take care of him—and she'd tried to hook him with a pretty face.

"Enough." He moved to slide off his stool, and Sloan raised an arm, blocking his exit.

She held up a single finger, silently beckoning him to wait, then asked Clancy, "You'll have time for this trip now?"

Clancy glanced between them, equal parts confused and amused. After a moment, he shrugged, giving up on understanding their dynamic as so many had over the decades. "Aside from some calls for this charity thing I'll have to take, all during the day, of course, I'm free until I join my father's practice in the new year. My parents gave me this trip as a gift, a sort of last hurrah. The timing's perfect for me, and my mom's offered a company jet."

"Company jet?" Miller couldn't help asking.

Clancy pushed his blazer aside and pulled his wallet out of his back pocket. He extricated a black business card from his billfold and pushed it across the table. On one side, ESSLEY TRAVEL ASSOCIATES was engraved in plain silver script and on the other, Miranda Essley, Owner, with a phone number beneath the name. Chicago, if Miller remembered his area codes correctly, which made sense given Clancy's earlier comment.

"Mom runs her own concierge service," Clancy explained. "Flies rich people around the world and makes all their reservations. Wherever they want to go, whatever they want to do. She'll book the hotels too."

"And do you have any dietary restrictions?" Sloan asked.

"Not a one. I eat it all."

Miller side-eyed his wife. Grinning like the cat who'd eaten the canary, she was no doubt smug at having delivered him a pretty face, an open culinary mind, and a blank check. She'd made this one hard to refuse. He turned back to Clancy, and their gazes caught, sparked, and fired. Maybe also interested? Miller had to blink several times to shake himself loose. "Clancy, could you give us a minute?"

"Oh, yeah, of course." He grabbed his wallet from where he'd set it on the edge of the table. "How about I get us another round?"

"Negroni." Sloan held up two digits.

Miller batted them down. "She'll have water. I'll have another Negroni."

Clancy laughed, amusement outweighing confusion. "Coming right up."

Sloan waited until he was at the bar before twisting on her stool and lowering her voice. "You're a goddamn fool if you turn this one down. He can pay the fee, and the travel will be covered."

"He didn't say that. He said they'd arrange for it."

"Miranda told me it's covered. Fully paid. It's no cost to you."

"Nothing is no cost to me at this point."

Her bulldog posture crumbled. "That's not what I meant."

"I know it's not." He propped his elbows on the table and scrubbed his hands over his face, his calloused fingertips catching on his beard. When he opened his eyes again, it was to the sight of Clancy at the bar, his head in one hand, nodding off as he waited for their drinks.

Stunning and so young. "He's just a kid, Sloan."

"I've already told you he's not, despite appearances."

"He's a doctor too. He'll figure out what's really going on."

"At least there'll be someone with you who knows what to do if, God forbid, you take a turn for the worse."

Miller dropped his arms on the table and glared. "I knew that's what this was about."

"And what if it is?" she snapped, voice hardening, going lawyer again. "You want to make this trip, and I want you to make it, but I can't send you out there alone. I love you too much."

"What if he tells someone?"

"If you don't get treatment, you're going to be dead in six months. Everyone's going to know anyway."

He turned his face away, as if struck. Hearing himself say it was one thing, hearing his best friend say it was another. And hearing that thread of anger in her voice. Would she ever forgive him for his decision? Could he die with that on his conscience? Could he live with the other potential consequences? It seemed a kinder cruelty to ask her for the next six months than to ask for God-only-knew how many years as he underwent treatment. Treatment that had less than a fifty percent chance of working, and if it did, had a more than a fifty percent chance of stripping him of the person he was, the person she loved.

She twined her fingers around his biceps and leaned into him. "Shit, baby, I'm sorry."

"No, you're not the one who needs to apologize. And you're right, as always." At least about the immediate situation. "Twenty-plus years, I should know better than to argue with you."

"So don't." She nuzzled his shoulder. "Your options are the apron-chasers, the old-timers, or the super cute doctor standing at the bar. This is the point at trial where I move for summary judgment and wrap this puppy up."

Laughing, he kissed the top of her head. "I love you too, by the way."

She propped her chin on his shoulder, grinning. "Who doesn't?"

Clancy was smiling too, albeit sleepily, when he rejoined them. "Negroni, water, coffee," he said, passing out their drinks. "So, did I pass the test?"

Miller stared into his glass, contemplating a very short cons list versus a growing pros one. The past six months had been the darkest in Miller's life; the next—last—six promised more of the same. But for two weeks he had the chance to travel well and relive some of his favorite meals in the company of a beautiful, bright young man who seemed every bit the antithesis of darkness. This was a no-brainer.

Lifting his eyes, he met the doctor's eager green ones and smiled. "Can you be ready for the first meal next Saturday?"

"I can be ready tomorrow," Clancy said, fully awake now. "Where are we going?"

"Saturday, a week from today," Miller said. "As for the locations, those will remain a secret to be revealed as we travel. You good with that?"

"I can't promise not to make guesses."

"I can promise not to tell you," Miller replied with a laugh.

"Can't fault me for trying." Clancy raised his mug, almost spilling the contents as he bounced on his toes, his excitement brimming over. "Saturday, then."

Miller clinked his glass against Clancy's. "Saturday."

The seat belt light dinged off and Clancy's first instinct was to stand and retrieve his case tablet from his luggage. It'd been practically attached to his hand the past five years, on the go access to all his patient files; he felt naked without it, despite his multiple layers of clothing. But then reality and memory caught up to instinct. Sans glasses, Clancy could barely see the forward luggage hold, and even if he managed to get there without tripping over his own two feet, his tablet wouldn't be in his bag. He was no longer a resident, no longer had his patients.

Laughter echoed from across the plane's aisle. "The appendage will grow back, darling. I'm surprised your father didn't give you a shiny new one before you left."

He swiped his glasses off the polished wood table, slipped them on, and eyed his mother. Judgmentally. In her hand was the latest and greatest mobile device. The shiniest of them all. "You're one to talk."

She winked and blew him a kiss before returning her attention to the phone, typing as she talked. "Just making sure the other jet is ready to go when we land in Napa. I have an early meeting in Chicago, and the plane I'm flying in on leaves again at noon to take clients to London."

Clancy unwound his scarf and removed his coat,

tossing both in his seat. He stepped across the aisle and sank into the chair opposite his mother. "You didn't have to come all this way to ferry me ninety minutes north."

Email sent with a *whoosh*, she dropped the device into the chair's side pocket, kicked off her heels, and stood. She crossed to the minibar fridge and pulled out a bottle of Dom, along with two chilled flutes. "This might be the last chance I get to see you before Christmas." She handed him the glasses, then used the jagged hem of her cashmere sweater to pop the cork. Once she'd filled the flutes, she set the bottle aside and took a glass from him. "Happy holidays, my beautiful, smart boy."

"Thanks, Mom." He tapped the crystal rim against hers. "And happy holidays to you too."

Her green eyes, the same as his, sparkled with joy and the same pride that had shone in them at the party last week. Clancy's chest warmed with more than just champagne bubbles. He'd worked so hard to please his parents, wanting to live up to the kid-sized UCLA Med scrubs his dad had dressed him in for his third-grade picture. Two decades later, he was finally there. He even had a picture of his office door nameplate saved on his phone and emails from the charity organizers in his inbox.

His smile waned and barely a second passed before red toenails nudged his knee. "What's that about?" his too perceptive mother asked.

"What's what about?" He ducked his chin and guzzled more Dom, snorting when the bubbles fizzled up his nose.

She wouldn't be deterred. "That frown you tried and failed to hide."

He toed off his own shoes and folded his legs under him, sliding all the way back in the cushy leather seat. The demands of an accelerated undergrad program, med school, and then his plastic surgery residency and volunteer oncology rotations had left him little time to take advantage of this particular parental perk. Despite having multiple planes at his mother's disposal, he'd only flown on them a handful of times. More often, Miranda and Robert had flown to him.

"Just bummed I'll miss Christmas with you," he said. Also true, if not what had caused his mood to dip.

She saw right through him. "You did not inherit your father's talent for bullshitting."

"That was one of the things my oncology attending in med school commended." He tried not to sound too wistful. "I didn't bullshit our patients."

She tilted her head, long brown strands falling out of her chignon. "How's that going to work out for you in plastic surgery?"

He sipped his champagne, drowning the doubts he didn't dare speak, and stared out the window, watching the plane's wing light blink in the inky darkness.

Five blinks later. "Darling, are you sure—"

He swung his face back to her, smile plastered on. "What are you and Robert going to do without me this Christmas?"

Her concern faded, eyes growing bright again. "He's planning a surprise." She blushed, pale skin turning lobster red, same as his was prone to do. Miranda was ever the blushing bride when it came to her commodities-trader second husband, who she'd met ferrying to Paris five years ago. The both of them frequently on the go for work, they cherished their time together when they could steal it.

"I'm really happy for you, Mom."

She reached out and laid a hand on his knee. "And Robert, Alan, and I are happy for you too." She squeezed his knee, then scooted back in her chair. "We're also happy you're taking this trip. You deserve it."

"I'm glad your efforts didn't go to waste." Clancy grabbed the champagne bottle and topped off their glasses. "Speaking of surprises, you want to tell me where I'm headed on this tour?" It kicked off in Napa Valley, where he'd met Miller and Sloan last week, but that's all they'd disclosed so far. To him. They'd had to give the entire itinerary to his mother, however, so she could record flight plans and book hotels.

She shook a finger at him. "Nuh-uh-uh. I've been sworn to secrecy."

"By Miller?"

"Sloan, actually. She's my kind of woman."

Clancy didn't doubt it, even just from his brief interaction with Miller's wife at Goose & Gander. And from what he knew of their history from the press and gossip blogs. She was an ambitious, talented attorney and the vibe between her and Miller reminded Clancy of his parents, Miranda and Alan—still close, even after their divorce. "You two would get along."

"And you and Miller?"

He guzzled more champagne. How many glasses were too many? Thank God all he had to do tonight when he arrived in Napa was fall into a town car, then stumble into his hotel room. Those emails would wait until morning.

"Tell me about him," his mother pressed.

"He's one of the best chefs in the country."

"Yes, Clancy, I looked that much up myself. Your dad raved about him too." She sipped her drink, eyes taking on a devious gleam. "Saw his picture too. He's handsome, in that giant burly man sort of way." Totally Clancy's type, as far as guys went. And she knew it, having witnessed his bumbling high school crushes and failed college dating attempts, mostly with jocks, too many of them closeted. He'd given up on relationships during med school and residency, quickie hookups all he had time for.

"Stop your meddlesome matchmaking, Charlotte," he said with a wide grin. Samantha last week, Charlotte this week. He was waiting for Carrie to appear. Ever since they'd marathon-watched *Sex in the City* one holiday, he'd call her by the other character names whenever she started acting outside her too-fitting Miranda mold. "I'm on this tour for the food and the experience. And he's married."

"Yet his wife asked me about flights and hotels for a honeymoon."

Clancy didn't have time to rein in his surprise, the words tumbling out as he tilted forward in his seat. "What now?"

"She didn't swear me to secrecy on that part."

"Maybe they're taking a second one?"

"I didn't get the impression Miller was the other part of that 'they.'"

Clancy slumped back in his seat and stared out the

window again, mind connecting the dots. Maybe the vibe he'd picked up between Miller and Sloan was even more like his parents' than he thought. Best friends who had fallen out of love, but who still cared deeply for each other? Amid his confusion, Clancy felt a twinge of sympathy for Miller. He obviously loved Sloan; Clancy had witnessed that with his own eyes at the tavern. Even if Miller wasn't in love with her, Clancy had to imagine losing her would hurt. That sort of loneliness weighing on Miller, on top of his restaurant closing, as reported in all the food blogs, couldn't be easy. It had been a rough year for Miller Sykes. He probably needed this trip as much as Clancy.

"What's going on in that head of yours, Clancy Rhodes?"

He rolled his eyes. "This might be the strangest conversation we've ever had."

"I can't wait for the one two weeks from now." She winked at him and poured the rest of the champagne into his glass. "Drink up, darling. I have a feeling you're gonna need it."

Clancy couldn't shake the feeling she was right. He sensed it too. Something in his life was about to change, big-time.

Chapter Two

YOUNTVILLE

Miller stood by the side of his hotel bed, phone to his ear. "We'll be there in two weeks. You'll be back by then?"

"Yes, for the umpteenth time." His mother sighed dramatically. "Are you losing your memory in your old age?" Her Southern drawl made the question sound sweet and genuinely concerned, not like the joking dig Miller knew it was.

"Ma, forty is not old!"

"You keep telling yourself that." She chuckled. "And this cruise was a retirement gift from you and your sisters, or did you forget that too?"

No, he hadn't forgotten. It was one of the reasons he hadn't yet told his parents about his diagnosis or how he intended to deal with it. His parents had worked their asses off raising him and his three sisters. They deserved to enjoy at least one holiday free of work and worry. The other reason he hadn't told them was because he needed to do it in person, and he'd planned the last stop on this tour accordingly. He and Clancy would share their last meal together in Miller's hometown, then the next day, after Clancy left, Miller would have the hardest conversation of his life, with his family.

His melancholy silence went on too long, prompting Michelle to ask, "Are you okay, sweetie?" Her mother's intuition had pinged—accurately—from three thousand miles away. "With Sloan moving on and the restaurant closing, I know things have been tough lately."

"You don't have to worry about me, Ma." Ever again. She'd worried and sacrificed more than enough already. "Enjoy your cruise, and just promise me a pecan pie when I get home."

"It's a deal. Love you, sweetie."

"Love you too."

He pocketed the phone and reached for the bottle of pain pills on the bedside table. The knot in his throat, real and emotional, didn't make getting the meds down any easier, even with a giant slug of water. He twisted the lid back on and set the bottle on the table, hoping the meds would be enough to get him through tonight's meal. He glanced at the bedside clock. Five minutes until he had to walk next door to get Clancy, five more to walk across the street to the restaurant, fifteen until their reservation. He'd never cut a departure this close before, hyper-aware of what late and missed seatings did to a kitchen, but staying this close, they had more than enough time to reach their destination. He'd told Miranda and Sloan he didn't need a hotel room—his place was just down the road in Napa— but the two women had insisted he stay in Yountville too.

Miranda had told him in no uncertain terms that a town car would pick him up that afternoon. Then Sloan had tacked on, "The trip should start there, for both of you. Check in, get some rest, and enjoy your dinner," in that half pleading, half order voice still so much like it had sounded when she was sixteen, asking him to marry her so they could leave town after he graduated. She'd had a bright red handprint on her cheek and purple finger bruises on her arms and wrists, but in that moment then, she'd been more concerned with reining in his seething, protective instincts, hungry for vengeance on her behalf, than on her own trauma.

Shaking off the unsettling memory, and the last of the melancholy from his call with his mom, Miller looked instead to the night ahead. In retrospect, staying at the hotel worked out better. Entering the restaurant with Clancy would forestall any questions from the staff, many of them friends and colleagues, about his own restaurant closing or about why his charcoal plaid suit fit a little loose. That awkwardness avoided and hoping that none cropped up between him and Clancy either, he looked forward to tonight. There was something special about introducing a true foodie to one of the best restaurants in the world.

Knock, knock, knock.

Miller glanced again at the clock. Five minutes gone while he'd been stuck in his head. Five minutes lost. The quick rap against the door came again.

"Just a minute." Miller tweaked his whiskey barrel cuff links and patted down his pockets. Phone, wallet, keys. Panic crashed through him; keys were missing from the ring. Emptiness followed; he'd met with the attorney yesterday to turn over the restaurant keys and sign the divorce papers.

Two endings, one more to go.

But not tonight.

With a sharp shake of his head, he buttoned his jacket, picked up his overcoat, and headed for the door, slapping off the gas fireplace on the way. He opened the door and failed to restrain his smile.

Whereas Miller had gone with a more casual, admittedly flashy suit—to distract from the weight loss, and to avoid a tie, because evil—Clancy wore a three-piece number that was dark and sharp, befitting a Hollywood plastic surgeon, as was the slim-fitting cashmere trench he wore over it. It hung well on his tall, lean frame, fitted to a T over his broad shoulders, tapered waist, and long limbs. He looked closer to his thirty years dressed up like this, but the elegant suit and coat couldn't contain the exuberant kid inside. From the black bow tie decorated with champagne bottles, to the bright green eyes behind black-rimmed glasses, to the big grin that split his clean-shaven face in two.

"I know you said you were coming by my room, but I couldn't sit still any longer. I mean, honestly, I haven't sat still since check-in when you told me where we were going tonight."

No shit. Clancy was bouncing on his toes again, the shiny patent leather of his Oxfords squeaking.

Miller was amused but also cautious. He didn't know Clancy, didn't know how he'd react at the restaurant, among people who were Miller's friends and colleagues. And while maybe he considered Clancy's exuberance charming, Miller could also see it being regarded as over-the-top. Granted, The French Laundry staff knew how to read a room and table better than any place, but to some extent, this was still Miller's reputation involved. Clancy was his guest, and with Miller's name taking a hit already from the restaurant closing, caution was warranted.

Miller beckoned Clancy to enter and closed the door behind him. "Couple of ground rules," he said. "And I mean no disrespect in putting them out there. This would go for anyone."

Clancy shrugged one shoulder, smile unfaltering. "None taken, Chef."

"One, don't call me Chef." It hadn't been the first rule Miller had in mind, but as soon as the word was out of Clancy's mouth, the rule was out of Miller's. Clancy had called him "Chef" at G & G last week. Miller should have put a stop to it then, but he'd been too tongue-tied by the unexpectedly attractive prospect standing beside his table.

Clancy was similarly tongue-tied now, though more from confusion, judging by the deep groove between his dark brows.

"I know that's what's been advertised here," Miller said. "A culinary tour with a chef, and people tonight and along the way are going to refer to me as that. But for you, I want the food and destinations to be the star, not me. Ask me all the questions you want about the food, cooking, restaurants, et cetera, but I need to know you're on this tour for that experience, not for me."

The confusion on Clancy's face cleared, the lines and brows smoothing out. "I can do that, Ch—" He paused and smiled shyly. Far too attractive. "Sorry, it's a respect thing on my part too, but I get it. Miller, then?"

He chuckled. "Yeah, 'Miller' is good."

"Second rule?"

"Respect the service staff's time." Too often, guests didn't fully appreciate the mechanics of the restaurant, or how different the experience was for diners and staff. "You're a foodie and a doctor. You're gonna have questions." Clancy made a head exploding gesture with his hands, and Miller couldn't decide whether to laugh or cringe. This could go either way. "They'll be more than happy to chat and answer them, but remember, they've got a job to do. And like I said, you've got me to fill in the blanks."

"Easy enough," Clancy said, and Miller's worry eased. That potential speed bump had been Miller's primary concern. He didn't want to dampen Clancy's fun and enjoyment, but there had to be some limits, which Clancy seemed perfectly fine with. "Any other rules?" he asked.

There was one other, though not a rule so much as dispelling a myth that Miller, as a chef, fucking loathed. "If someone has ever told you to leave a tiny bit of food on your plate as a gesture of respect to the kitchen, don't listen to them. And don't do it. It's a load of horse shit. If you're full, then fine, don't force yourself. But if you want to eat it all, by all means, eat it all. Nothing I liked better than seeing empty plates come back to the kitchen."

"If someone ever told me that, I didn't listen. It's fucking idiotic."

"Good," Miller said with a sharp, satisfied nod. "I'm glad we have an understanding there."

"I understand that every bit of food I can get in my belly is going in there."

Miller had no idea where it was all going to go in that trim body, but he looked forward to seeing Clancy try. "Then we're all set." He shrugged into his overcoat and opened the door for Clancy. "Shall we get the belly stuffing underway?"

"Two and a half hours of it." Clancy patted said belly as he stepped into the hallway. "I can't wait."

"Revise that." Miller pulled the door closed behind them. "Four hours."

"Four? All the reviews I read said to plan for two and a half."

"Those people received menus. We won't. Think you can handle it?"

"I'm game." The eagerness in Clancy's eyes was a good sign. Miller's experience with people who said they "eat it all" was that their no-no list was in fact a mile long. He didn't sense that was the case with his companion, which boded well for tonight. And the trip as a whole. If it was true.

He gave Clancy a wink. "You're in for a treat."

Treat was an understatement.

As Clancy coveted his last bite of The French Laundry's famed oysters and pearls—two trimmed, meaty oysters in butter, eggs, and tapioca pearls, and topped with a giant dollop of caviar—*semi-orgasmic* seemed a more accurate description than merely *treat*. Each spoonful of yummy exploded with texture and flavor in his mouth. Luxury in every bite.

Same as the tiny bites that had preceded it—a medley of amuse-bouche plates and a sunchoke soup Clancy would sell his soul for. Like he'd sell his soul for the blissed-out look on Miller's handsome face. Long lashes lowered, blue eyes slitted, and a secret satisfied smile hidden in his beard. He'd been uptight earlier at the hotel, then relaxed as they'd laid down the ground rules, but the tension had returned as they'd neared the restaurant—eyes, forehead, and mouth corners creased, jaw tightened, and shoulders reared back. But all those battle-ready tells disappeared with a bowl of shellfish, eggs, and caviar.

Clancy likewise surrendered, using the delicate mother-of-pearl spoon to scoop the last bite into his mouth, humming contentedly.

Miller smiled from across the table. "Live up to the hype?"

"More than." Clancy wiped his mouth with the linen napkin and had barely placed it back in his lap when two suited servers stepped into the room off the main dining area where they were seated. With just three tables, a slanted roof, and a view of the reserve cellar through a window in the stone wall, the intimate antechamber was quieter than the main dining room, though even that space was smaller than Clancy had imagined. As a whole, the area for servers to maneuver was minimal and yet they moved about with effortless coordination, like they were on a wide-open football field instead.

Or on a stage, more precisely.

The two servers at their table cleared the plates and moved back out of the room, the maître d' who'd greeted them at the door stepping in after. "Satisfactory, gentlemen?" Lucy asked, her smile genuine and friendly.

"Excellent," Miller said. "As always."

Another suited man, older with a kind face and stylishly coiffed salt-and-pepper hair, appeared around the corner and clasped Miller's shoulder. "Chef, good to see you.'"

A passing server double-tapped Lucy on the shoulder. "I'm needed in the kitchen," she said, then to Clancy, "We'll be sure to get you back there before you leave, so you can see it too."

Lucy ducked out and the older gentleman moved farther in, holding out his hand. "Ben Turner, it's a pleasure to meet you, Dr. Rhodes."

"Clancy, please," he said, returning the handshake.

"Ben's the manager here," Miller said. "He and Lucy keep the front of house running smoothly."

Clancy adjusted his glasses and looked over Miller's shoulder to the dining room again. "It's like a ballet. They all know their steps, when and where to turn, and when to exit stage right or left." He thought to mention the chef's partner, who he knew from articles he'd read had enlisted a dance choreographer to train the servers to move so gracefully, but then he remembered the rules, and simply said, "It's incredible."

Ben squeezed Miller's shoulder. "Can you believe this big guy used to dance?"

Clancy's attention shot back to Miller. "You were a server?"

Miller nodded. "I was out here for a year before moving into the kitchen." He shifted in his chair, body and gaze angled toward the dining room. "Chefs should have this experience too. It's important to understand how every part of the beast operates."

"He was a favorite in the dining room and the kitchen," Ben said fondly. "Seven years ago now and the regulars still ask about him."

Clancy didn't doubt it. Miller's love of food and the industry was obvious already and to a guest, that translated. As did blue eyes, chestnut hair, a sexy smile, and the touch of Southern drawl.

Ben's voice broke through Clancy's inadvertent staring, and blushing, if the heat hitting Clancy's cheeks was any indication. But neither Miller nor Ben seemed to notice as they discussed wine for the rest of the meal. "Sloan said you wanted to open the Conterno."

"Yes, with the truffles, please."

Truffles. Clancy suppressed an excited shiver.

Ben's response chased it the rest of the way off. "You sure about that?" he asked Miller. "You've had it in the cellar for years."

"It's time," Miller replied.

"All right. We'll get it decanting while you continue

through the first half." Ben smiled again at Clancy, but something in his expression was too practiced this time. "I hope you continue to enjoy, Clancy."

"Thank you." He waited for Ben to leave, and for the approaching pair of servers to lay out the next course in front of them—crispy frog legs with an egg-shaped dollop of creamed spinach and round drops of sweet and peppery condiments—before asking Miller, "Exactly how many years have you hung on to that bottle?"

"I bought it with my first paycheck from here."

"You really don't have to break out the good stuff for me."

Miller crunched through a small bite of frog leg, chewed, and swallowed, his satisfied smile reappearing once more. "It's not just for you."

This meal wasn't either, Clancy sensed, even if it was part of the tour. He let the matter of the wine go—distracted by the frog legs, then the crab wrapped in fluffy layers of pasty, then the roulette of "tête de cochon" topped with a fried quail egg abed a float of sauce gribiche. Moat was more like it; he had absolutely zero objections.

Despite the couple of earlier speed bumps, conversation flowed more easily as the meal progressed, the both of them trained to talk to strangers, yet to Clancy, this didn't feel like sitting across the table from someone he'd just met. As promised, Miller gamely answered all his questions about how this or that was prepared, about working with the local purveyors, and about the white wine—a sauvignon blanc from Pouilly-Fumé—that he'd selected to go with this portion of the meal. All of it, every bite, every sip, was a taste bonanza in Clancy's mouth.

Especially the seemingly simple, divine dish that came next. Two razor-thin potato slices had been pressed together to form a sort of potato Lik-A-Stix that was stuck in layers of truffle custard and truffle gravy, all in an eggshell with its top removed. A moan may have slipped out as Clancy finished it in three bites.

Miller smirked. "You want to ask for another, don't you?"

"Who wouldn't? It's so simple and yet not."

"And yet not. Just getting the damn top off the egg is a skill."

They shared a laugh as the servers removed the plates, then Clancy, giving up the ghost on manners after a bottle of champagne and two glasses of wine, rested his elbows on the table and sank into the comfort that was emanating from his stomach. "Are we starting here because it's close to home?"

"In part." Miller sipped from his glass and sat back in his chair, crossing one leg over the other. "It's also the place every foodie wants to visit, isn't it?"

"Well, yeah, but *you* have to enjoy it too." Surprise flashed across Miller's face and Clancy added, "You're schlepping all over the country with a stranger at the holidays. I could have been a total dick."

Miller raised a brow. "Who says you're not?"

Clancy put a hand to his chest in affected outrage. "Me?"

The bushy chestnut brow dropped on a grin.

Clancy carried on, smiling too. "But if I was, which I'm not, at least you would enjoy the food."

Miller shifted forward again, matching Clancy's posture, bringing them nose to nose over the table. "You're just trying to get the list out of me."

Clancy thought to shrug a shoulder but he was too caught up in the flecks of gold he'd only just noticed in Miller's eyes. His admiration was interrupted, however, by servers entering with their next course, Lucy trailing behind them with a polished wooden box. Laughter bubbled out of Clancy as he got a good look at the plates. "They look like—"

"We call it the Flying Nun," Ben supplied, as he slipped in after the servers, balancing a tray of wine things. He placed two giant glasses on the table and held out the bottle of Barolo for Miller to inspect. Miller nodded, and Ben, after handing off the tray to the departing servers, filled their glasses with the wine from the decanter. "We actually retired these dishes, but they were Miller's favorite so I dug them out special, just for him."

Hands over his face, Miller groaned. "I dropped so many."

Eyes on the amusing plate that looked like a nun's habit, Clancy didn't notice Lucy approaching until the overwhelming scent of *earth* hit his nose. "White truffles from Alba," she said, displaying the delicacy in the open box. "Pairs perfectly with the wine and pasta."

By the time she was done shaving God-only-knew how many grams of truffle over his plate, Clancy couldn't even see the pasta.

A knee knocked his under the table. "Stay with me," Miller whispered.

Clancy wasn't sure what was more intoxicating—the earthy aroma that filled the room, Miller's gravelly voice full of humor, or the heat radiating from the leg next to his.

Lucy tapped the last shaving off onto Miller's plate and Ben set the decanter and bottle on the table. "Enjoy," he said, squeezing Miller's shoulder once more. Clancy could sense the friendly affection there.

Clancy picked up his fork and wound strands of the brown butter drizzled tagliatelle around the tines. Spearing extra truffle shavings onto the end, he raised the fork to his mouth and took the single best bite of food of his life. He closed his eyes, savoring the decadence on his tongue. "Okay," he said, eyes half-slitted. "This is just flat-out orgasmic."

Miller laughed out loud, drawing stares from the nearby tables. He lowered his voice and whispered, "Don't make a mess in your pants."

Clancy muffled his laughter in his wineglass. It truly was a great pairing, the dry wine wiping clean his palate so he could experience that first rich, silky taste of pasta and truffle over and over again.

After a few bites, he slowed himself by asking Miller again why TFL first.

Miller laid down his fork and sipped at his wine, looking around wistfully. "They know how to treat their diners. How to read a table like that." He snapped his fingers. "Interact or not, pacing, portions, without the diner having to say a word. It's customer service at its finest."

Clancy could see that, just in the different way the servers handled the three tables in this room. Social and familiar with theirs, polite and friendly with the second-time guests next to them, and practically invisible to the business dinner of four behind them. "And the food is damn good too."

"That too, though it's not for everyone. No restaurant is."

"Fools," Clancy said, and shoveled in another forkful of decadent pasta.

"It's also one of the more civil kitchen environments I've worked in. I wanted—"

He cut himself off, the stiffness from earlier in the night returning. He didn't have to say the words for Clancy to hear them. He'd wanted to run his own restaurant this way. With kindness, civility, and attentiveness. Though he was just getting to know the man, Clancy suspected Miller had done just that, for the time it'd been open. Clearly that hadn't been enough. Clancy wanted to ask more, but Miller had cut himself off from going there and he wasn't supposed to be the focus; the food and this experience were. Clancy wouldn't go there either, at least not now. They were here tonight to enjoy themselves, both of them. "I'll tell you what I want," he said.

"What's that?"

Clancy cut his eyes to the decanter. "More wine."

Miller picked it up and topped off their glasses. "Pace yourself. We have a ways to go still."

Clancy may have been imagining things—there'd been three bottles of wine already—but to his ears, it didn't sound like Miller was only talking about tonight's meal. "I'm looking forward to it."

The food orgy didn't stop with pasta and truffles. Buttery lobster claws on risotto enriched with mascarpone cheese—how was that even legal? Roasted squab served with young strawberries and rainbow chard. Dry-aged rib eye with fall vegetables and the best bordelaise sauce Clancy had ever tasted.

After a cheese course of Tête de Moine, the aroma of the fragrant cheese filling the room as Lucy shaved florets off the wheel table-side, they were treated to a dizzying array of desserts. The Laundry's signature coffee semi-freddo and cinnamon-sugar doughnuts, a pecan tart with bourbon-laced Chantilly cream, and a decadent white truffle sundae, because nothing said "OTT Luxury" like truffle-steeped milk churned into ice cream and served with a dessert wine that tasted sweet and smelled like truffles.

And after all that, Lucy and Ben had the nerve to send him off with a bag of snacks—cookies, chocolates, granola, and fruit—"in case he got hungry." He was still giggling at that absurd statement as Miller shooed him out the door. He'd be lucky if he ate again this week, which was prob-lematic, as they were flying to their next destination tomorrow.

"Did you walk through the restaurant's garden today?" Miller asked.

Clancy shook his head dramatically, then had to adjust his glasses. "Was too busy enjoying my lie-in on the Egyptian cotton sheets."

"Your lie-in?" Miller laughed. "Were you watching BBC all day?"

"It was raining outside."

Miller laughed and nudged him across the street toward the garden. "Walk, then. It'll help the digestion."

Clancy buttoned his overcoat and patted his belly. "I'm not sure how I got it all in there."

"Never had a meal like that before?"

Even with the moon shining bright, Clancy had to watch his step over the curb and wood mulch, then onto the grass and level ground again at the edge of the garden. It was mushy from the earlier rain, but the thick grass kept his Oxfords out of the mud, mostly. "I've been to places with tasting menus before, but nothing quite like that."

Miller shoved his hands in his coat pockets and turned right, down the first row. "Around LA?"

"There and Chicago." Clancy stopped at each placard they passed, reading what winter vegetables grew in the neatly maintained plots.

"Alinea?"

"That was my last Michelin-star meal, before this one."

"The flavor Grant packs into those courses is incredible."

"Right!" Clancy had talked incessantly about that meal for weeks after. "That truffle explosion course."

"One of the best," Miller agreed.

At the end of the row, they peeked into the chicken pen

where all the residents were tucked into their coop or hay for the night. They turned the corner and headed down the next row. Clancy hung back, taking in the impressive scope of the cultivated garden, alight in the moonlight. And the impressive backside in plaid pants that walked ahead of him, sure-footed, like he'd traversed this particular ground countless times.

"How'd you get into food?" Miller asked. "Especially with all those years of schooling and residency."

"LA's a big town, you know." Clancy thanked his long legs, able in just a few strides to catch up with Miller, who'd stopped next to a half-harvested plot of willowy, leafy stalks that towered over them both. At least eight feet high, they looked like corn stalks, but not. "Holy shit, what are these?"

"Remember that soup you were moaning over at the start of the meal?" Miller laughed when Clancy stuck his tongue out at him. "All that"—he waved a finger up and down at the stalks, then pointed at the ground—"for a bulb down there. Jerusalem artichoke, also known as—"

"Sunchoke. I had no idea this was how they were grown."

"Bitch to clean," Miller said, as he led them on down the row. "And you didn't answer my question. Were you always a foodie? Because you look like you barely eat."

"Hey!" Clancy backhanded Miller's gut. "We can't all be bears."

Miller feigned injury, clutching his belly, and trapping Clancy's hand underneath. Their hands tangled briefly, so did their gazes, sparking like they had at their first meeting.

Clancy hoped like hell his blush wasn't noticeable in the moonlight. He drew his hand out from under Miller's big warm one.

"I liked food well enough as a kid. Mom could cook, and we had a chef that came in once a week to prepare meals and such. I'd hang out with her, watch what she did on those nights when my parents would take their night out on the town. That is, until Mom left."

"I'm sorry, I didn't—"

"Nothing to be sorry about," Clancy said. "They all still get along. My dad and stepdad even golf together, if they're in the same town. My parents still love each other, but they weren't in love any longer."

It wasn't exactly tension that rippled through Miller, but a sort of pensiveness that made Clancy wonder again about what his mother had mentioned on the plane. About Miller and Sloan. But not wanting to destroy the happy bubble cast by the meal and moonlight, Clancy didn't poke. "Anyway, when she left, he lost his weekly dining companion."

"So you filled in?"

"It was the only thing I could do to get him out of the house those first few months, aside from when he went to work."

"I thought you said—"

Maybe not poke directly, but Clancy could offer Miller his sympathy, vague as it was. "Didn't mean he didn't miss his best friend."

Miller glanced his direction, curiosity, fear, and hope

all swirling in his blue eyes that looked ghostly in the pale light. "He's okay now?"

Clancy jostled a shoulder against his, grinning. "He's dating a pastry chef we met on one of our dinners out."

"And you're going to work with him?"

"After this trip." A small cringe slipped out before he could stop himself. "Did I just do that?"

Miller chuckled. "Yeah, you did."

Clancy pushed his glasses up and got them moving again. "Too much wine. And a story for another dinner." They stopped at the edge of the garden, close together as they waited for a car to pass. "Speaking of, you want to tell me where we're going next?"

Miller's eyes flickered down to his mouth, and in the flash of passing headlights, there was no way he didn't notice the blush burning up Clancy's cheeks. "I'll tell you where we're going next."

"Where?" Did he sound breathy?

"To bed."

Did he have any breath left?

"To sleep," Miller added.

Clancy stuck out his bottom lip, pouting, and got the reaction he wanted. Miller's deep, sexy laugh played on in his dreams all night long.

Chapter Three

NAPA

Miller waited in the back seat of the town car, sipping a coffee and listening to the rain patter on the roof overhead. When his travel companion finally appeared, Miller had to grin at the stark contrast from last night. Clancy trudged out of the hotel, a half hour past late checkout, carrying his TFL goodie bag in one hand and dragging his rolling suitcase behind him with the other. His mop of thick brown hair stuck out in every direction, his eyes were hidden behind a pair of battered Oakleys, and he was dressed in a mishmash of layers—last night's cashmere overcoat, a gray hoodie, a navy tee with a giant rainbow Psycho Bunny logo, together with tattered jeans and a pair of Chucks.

He looked an adorable, hungover mess. And yet still stunning.

While the driver loaded Clancy's bags into the trunk, Clancy opened the door and fell into the back seat.

Miller mimicked taking his photograph. "Clancy Rhodes, cover model."

"Don't judge. It's a travel day." He ducked his chin and peered over the top of his sunglasses. "How much plaid do you own?"

"Don't judge," Miller parried back, as he unbuttoned his pink plaid blazer. "I promise the hangover won't be as bad after the other stops."

"I'm not hungover."

Miller reached into the paper bag at his side, pulled out a muffin, and waved it under Clancy's nose.

Clancy rolled down the window and stuck his head outside, sputtering as raindrops splashed his face.

Laughing, Miller set the muffin on the armrest between them and loosened the extra coffee from the holder. He waited for Clancy to wipe off his glasses. "Let's try this first," he said, holding out the cup to him.

Clancy accepted it and took a long swallow. "Ah, humanity."

Miller nudged the muffin toward him. "Get something in your stomach. It'll make you feel better."

After another gulp, Clancy traded his coffee for the muffin. He peeled back one half of the wrapper and broke off a nibble. He chewed slowly, like he was solving a puzzle, then held the muffin up, close to his face. "It looks like a bran muffin." He passed it under his nose. "Smells like a bran muffin." He popped in another bite. "But it tastes better than any bran muffin I've ever had."

"From an LA boy, that's high praise."

He continued to gobble up the muffin. "Where's it from?"

"The Model Bakery. When you texted you were

running late, I snuck out right quick. Just wait for the English muffin."

"Oh!" Clancy shifted suddenly in the seat, then cringed, as if his exclamation and abrupt movement reminded him of his hangover. "I've heard about those," he said more quietly. "The doughnut ones?"

Miller nodded. He'd already indulged in the fluffy, buttery goodness, slathered in apple butter, sweet with a hint of spice. How could he ever risk that? The simple pleasures of fresh baked bread, homemade jam, and an exceptional cup of coffee. Or the splash of salty sea in an oyster or dollop of caviar. The heady richness of classic sauces like hollandaise and bordelaise. The pure umami smell and taste of white truffles, shaved over pasta or in a sundae. The way wine could pair so perfectly with food, the Conterno last night worth every penny he'd spent on it. He didn't go a day, a meal, a snack without analyzing flavors, without losing himself in thought over it, without thinking of new ways to work with it. It wasn't just what he did for a living; it was who he was. A life without taste and flavors, for a chef, for him, would be no kind of life at all. He wouldn't recognize it, wouldn't recognize himself, and that was not how he wanted his life to end, in six months or in sixty years. The cancer would kill him, but it wouldn't kill who he was—a chef. The treatment might and that thought was scarier than even death.

Long fingers gently clasped his arm. "Hey, Miller, where'd you go?"

He cleared his throat and thoughts with a wash of coffee. "Just thinking about our next destination."

"You gonna tell me where that is now?"

He glanced again at Clancy, whose color and energy were returning. Good, he'd need the latter especially. "How about when we get on the plane?" Miller offered. "Maybe."

"Only if you give me that English muffin," Clancy bargained.

"Deal." He dug one out of the bag, together with the knife and container of apple butter, and passed it to Clancy. "Go easy, though, if you get altitude sickness," Miller warned. "And that's all you're getting out of me," he added before Clancy could ask for more details.

Clancy scrunched up his nose. "You sit on a throne of lies."

They were both still laughing when the car reached the Napa County airfield a few minutes later. By the fretful look on the waiting flight attendant's face, Miller guessed they wouldn't be laughing much longer.

"Wonder what's going on?" Clancy said.

All this rain had probably complicated matters at their destination.

Sure enough. "Dr. Rhodes, good to see you again," the attendant said, then hand out to Miller, "Mr. Sykes, I'm Toby, I'll be taking care of you and Dr. Rhodes on this trip. Unfortunately, we've hit a bit of a snag. It's white-out conditions in—"

"Where we're going," Miller said, cutting him off.

Toby blushed and put his fingers over his mouth.

"Someplace with snow?" Clancy said, brow raised in campy fashion again. "And with high altitude. Hmm." He faked a Rodin pose and everyone laughed, even poor stressed-out Toby.

"Truly, sir," the attendant said. "My apologies. Won't happen again."

"No worries," Miller replied. He knew the circumstances of this trip were unusual. "I already gave away the high altitude bit."

"Well, we can't get in there at the moment," Toby said. "Things may clear up later tonight, but probably not until morning."

An inconvenience, but not one that would throw off the trip too much. A little less time for Clancy to sightsee tomorrow before dinner, but if they left early enough, only a few hours would be lost. "We don't have dinner reservations until tomorrow night, so we're clear there."

"Should I contact Ms. Essley about arrangements for tonight?"

"I'll take care of it," Clancy said, already pulling out his phone. "How many rooms does your crew need?"

"We're fine, sir," Toby said. "We'll check back in to the hotel close to the airport here so we can ready the jet when it's time to go. We'll give you a heads-up an hour or so before wheels up?"

"Sounds good."

Toby ascended the steps into the plane, and Clancy turned to Miller, phone raised. "Let me call Mom. She'll work something out for us."

Miller covered his hand. "Just ask her to give our next stop a heads-up. I don't want to lose the reservation. As for today, here, I'll handle that." Twenty years in unpredictable kitchens had taught him to think fast on his feet. They were on his home turf, there were a wealth of options for him to treat Clancy too, but with the chance, albeit slim, that they could still depart tonight, he needed something flexible. Sounded about right for a picnic. "Think you can eat some more?"

Clancy smiled gamely. "Isn't that the point of this trip?"

Picnic on, and Miller knew just where to get everything they needed.

Clancy didn't know where to look. The riot of color pouring from the vegetable-filled crates to his left, the giant pink wall and cases of cupcakes directly across the space, or the bowling alley length of culinary vendors to his right. And there was a second aisle with more vendor stalls down the other side of the space. "Holy shit."

Miller nudged him out of the way of the entry doors. "Don't tell me you've never been to a farmers market before."

Sure he had. Year-round farmers markets were a major benefit of living in California. But this—Oxbow Public Market, according to the sign atop the long brick and glass building—was not rickety stands and pop-up tents. "This is a farmers market on steroids."

"Welcome to Napa."

"I could spend days here." Ogling the Italian pastry case within arm's reach, tasting the olive oils on display at a stall halfway down the aisle, and was that an oyster bar at the far end of the building? "Holy shit."

Miller laughed. "I'll give you an hour."

Clancy swung his gaze back to his tour guide. "Rude."

Also rude, the satisfied grin on Miller's face, the way that pink plaid blazer fit him just so, and the determination that lit his blue eyes and the deep lines that crinkled around them.

"Come on." Miller grabbed a basket and started toward the vegetable stand. "We have provisions to get."

"Do provisions include cupcakes?"

He'd taken two steps toward the pink-branded Mecca when Miller yanked him back by a handful of jacket.

"There's a reason the cupcake place is at the front, in the far corner. You have to make a loop first—check out everything else—before dessert. Last stop, promise."

Point taken. Didn't stop Clancy from pouting as he pushed up his glasses and followed Miller into the stacked crates of produce. "So, what's the plan?"

"Well, since we may still have to jet at a moment's notice, I thought we'd grab some things here and have a picnic. No reservations needed."

Clancy covered his excitement with a gruff, "Not bad, Sykes, not bad." He played like he was only mildly impressed when in fact it was a genius idea. And perfect after the twenty-course feast last night.

Miller saw right through his charade. "Not bad?" Laughing, he shoved the shopping basket at him. "You hold while I work."

And work he did, all of it fascinating to Clancy.

Peeling back corn husks and smelling the ears until he gave up, bypassed the "fucking out-of-season corn" altogether, and moved on to the peppers, testing firmness and comparing colors. He was less picky about the bunches of rainbow carrots, radishes and endive he added to the basket. A handful of assorted greenery later, they checked out and started down the aisle.

Easily distracted, Clancy lagged behind often—tasting olive oils, sampling locally-made gin, drooling over a display case full of chocolate truffles, and staring longingly at the coffee importer's selections. He exerted all his willpower to not buy a pound of everything and caught up with Miller at the cheese merchant.

"Tell the truth." Miller gave Clancy a stern look as he dumped the lot of wedges and rounds he'd already collected into the basket. "Anything goes? Nothing on the no-no list?"

"Nothing." Clancy swept a hand over the refrigerated case. "Do your worst. Bring on the stinky cheeses." In his experience, the stinkier the better.

Miller shot out a hand and grabbed one of the circular wooden boxes labeled *Époisses*.

Clancy grinned. "My favorite."

One corner of Miller's mouth ticked up. "Good to know." He dropped the cheese into the basket and turned back to his hunt.

Thank God because Clancy's knees had gone liquid in the wake of that sexy leer. It took a good minute to get his legs back under him, and by then, Miller had returned with more cheeses, almonds, and fruit paste.

"I take it this is the basis of our picnic?" Clancy asked.

"The best kind." Miller claimed the basket and headed to the counter. "We'll grab some meats and bread to go with next door."

"Which of these is your favorite?" Clancy asked, as they unloaded the basket for the cashier.

Miller held up a wheel wrapped in wax paper and twine. "O'Banon."

He peeled back a flap so Clancy could see inside. Expecting cheese, Clancy was surprised to see green leaves instead.

"Goat's milk cheese from Indiana that's wrapped in bourbon-soaked chestnut leaves," Miller explained.

"Very cool. Why that one?"

"It's the most well-rounded goat cheese I've tasted. The bourbon-soaked leaves mellow out the bite without making it too sweet." Miller handed the round to the cashier. "Why the Époisses for you?"

"Funny story." He took the insulated bag from the cashier and followed Miller toward the rear exit door. "I didn't date much in school."

Miller's brows raced north. "Really? Social guy like you? I figure you could talk to a tree."

"Talking takes energy, and I had none." Rain reduced to a light mist, they leisurely crossed the parking lot to a set of adjacent buildings. "I did undergrad in three years but even accelerated, it was easy, compared to medical school. That was the first time I really had to work. Add rounds on top of that and..." They turned the corner and Clancy momentarily lost his train of thought, distracted by the smell of fresh bread.

"And what, Doc?"

The nickname brought him back. Or was it the swooping sensation in his belly? Clancy couldn't tell, the two so closely connected. He locked his knees, fending off weakness, and distracted himself with the rest of his story. "I would've rather gone to dinner with my dad or gone to a club to pick someone up. No pressure, either way."

Miller rested a hip against one of the picnic tables. "Do I want to know how gooey cheese fits in here?"

"Gooey, *stinky* cheese."

"Sykes!" A shout rang out, interrupting them. "What'll it be?" A hipster-looking fellow in a rubber apron stood in the doorway of The Fatted Calf, the butcher shop next to the place where the heavenly fresh bread smells were coming from.

"Doing a picnic," Miller replied. "Little bit of this, little bit of that."

"I got you," the young man said.

"You want bread too?" came a woman's voice from the neighboring bakery.

"Yes, please," Miller called back. "And a few more English muffins."

Clancy's gaze darted to the sign above the screen door. The Model Bakery. More doughnuts. "Best. Picnic. Ever."

Miller snapped his fingers in front of Clancy's face, yanking back his attention. "Only if you tell me the rest of the Époisses story."

"Fine," Clancy groaned, resting against the table next

to Miller. "So, second year of med school, this girl I dated first year and was still friendly with sets me up on a date with her cousin who's new in town. He's cute and nice enough, but he keeps going on and on about venture capital—for med devices, mind you, so he was trying to be relevant to my interests—but I was literally two seconds from falling asleep in my soup. I had three hours before I had to be back at the hospital. All I wanted to do was sleep. You want to know how to end a date real fast?"

Miller laughed out loud. "Order the stinky cheese."

Clancy held up nine fingers. "Works nine times out of ten."

"Count me as the one time it doesn't," Miller said with a wink, before pushing off the table and entering the butcher shop.

Clancy stood frozen by the table, needing the extra support as he coached himself not to read too much into Miller's teasing words, into the nickname and earlier leer. Reminding himself of the ground rules. This tour was about the food, not the chef, no matter how interesting Miller Sykes continued to be.

Some lessons were harder to learn than others, especially when the promised picnic turned out to be at Miller's house. At least that's where Clancy assumed they were. Pink box of cupcakes in hand, he followed Miller up an internal staircase that was decorated with framed, signed menus—many *To Miller and Sloan.* The French Laundry, Alinea, Le Bernardin, El Bulli, among a dozen others.

"This is your place?"

"For a little while longer." Miller unlocked the door at the top of the stairs while, behind them, the driver was unloading their bags into the downstairs rooms Miller had opened directly after entering.

"Is Sloan here?" Clancy asked.

"She lives in San Francisco."

Not a direct answer, and even more confusing. Those menus indicated she did once. Clancy wanted to ask where exactly Miller and Sloan's relationship stood, wanted to get clarity on this mystery that seemed essential to something else he was also missing. He bit his tongue about that, but not about the other tidbit Miller had dropped.

"You're moving?"

"Selling this place." Miller pushed inside, arms loaded down with their shopping bags. "We don't need this much space here anymore."

"Are you also moving to—" Clancy's question dropped as he crested the stairs and got a look at the top floor.

He would've dropped the cupcakes too if Miller hadn't saved them. "Chin off the floor, Doc," he said, slipping the box from Clancy's hands.

"Sorry, it's just..." He flapped his hands, trying and failing to summon an adequate word for the upper level. Tuscan tile flooring ran the length of the open space, from the gourmet kitchen at one end, with its massive cooktop, butcher-block island, and hanging pot rack, to the farm table in the middle dining area, to the living room with its leather sectional facing a huge stone hearth. And across the back wall, floor-to-ceiling windows and doors offered stunning vineyard views. There was a hallway on the other side of the kitchen wall and Clancy peeked down it—a bathroom and bedroom, a plaid blanket over the end of the bed. It was homey, same as the living room. Lived in. The pots weren't shiny, the leather couch had creases, and the farm table had more than a few dings. It was comfortable; it was a home. And Miller was selling it?

"We were barely here anymore," Miller said, as if reading his mind. He began unloading their haul onto the island. "Someone else will get to enjoy it, more than we were able to lately. The Realtor will be showing it while I'm gone. I'd cook"—he pointed to the pots overhead —"but I don't want to mess too much up. Picnic is relatively contained."

"You call this contained?" Clancy said, as Miller covered the island from one end to the other with meat, cheese, and bread.

"You haven't seen me cook." He snagged a colander from the overhead rack and tossed in the vegetables. "Go pick a room downstairs, in case we have to sleep here. I'll get these washed and cut, then we'll be ready to eat." He turned toward the sink, washing with one hand, grabbing a cutting board and knife with the other. Totally focused, even just for a picnic.

Clancy let him be, wanting to explore more himself. He read all the menus on the way down the stairs and snapped a few pictures. He texted them to his dad and was unsurprised when his phone rang less than a minute later, Alan's face lighting up the screen.

"Hey, Dad."

"You think any of those places are where you're going?"

"You tell me."

His dad laughed. "Nice try. Now tell me everything about The French Laundry. What'd you eat, what'd you drink, what was it like?"

"You do know where I'm going!" Clancy said, as he poked around in the first of the downstairs bedrooms.

"Never denied that." A desk chair squeaked in the background. Loud and familiar.

"Are you in the office?" Sunday was usually his dad's day off.

"Just trying to get caught up on case notes. No time during the week with the influx of patients. You'll see soon enough. It's hard to keep up."

Clancy leaned back against one of the bed's four wooden posters. He missed his case files. They'd been his life for almost a decade—each a story, each a puzzle, each a chance to make a difference in someone's life. It was weird not having them to dig into, not having that sense of purpose. It would come again, soon enough. Wouldn't it? Would he still feel that spark of interest digging into the case files of the patients at his dad's practice? His reconstruction cases, sure, but the others? He didn't have an answer, so he stared out at the vineyards instead.

"Son?"

"Right, so it started with this amazing soup." Clancy

distracted them both with descriptions of each course—the food, wine, and service. As he talked, Clancy checked out the other downstairs bedrooms. This one, like the other bedroom on this level, held no clues. Closets were empty, pictures were gone, and it appeared staged by the Realtor. Or maybe Miller had been renting out the bottom floor? Or maybe these rooms where for guests? Visiting chefs? The hot tub out on the patio would no doubt draw rave reviews.

"Where do you *think* you're going next?" his father asked, bringing Clancy back to the tour, not the man.

"Someplace with high altitude and a lot of snow. That's all I've got."

"You're gonna love it." The smile in his dad's voice rang as loudly as the squeaking chair.

"Dad!"

"Doc!"

Clancy lowered the phone and glanced at the call time. *Shit*, they'd been chatting for twenty minutes.

"Doc, you get lost down there?" Miller called again.

"Dad, sorry—"

"You gotta go. Keep me posted. I want to see menus."

"You got it."

Hanging up, Clancy pocketed the phone and rolled his suitcase out of the downstairs foyer into the first bedroom. He bypassed the internal staircase and exited onto the patio. He wanted to get a better look at the hot tub. Maybe take a dip after their picnic, if the rain stayed away. Would Miller join him? Just to chat, that was all. He ignored Miranda snickering in his head and climbed the outside steps to the living room, tapping against the glass doors.

Miller loped over, corkscrew in hand. "How'd you get out there?"

"There's a hot tub."

"It's a house in Napa. There's a hot tub." He laughed and closed the door behind him. "Come on. I was just about to open the wine."

"We didn't buy any wine."

"Because I had it here already."

Wines, as in plural. A bottle of white and a bottle of red set in the middle of their spread, which had been moved from the island to the table. No way it would've all fit on the island. "I think our eyes were bigger than our stomachs."

"This is nothing," Miller said, as he uncorked the wines. "This was our go-to meal after long weeks or a tough day. I remember this one time Sloan had been prepping a case for months, and it unexpectedly settled, very much in her client's favor. I told her I'd take the night off, come in to San Francisco, and we'd go out to celebrate. She just wanted to come up here and veg. I left work early and came home to find the entire table covered and two bottles of champagne in the bucket. We had a hell of a night in our sweats."

"That sounds wonderful."

Miller's smile was genuine and wistful. "It was."

Why always the past tense? Clancy wanted to ask, but he asked about their meal instead. The wine—Arbe Garbe, a white blend of Italian grapes grown and harvested locally, and Lieu Dit, a bright red Gamay from the Santa Maria Valley. The meats—a local wild boar sausage, a French dry sausage, imported prosciutto, and half a dozen other meats and pates. The cheeses—O'Banon, Époisses, and several others from local creameries, Andante Dairy and Bellwether Farms. The bread—sweet and sour baguettes, a brioche loaf, and pretzel buns. And all the fixings—chopped peppers, endive leaves, quince paste, honey, and almonds.

They dove in, Miller's stories about working with the various local purveyors carrying them through the first bottle. The white wine was fresh and delightfully different, nothing like Clancy had ever tasted before. As they moved on to the red and continued to whittle down the food stuffs, Clancy proposed a round of twenty questions. Miller conceded to five, and Clancy had to answer them too.

"I can live with that," Clancy said, while considering his approach. Keep it light, try not to pry, but he wanted to learn more about the person he'd spend the next two weeks with. "Favorite color?"

"Plaid."

Clancy rolled his eyes. "You don't say." Two days and he'd figured that much out already. "Also not a color."

Miller flipped him the bird. "Your answer?"

"Dodger Blue, baby."

"Ugh." Miller threw an arm over his face. "If I'd known that, I would've disqualified you on the spot."

"Too late now," Clancy mumbled around a sourdough round slathered in Époisses and honey. "Favorite wine?"

"Ridge, Monte Bello, from the Santa Cruz Mountains."

"Not a Napa Cab, or something French?"

"I love a big, bold Napa Cab as much as the next Valley chef, and the French reds, especially the Grand Crus, are sublimely balanced. I love the Monte Bello most because it comes in right between those two. It's not so balanced that it doesn't pack a flavor punch, but the punch isn't so big as to overpower whatever you're eating. It's perfect."

Clancy swirled the wine in his glass. "Maybe we'll see the Monte Bello on the tour?"

Miller narrowed his eyes, the crinkles around the corners almost as attractive as when he smiled. "I see what you did there. Your answer?"

"I don't know. I haven't met my favorite yet."

Almost when narrowed, because the crinkling with the smile now was divine. "Good answer." He munched through a pretzel round with mustard, Manchego and prosciutto. "And that's four questions."

"Two were related to the wine question!" Clancy objected.

"Still, that's four total. One more, make it count."

Clancy huffed and nudged up his glasses, contemplating. Favorite vacation spot? Favorite food? Nah, those were questions he'd get answered on the tour. He wanted to know something more basic, more elemental. "Favorite flavor? Sweet, sour, bitter, salty or umami?" He figured the answer would be umami.

Miller didn't hesitate to answer, "Salt. It's the most

useful and one of the hardest to master. Did you see salt on the table last night?"

Clancy thought back through the meal. "Not once."

"Exactly, if a chef is good—confident—there won't be salt on the table. It only comes out at TFL with the foie gras, which we didn't have. Otherwise, everything was seasoned so you didn't need to add it."

There wasn't salt on the table here either.

"Let me guess yours." Miller stood from the table and fetched the pink box of cupcakes.

Clancy groaned.

"Am I wrong?"

"You're not wrong. I just don't know where I'm going to put that."

"Oh, come on," Miller teased. "Don't surrender now."

"I'm used to meager medical round snacks. Day after day of this good stuff, how do you do it?"

"Balance." Miller cut several of the cupcakes in half, splitting them to share. "Which admittedly, I was not always good at. Much like you, I was more often grabbing the easy stuff between services."

"So, maybe not just me struggling on this trip?"

"I think you'll find the rest of the stops not so daunting."

"Oh, like this 'picnic'?"

"My definitions might be a little skewed."

Clancy held up his thumb and forefinger, an inch apart. "A wee bit."

Miller balled up a sheet of wax paper and tossed it at him. "Eat your cupcakes, Doc."

"Then a dip in the hot tub?" Clancy hadn't meant to ask that, even though the idea had continued to play at the back of his mind through dinner. With it out there, though, Clancy went with it, cocking a brow.

Miller laughed. "You look like Dr. Evil's son."

"You didn't answer my question."

"*You* ran out of them," Miller reminded him. The lines around his eyes reappeared, together with a mischievous glint in the blue-gold gaze. "But I think we could do that."

Mischievous or flirtatious? Either way, the same rush of warmth and tangle of confusion that'd first struck last night fluttered in Clancy's belly. He still wasn't sure what was going on with Miller and Sloan. Clancy needed to answer that before he put a toe into that hot tub. He opened his mouth to ask, and Miller's phone rang.

Several rings they stared at each other, until Miller broke the connection and leaned back, lifting the phone to his ear. "This is Miller." Intensity morphed into surprise, into happiness, a trace of relief, as a smile stretched across his face. "That's good to hear. We'll be ready to go when the car gets here. Thanks, Toby." He lowered the phone and glanced back up at Clancy. "We're cleared to fly out tonight. It'll be worth it to have the whole day tomorrow, promise."

Hot tub fantasies died, but Clancy couldn't lie. He felt a bit of relief too. And excitement at seeing the same on Miller's face. He was looking forward to the next stop. Clancy couldn't wait to find out why.

"As long as I can take the cupcakes with me."

"Fuck" was the only word Miller could mutter as he stepped onto the plane that would fly them across the country the next two weeks. Other words came to mind but getting them out past the shock and awe was problematic. *Sleek*, with light interior walls, herringbone patterned carpet, and gleaming mahogany tables. *Comfortable*, not usually associated with the first, but the bench seat looked long enough for his six-foot-three frame and the chairs were the cushy kind of leather you could get lost in. *Rich* blinked like a neon bar sign, brightest of all.

He could only imagine what his family back home would think if they could see him now aboard a private plane. He'd flown them out for the restaurant opening—in commercial business class—and they'd thought that had been the ultimate in high class. This was a whole new level, and Miller wasn't quite sure what to do with it. It made him both comfortable—at the prospect of traveling well on this trip—and uncomfortable—at the thought of living, even for two weeks, and even on someone else's dime, way outside his means.

Clancy, by contrast, didn't seem the least bit fazed. He'd said before he didn't travel on his mother's planes much, but it was often enough he knew where to stash their overcoats and where to find the bottles of water. He handed one to Miller and gestured to the set of chairs mid-cabin, a table between them. He moved his box of cupcakes onto the table and sank into his seat. "Mom's letting us use her best bird."

Miller's head was still on a swivel, taking it all in, as he lowered himself across from Clancy. "She didn't need it around the holidays?"

"She's got two more."

He swung his gaze back to Clancy. "Three total?"

"For now. She's thinking about expanding." He seemed to debate the cupcakes for a moment before choosing two different halves—a lemon one and a red velvet.

Apparently, Clancy's stomach had expanding powers too. "So much for not being hungry."

"Moving around made room."

He had one half eaten when Toby appeared from the front of the plane. "Dr. Rhodes, Mr. Sykes, we've been cleared for takeoff. If you'd please buckle your seat belts, we'll be up in the air soon."

True to his word, they were airborne in less than ten minutes, another advantage of flying private. Leaning back in his seat, Miller nursed his bottle of water and stared out the window, watching the place he'd grown to love as home disappear. The San Francisco Bay that stretched farther north than tourists realized. The clash of fall colors he hadn't expected and that never ceased to amaze him, the greens coming back to life with the rain and the vines dotting wine country bursting with reds, oranges, and yellows. And though he couldn't smell it way up here, the sense memory of fermenting wines, the fragrance so strong at the intersection of Whitehall Lane and Highway 29. It hadn't worked out like he'd wanted here, but it'd been home for ten years. A good one where he and Sloan had been safe. That much he'd done right. He had no reason to think he wouldn't be back here—the doctors had given him six months to a year—but he couldn't say that with absolute certainty. There was something in his body he couldn't control. A variable he couldn't predict or plan for, other than knowing its eventual result. So he'd decided to let it play out as it would. He hadn't been very good with variables lately anyway.

A series of bumps shimmied the plane, and he clutched the armrests. More variables he couldn't control. Why the fuck had he thought this was a good idea? He usually had Sloan on flights with him to talk his ear off and distract him from the turbulence.

Clancy was game to try. "Can we play twenty questions again? See if I can guess where we're going?" He shoved another cupcake half into his mouth.

"All right, but same conditions as before." Miller shrugged out of his jacket, tossed it onto the bench seat, and rolled up his shirtsleeves. He didn't miss how Clancy's eyes strayed to his tattooed forearms, but Miller wouldn't let his own mind stray to what that might mean. Food and destinations, that was all Miller could offer and afford. That's all this trip was supposed to be about. "Five, not twenty, and for each question you ask, I get to ask a different one this time," he proposed. "And you can't ask point blank where we're going. I made you a promise."

Clancy pouted, his kissable lower lip thrust out. Miller's mind and body gave him the middle finger, straying as they pleased after an evening and afternoon full of temptation. Stirrings he couldn't acknowledge and couldn't reciprocate. He wrenched back control, telling Clancy, "That's the offer, take it or leave it."

"Fine, so we're going somewhere with high altitude?"

"I already told you that. Wasted question." He kicked his shin under the table. "You're terrible at this game."

Clancy threw a balled-up napkin at him in return.

Chuckling, Miller snatched it out of the air before it collided with his nose. "How long have you been flying around on these fancy planes?"

"And you made fun of my questions."

"Answer it, smart ass."

Clancy curled his legs up under him, getting comfy. "Mom bought her first one with the divorce settlement, right after my freshman year of college. She bought the second and third a few years back. Like I said before, she's very good at what she does."

"That's what Sloan said."

"We should watch out for those two. Trouble together."

Miller kicked his shoes off and propped his feet on the bracing bar beneath the table. "I got the same impression."

"They seem a lot alike."

Miller sensed a question in there, but when he didn't bite, Clancy moved on to another.

"How long is the flight time?"

"Now you're smartening up. About two and a half hours."

Contemplating, Clancy rubbed his hand over the bit of scruff growing in along his jawline.

Miller asked another question before the unwelcome stirrings started again. "Why didn't you leave LA for undergrad or med school?"

"Los Angeles gets shit on a lot, and I concede, it's not perfect, by a long shot. The traffic is terrible, there's too much emphasis on appearance, and too much disparity of wealth. But it's my home. One that's relatively diverse, where the beach is only a traffic jam away, and where a foodie can get decent fine dining or a killer fish taco."

Good. Very good. Clancy would appreciate some of the more unexpected stops on this tour. "And staying in LA kept you close to your dad."

"Is that one of your questions?"

Miller nodded.

"Like I mentioned, it took Dad a while to bounce back after Mom moved to Chicago. I wasn't going to leave him in LA all by himself."

But what of that cringe last night? When Miller had asked him about going into practice with his father. Clancy clearly loved his parents—he'd gone out of his way to be there for his father when he'd needed him—but some puzzle piece no longer fit. Before Miller could decide how to ask the question delicately, Clancy spoke.

"Why are we going to this next stop?"

Easy answer. "It's my favorite view while dining."

"Is it in a building with a giant needle on top?"

Miller chucked the napkin back at him. "Cheater. That's as good as asking if we're going to Seattle."

He shrugged, not looking the least bit chastened. "Are we?"

"No, and no more questions for you."

"You got anymore for me?"

Yes, but those could wait. "Are you enjoying yourself so far?" Miller asked instead.

Clancy snatched an entire cupcake and reclined in his seat, kicking his Chucks up on the table as he bit through the banana caramel decadence, humming contentedly.

Miller laughed. "I'll take that as a yes."

Chapter Four

JACKSON HOLE

Miller's only tour obligation was to attend each dinner. He'd blown right through that boundary yesterday with the impromptu picnic. And he'd known he'd do it again when they'd stepped off the plane last night in Jackson Hole, Wyoming. The LA boy beside him had glimpsed the snow-covered Tetons and begun bouncing on his toes. By the time Miller had returned to the hotel lobby from accompanying the luggage valet to their two-bedroom suite, he'd found Clancy at the lobby bar with a stack of activity brochures. There was a winter wonderland to see and experience in and around Grand Teton National Park. Miller remembered that sense of wonder, that excitement from the first time he'd visited here. It was unlike any place he'd ever seen, and he'd wanted to see it again, one last time. And Miller wanted to be there with Clancy as he experienced it the first time.

The day went as they'd planned for Clancy, Miller made sure of it. For himself, it was a roller coaster of sight-seeing and ducking out of view to heave. When he'd warned Clancy to go easy, in case of altitude sickness, Miller hadn't thought he'd be the one affected. It'd never given him fits before at higher elevations, but he'd been perfectly healthy those other times. Not so much anymore. But he'd soldiered through, doubling up on pain meds and cursing the anti-nausea pills that did little to settle his roiling stomach. Brief moments of reprieve had come in the form of Clancy-induced distraction—the surgeon's full-body shiver each time a wolf howled, his bushy brow furrowing as he observed a master craftsman carve a bear out of wood, his laughter as their sleigh sped among giant elk in the Park's National Elk Refuge.

By the time they returned to the hotel, however, not even Clancy's babbling recount of the day to his dad on the phone was enough to distract Miller from the world swaying around him. Sweat had gathered at his temples under his plaid skullcap, pots and pans clashed in his head, and his stomach was knotted worse than that time he'd eaten bad oysters. Take Clancy's hungover state from yesterday and multiply it by a hundred and Miller suspected that's about where he was right now.

He ditched his gloves in the hallway, dug his room key out of his pocket, and swiped it over the electronic lock. He pushed open the door and had to catch himself on the jamb to keep from falling through into the room.

Clancy's voice echoed from the far end of a darkening tunnel. "Dad, I gotta go." The next instant, he was there next to Miller, shoving a shoulder under his and throwing an arm around his waist.

"Hey, big guy. I got you. Steady now."

Clancy shifted them off the door, and it slammed shut, the sound a tower of plates crashing in Miller's head.

"I've been fighting all day not to go into doctor mode," Clancy said. "But if I ignore this any longer, I'll be compromising my oath."

"Bathroom," Miller croaked.

Clancy didn't question, just hustled them through Miller's bedroom to the attached ensuite bathroom. Miller's knees hit the marble floor a second before his stomach went for the final KO. He clutched the sides of the toilet bowl, heaving nothing but bile. The pain that shot through his throat made him retch more. Clancy was moving around him, and Miller didn't bother shooing him off, especially not when the nausea eased and he fell back into a body strong enough to hold his up. Clancy helped him out of his jacket and cap, and Miller craved the cool marble floor, despite his teeth-chattering. Clancy wrapped a robe around him first before laying him down, a rolled towel tucked under his head.

"Fuck, Miller. Do I need to call—"

"You are a doctor. It's just altitude sickness."

Soothed by Clancy's long fingers combing through his damp hair, he closed his eyes. He tried to blink them open again when the soft touch disappeared, but his lids were too heavy. The toilet flushed, water ran, and a cool, wet towel was laid against his neck.

Heaven.

A shadow fell over his face, a hand brushing back his

hair that was too long in the front. He opened his eyes and looked up at Clancy.

No, not Clancy. Dr. Rhodes.

Hell.

"I like the fanboy better."

Dr. Rhodes ignored him, shoving his sunglasses on top of his head and peering at him close-up. "This has happened before?"

No. "Yes."

"Are you telling me the truth?"

Nausea threatened again, but Miller didn't have the energy to force himself upright. He swallowed it down, wincing as razors of acid lanced this throat. "Some bedside manner," he said once he had his insides under control, relatively.

"There's really no time to dick around with my patients."

"In plastic surgery?"

Clancy's hand drifted from Miller's hair to his cheek. "Not exactly."

Miller closed his eyes against the assessing green gaze.

"You gonna be okay for a minute?" Clancy asked.

Miller wet his lips with the tip of his tongue. "Yeah, Doc."

Clancy's soothing touch disappeared, as did the bright vanity lights, *thank fuck.* The kitchen in Miller's head quieted, enough that he could hear Clancy on the phone in the main room.

"Ms. Thatcher, please."

Sloan.

Panic seized Miller. Maybe this wasn't just altitude sickness. He was supposed to have more time, but supposed to didn't mean much when there was a death sentence hanging over his head. If this was the end, he needed to talk to his best friend, one last time. Needed to beg for her forgiveness. Needed to tell her that he loved her, to be happy, and for fuck's sake, don't name the cannoli after him.

He tried to push himself up, but he was so weak, so tired.

"Please," he croaked, barely a whisper.

Darkness answered.

Clancy hung up with Sloan and tossed his phone on the dining table. He shucked off his outerwear, swapped his sunglasses out for his regular frames, and circled the dining bar into the kitchen to fill a glass with water. He wasn't completely buying her or Miller's claims that this was just altitude sickness, or that it'd happened before. Granted, all of Miller's symptoms were consistent with acute mountain sickness, but something was tickling Clancy's Spidey-senses.

On the flight out yesterday, Miller had intimated that Clancy was the one likely to get sick, cautioning him against eating too much. Miller hadn't spoken like he expected to get sick. Then again, maybe he'd been cautioning Clancy because of his own experience. And maybe Clancy's guilt was talking, making him think this was worse than simple altitude sickness.

He'd noticed something was wrong. He should have brought Miller back to the room instead of keeping them out all day. But Miller had insisted they keep going, and Grand Teton National Park had been like nothing Clancy had ever seen. Yes, he'd trudged through snow before in Chicago, but it was banked and blackened with sludge by sunup. Not fluffy and white, untouched in its natural habitat. And never had he seen elk roam, heard wolves howl, or seen a wrinkled old man, likewise in his natural habitat, use similar skills as Clancy's—a sculptor with a knife—to create art out of wood.

Clancy patted his pants pocket, feeling the carved block in one and the uncarved piece in the other. He dropped both off on the table, next to his phone, before heading back to Miller's bathroom with the glass of water. He quickened his pace when he heard the toilet flush and spied a big shadow straightening.

Miller was staggering around, tossing back a pill and leaning heavily on the vanity, struggling to hold himself up, when Clancy entered. "Hey, big guy, just a second." He set the glass on the vanity and scooted under Miller's shoulder. He flipped on the vanity light, needing to get a better look at his patient now that he had his glasses on. The sunglasses were prescription but shade, in this case, was not his friend. Neither was the sickly pallor and clammy feel of Miller's skin.

"Your wife says you're a big baby in the altitude," he said, trying to distract Miller from his cursory examination.

"Best friend," Miller said, voice barely a whisper. "Can't keep calling her my wife."

"But she is."

Miller winced and shot out an arm, slapping off the light. "Not anymore." He swayed, eyes fluttering, and gave Clancy more of his weight. "She loves Tyler. They're good together. Made a cannoli."

With his free hand, Clancy snatched the two pill bottles off the vanity and carried them with him into the bedroom where the curtains were open, letting in the waning rays of orange and red. He read the labels. A mild painkiller and an anti-nausea med frequently prescribed for motion sickness. Disorientation wasn't usually a side effect of either, but every patient's drug interaction profile was different.

He pocketed the bottles and shuffled Miller toward the bed. "Sit, Chef." Clancy regretted the slip immediately, his professional demeanor on overdrive, but Miller didn't seem to notice, plopping onto the bed without comment. Clancy fetched the water and handed it to him with an order to drink, then knelt to pull off Miller's boots and socks.

"I'm gonna miss her," Miller murmured above him.

"Because you're in love with her."

"No, I'm gay."

Clancy's hands froze where they were on Miller's calf, checking to see if his pant leg was dry. Clancy had suspected Miller was bi, like him—he hadn't missed the sparks between them, and he hadn't been able to shake the conversation with his mother—but he'd figured Miller and Sloan's relationship was more like his parents, once in love if not now. It seemed he'd figured wrong, not that he could or would ask Miller to clear things up in his current state.

Especially not when Miller singsonged, "But she was mine, and I was hers," above him.

Pants confirmed dry, Clancy stood and yanked the covers back for Miller to crawl in. "That's from *Game of Thrones*."

"Our favorite books." Shivering, Miller handed off the half-empty glass and stretched out, pulling the covers up and closing his eyes. "Doesn't matter now anyway. I'll be gone."

Gone from her life, Miller must mean, but surely not. They were best friends, for a long time Clancy was coming to understand. He didn't think that would change. Married or not, surely Sloan would always be in Miller's life. Clancy should get her back on the phone and have her tell Miller that so he'd feel better. If Clancy was going to do that, he needed to do it fast, before Miller fell sound asleep. He moved to stand, and Miller flailed a hand his direction. Clancy grabbed hold of it. He looked back at Miller, whose eyes were open and lucid. More so than they'd been since returning to the room. "I don't think I can eat tonight."

"It's fine, Miller."

"I'm sorry." He pushed up on one elbow. "Not what you paid for."

Clancy lowered Miller back down and brushed the hair off his forehead, a few strands of silver peeking through in the fractured light of dusk. "I heard wolves, saw elk, rode in a fucking sleigh as the snow fell. That's more than this LA boy could have hoped for."

Miller shook off his hand and turned his face away. "Not the point."

Clancy smiled, even as Miller's eyes closed and his breathing evened out in sleep. "It kinda is."

Miller woke and wondered where the Mack truck was that had hit him. *Flattened* was the only way to describe the pancaked feeling of his head and body, the utter heaviness of his limbs, and the lack of energy to peel himself off the superfine sheets.

Superfine sheets.

In his hotel room.

In Wyoming.

With Clancy. Who'd had to take care of him when a day of thin air had wreaked havoc on his already weak—dying—body.

Oh, there was the Mack truck.

He opened his eyes to darkness, shot through with moonlight, and he'd never been so happy to see a fucking ceiling fan in his life. The last thing he remembered was lying on the bathroom floor, afraid the darkness would be forever. No, wait, he remembered Clancy sitting on the side of the bed. Remembered apologizing for not being able to make tonight's meal.

Shit.

Miller twisted his head, checking the digital clock on

the bedside table. 10:30 p.m. Way past their seven o'clock reservation. He glanced toward the door that was ajar to the living area. From the other side, a dim firelight flickered, casting wavering shadows on the walls, out of sync with a steady scraping sound Miller couldn't place. Clancy was still awake out there.

Miller needed to get up. Go apologize again for missing dinner and go make sure his cover story was intact. It was just altitude sickness. Clancy didn't need to know it'd hit him harder because his body was preoccupied losing the battle to the cancer in his throat. The doctor might overreact; the stranger might tell someone. Neither were an acceptable outcome.

He pushed himself up, biting his lip against a grunt, and moved as quietly as he could to the bathroom. He didn't want to draw Clancy's attention just yet. The awful taste in his mouth and the pressure on his bladder demanded a few minutes of privacy first. The latter handled, he flipped on the vanity light to take care of the former and recoiled at his reflection in the mirror. He looked like he'd been hit by a Mack truck—pale skin, bags under his eyes, and the hair atop his head a curly tangled mess. He cursed Sloan again for talking him into buzzing only the sides and leaving the top long.

Sloan. He'd wanted to tell her...

He hurried through the rest of his washup, changed into a clean pair of sweats and a tee, and snagged his phone from the charger where Clancy must have plugged it in. He expected a phone full of messages but there was only one, from Sloan. **Text me when you're awake.** Clancy must have kept her updated.

Awake, he texted her.

Are you okay? came right back.

I'm good.

Doc didn't seem to think so.

Exactly how much had Clancy told her? **Altitude got a hold of me.**

That's new.

Even over text, he could sense the lawyer setting her trap. **We're old now, dear.**

The middle finger emoji appeared. He returned the sentiment with the poop one.

When she didn't immediately respond, he second-guessed his sarcastic tone. She was worried about him, and before, when he'd thought he wouldn't get a chance to say a proper goodbye, he'd felt regret like never before. **Love you**, he texted back. **And I feel better, promise.**

No delay this time. **Love you too. Text me tomorrow.**

Yes, Mom. He couldn't help it.

Fuck you. And neither could she. It's how they'd always been.

He smiled, turning the phone over and leaving it face-down on the dresser. A cold draft tickled his ankles and arms, and he backtracked to his luggage for a sweatshirt and grabbed his skullcap off the dresser, yanking it down over his ridiculous hair. By the time he got back to the door, he heard murmured voices outside, the distinctive clink of plates and cutlery, and then the suite door clicking shut. The breeze was no longer just cold. On it traveled the aromas of fresh bread and soup, and Miller's stomach unexpectedly rumbled.

He stepped into the living area and found it rearranged—the bigger pieces of furniture pushed back, a rolling dining table set up in front of the fireplace, and two dining chairs situated catty-corner so they both had a view out the open patio doors. "What's this?"

Clancy spun where he stood, barefoot, leaning against the patio doorjamb. "We're a few floors above the restaurant. Same view, yeah?"

"Yeah," Miller answered, but his eyes quickly strayed from the moonlit view of the Tetons and the Valley floor to the stunning young doctor, dressed down in his jeans from yesterday and an LA Rams hoodie, his hands fidgeting with something in the front pocket. What was he nervous about? Something Miller had said? Going into doctor mode? Missing the dinner? The initial awkwardness from before their first meal began to creep back in, and Miller, tired and increasingly hungry, swatted it away with sarcasm. Since he was on a roll with that tonight. "Were you even born before the Rams left LA?"

Clancy crossed his arms and ducked his chin, glasses sliding down to the end of his narrow nose, his lips pressed into a stern line beneath it. "They're back now. That's all that matters!"

"I don't know him, but I feel like you're mimicking your father."

Clancy dropped the exaggerated outrage and pushed

his glasses back up his nose, grinning. "Because I totally am."

They both laughed, and the tension eased, making more room for the view, human and landscape. And for the smell. Miller's stomach gave another interested rumble.

"You up for some food?" Clancy gestured to the table. "I ordered some things that should be easy on your stomach, relatively. Bison barley soup, fresh bread, pasta with rabbit sugo. The bison will be a first for me, and the carbs will help you with the altitude sickness."

Sounded like he was buying that explanation or at least going with it. The last bit of tension faded and Miller collapsed into the chair closest to the fire. "Will dessert help too?"

Clancy claimed the other chair and started pulling lids off plates. "I don't know, but I also don't know the point of a meal without it."

Miller bumped his shoulder. "You might be all right, Doc."

He tried a few bites of the bread first, sinking his teeth into the thick texture of the country-style levain. For Miller, it was second only to New England's light and fluffy Portuguese-style sweet bread as far as mouth feel went. And this levain had a touch of sweetness too, honey in its making, that was a nice complement to the hearty wheat. And perfect for dipping. He broke off a piece and dunked it in the soup, testing that on his stomach. When he was sure a revolt wasn't in the making, he traded bread for spoon and was halfway through his own bowl before glancing over to find Clancy done with his.

"I take it you liked the bison?"

Guilty eyes shot up. "Sorry, I kind of got lost in it and my manners went poof."

"That's a compliment any chef would want to hear."

"It's just so much better than the vegetable beef soup I'm used to in hospital cafeterias."

"Shh!" Miller said, finger over his lips. "Let us never speak of such heresy again."

Clancy shrugged. "It's safer than the mystery meat."

Miller willed the images of graying meat away. "I'm thinking Campbell's in a pop-top can, as much as it pains me to say, is safer than both those options."

"Too right," Clancy said with a nod. "And this soup was a major step up from either version."

"How so?" He liked hearing how Clancy's foodie descriptions varied from his own more technical analysis.

Clancy swiped his bowl with a hunk of bread and popped it in his mouth, chewing and contemplating. "No one ingredient steals the show, but it's also not a mush like the hospital stuff. The barley gives it texture, the vegetables crunch and flavor, the bison is meaty, but not overly so, and not wild like I expected. Not sure about the peas, though."

Miller chuckled, then slurped his last spoonful, really concentrating on the flavors. "Bison isn't as fatty as cow, so you get more of the beef flavor without the grease. It's clean, so to speak, but expensive, so it's not used as often. As for the broth, it's pretty simple. Carrots, onions, and celery lend flavor to the beef stock, as does the bison itself. Basic seasonings—garlic, parsley, a splash of red wine vinegar, salt and pepper. Nothing fancy, just extremely well-balanced."

"And the peas?"

"The peas are there to look pretty." He leaned forward, dropping his voice to a conspiratorial whisper. "It's blasphemy for a chef to say, but I'm of the mind they don't serve much purpose once you pass toddler."

Clancy hooted with laugher.

"Tell you another secret," Miller said. "This is actually my second favorite view." He cast his gaze out the window, as he spun pappardelle pasta around his fork. "The place I wanted to go inside the park was closed for the season."

"How many times have you been here?"

"Only one other time, but it's special, for more than just the view." Miller reached up and pulled the cap off his head. "Got my first piece of plaid here."

"You mean they didn't wrap you in plaid the day you were born?"

Miller shoved his shoulder. "Hardly, my mom fucking hates it." He set the cap on the table and took another bite before continuing. "But being from the Southeast, on the coast, Sloan and I had no idea what cold really was until we stopped here on our way out to California."

"You drove cross-country? Was that when you moved out?"

He nodded. "It was the first time either of us had had a break in ten years, so we made a vacation out of it. Stopped in Nashville for the music and chicken, in Kansas City for the steak, then came up here for the national parks. It was September, so we didn't expect it to be so cold, but winter came early that year." He ran a hand over his top mop. "I had a full buzz cut back then, and the steam was coming off my head." Sloan had teased him mercilessly about being his own heat source. Finally, he'd stopped into the hotel gift shop for some sort of hat, desperate to keep the heat in. "The plaid called to me, what can I say."

"And thus the addiction was born." Clancy cracked up laughing. "It's a great story. And not at all what I expected."

Seemed to be a trend whenever Miller visited here. But even with the cold then, and the nausea now, both trips were turning out okay.

Clancy waved a hand at the view, the room, and the spread in front of them. And at the plaid cap. "I'm not complaining about any of it."

Neither of them complained about the rabbit sugo either. It took them a while to get through it, between the debate over how to eat pasta and another flavor breakdown, but it was enjoyable company, easy discussion, and Miller felt better than he had all day.

Until Clancy got up to retrieve the dessert from the fridge and Miller spotted the scalpel on a nearby table. Had he been that bad off before? "Did you think you were going to have to do surgery?" he asked with a nod toward the knife.

"On you, no." Clancy set down the two plates of cheesecake and fished something out of the front pocket of his hoodie. "And if you ever do meet my father, please don't tell him I used my graduation scalpels for this." He held out his hand, waiting for Miller to do the same, then dropped a carved block of wood into Miller's palm.

Carved in the shape of a wolf. No, not a wolf exactly. A dire wolf, with a mane like scales and a mouth full of fearsome teeth. The detail was amazing. "You made this?"

Clancy nodded. "House Stark's sigil, right?"

Another memory from earlier came floating back to Miller. Him sitting on the edge of the bed, rambling about losing Sloan, while Clancy removed his shoes and got him settled. He'd spilled more than he should to a guy he hardly knew. His and Sloan's relationship was complicated; not everyone got it. Maybe Clancy would, but with his stomach settled and happy, Miller didn't want to bring the food or topic back up. Instead, he ran his fingers over the intricate carving. Clancy had only just today seen the wood carving demonstration, and yet, it wasn't a wholly unfamiliar skill. "You'll make a hell of a plastic surgeon." Having glanced back up, Miller didn't miss Clancy's seemingly instinctive cringe. "There's that face again."

Clancy covered his face with his hands. "I have no talent for bullshit."

"That's not a bad thing. Don't be so hard on yourself." Miller set the carving on the table.

Clancy picked it right up, turning it over and over in his hands. "Honestly," he started, more quietly, "I don't ever remember choosing to be a doctor. My dad put me in kiddie scrubs for third grade picture day and that was it. I was always going to be a doctor."

"You don't want to be?"

"No, I want to be. I love it." Clancy's voice was a study

in contradictions. Miller believed that he did want to be a doctor, but the "but" was very loud. "And growing up, I always wanted to work with my dad." And louder still.

"But now?" Miller prompted.

Clancy set the carving back on the table and guilt of a different sort drifted through his eyes. "I'm not sure I want to do plastic surgery anymore."

"It's not all *Nip/Tuck* level bad, is it?"

Clancy chuckled, and Miller was glad for it. "Not at all. There's a lot of good in it, actually. I spent most of my residency specializing in reconstructive surgery, working with cancer patients. Dad's cool with me keeping up some of that work in private practice and he set me up to work on a big cancer benefit in the spring."

Miller fought not to squirm in his chair.

Clancy, lost in a memory, thankfully didn't seem to notice. "But working with cancer survivors, hearing their stories and what they go through, years of hell, I can't help but wonder if I could help more earlier. Maybe I could save them some of those hellish years. I've kept up a volunteer rotation on the oncology ward, broader than just plastics, learning and helping out as I can. It was my favorite rotation during med school."

Miller couldn't stand it any longer. He was sure the second Clancy glanced his way again, he'd see the truth in his eyes—that Miller was looking at the same hell in his future and had opted for a much shorter one instead. Standing, he avoided the quick whip of Clancy's gaze and skirted out between their chairs. "Cheesecake requires coffee," he said, heading toward the kitchen. Then diverted the conversation back to Clancy's decision, not his. "If you like oncology better, why are you going into practice with your dad?"

"Because it's what's expected, just like being a doctor was."

Miller finished filling coffee mugs and returned to the table. "I get it." Oh did he get it. He gathered huckleberries and cheesecake on the end of his fork and savored the velvety sweet bite and burst of tart flavor, before he spoke a more sour notion, one he'd only previously discussed with Sloan and his other best friend, Greg. But this Clancy would definitely understand, and if Miller could save him from making the mistakes he had, all the better. "Even before I opened my own place, other chefs and staff were talking about the fine dining restaurant I'd open."

"It's not the restaurant you wanted?"

Miller shrugged. "Honestly, I don't know. Like you, I don't remember making a choice. That's just the way it was going to be."

Clancy raised his mug, grim understanding on his fire-lit face. "Expectations, tough to live up to."

Miller clinked back in downtrodden solidarity. "Nothing great about them."

Chapter Five

CHICAGO

The snow was definitely not as fresh here in Chicago as it had been in Wyoming, but even mounded on the roadside and caked in grimy sludge, it made Clancy smile. Being back in the town he considered his second home always did. He'd never met friendlier people, never eaten better pizza, and never found a place that was more fitting for his social, jet-setting mother. Given his connection to here, Clancy hadn't expected Chicago to be on the tour. Silly of him. The Chicago food scene was ever expanding and finally getting the recognition it deserved. But the fact his mother hadn't mentioned it, hadn't even called him last night after they'd arrived at Midway and made their way to the hotel, had him looking around every corner, expecting her to pop out at any moment.

"You're all smiley but jumpy at the same time," Miller observed beside him, correctly.

Clancy glanced over at the too-handsome gentleman in the town car with him. Beard trimmed, blue eyes bright, the gold in them fetching, and color back in his cheeks, Miller looked a million times better than he had the night before last. They'd delayed their flight out of Jackson Hole yesterday until early evening, giving Miller more time to recover and Clancy time to buy plaid, Teton-themed gifts for everyone. They'd even snuck in a late lunch in the restaurant, and Miller had been right—the view was fucking spectacular, the snow-covered mountains and valley floor glistening under the bright midday sun. Then today, Clancy had woken early and gotten a jump start on his Chicago to-do list while Miller had slept in. Well-rested and altitude sickness passed, Miller seemed back to his usual self, dressed in the pink plaid jacket, a starched white shirt and dark jeans, ready for their next meal out. Looking like that, Clancy sure would like to make a meal of—

Mental brakes!

Wait, was he supposed to slide into a skid? Because yes, he'd skid into—

BRAKES!

"Hey, Doc." Miller's concerned voice supplied the roadblocks his own mind failed to. "You with me?"

"Just expecting my mom to appear out of nowhere."

Miller laughed. "It's a couple months past Halloween, and I wasn't under the impression she's a witch."

"She's definitely more the eccentric fairy godmother sort, kind of like Carol Kane in *Scrooged*, but with better clothes and an Amex Black Card. The fact she hasn't shown up yet should worry us both."

Miller laughed harder, and the deepening grooves at the corners of his eyes were vying for most attractive feature, though the beard and top mop of curls he'd woefully tamed into submission were all duking it out for spots on the medal stand. "You could have gone over there today."

"They had a trip planned for the holidays. I didn't want to interrupt, if she and Robert are even still in town. And I had other stops to make today."

"Such as?"

Clancy crossed his legs toward Miller and pushed his glasses up his nose. "I have this routine anytime I come to Chicago. Places I have to see, things I have to do, foods I have to eat."

"Of course you do."

"Hey!" He shoved Miller's shoulder playfully. "We don't have Garrett's fresh-tossed cheddar cheese and caramel popcorn in LA."

Miller shifted in his seat, likewise crossing a leg toward Clancy, and the back seat of the car seemed to shrink. "You can buy giant bags of multi-flavor popcorn at Costco."

"Not the same as Garrett's."

"Okay, I'll take your word for it," Miller said with a smile. "So, did you eat and visit everything you wanted today?"

"I've still got pizza and a hot beef sandwich on my list."

"You can knock those out tomorrow while I'm in meetings."

"So then, those aren't on the menu tonight?"

"I see what you did there." Miller tapped his foot against Clancy's. So close, it was all Clancy could do not to tap back. "You haven't figured out where we're going for dinner?"

"Only that we're slowing down way too early to be near Alinea." Granted by *slowing down*, it wasn't much slower than the usual rush hour crawl, but the five percent of his brain that hadn't been mooning over the handsome man next to him had noticed the town car cutting through traffic toward the curb after they'd just crossed into Gold Coast. "Not that I'd mind going there again."

"I got that from our garden walk the other night."

"Sorry." Clancy ducked his chin. "The foodie gets excited by the creativity."

"Hey." Miller tapped his toe again and waited for him to look up. "I want you to get excited about that. Isn't that why you're on this trip?"

Yes, it'd started that way but after five days with Miller, it wasn't the only reason for Clancy now. And it wasn't just Miller's handsome mug. Clancy enjoyed his company, even Monday night, over room service, conversation, and the view. He also wanted Miller to understand he'd enjoyed that soup and pasta at dinner, and the bison pastrami sandwich he'd had at lunch, as much as he'd enjoyed TFL's oysters and pearls.

"I know not every restaurant on this tour—no other restaurant, period—is going to be The French Laundry or Alinea."

"I know," Miller said, smile dimming. "Those expectations we talked about." His mind was clearly back there with him Monday night.

"Yes, but I wouldn't want them to be," Clancy said,

giving in and bumping Miller's foot. "A juicy, simple burger can be just as creative as molecular gastronomy, as long as it's done well."

Miller's face lit up. "Glad to hear you say that."

And made Clancy's stomach rumble on multiple accounts, two competing hungers, but the food one was barreling through the roadblocks now. "We're going to a burger joint?"

"Not yet."

Now Clancy was intrigued, though it appeared he was out of time for guesses. The car pulled into a turnoff and came to stop.

"Not a burger joint," Miller said, "But this place does simple extremely well." He shot a smile over his shoulder as he stepped out.

Clancy followed and saw the sign as he straightened.

Morton's The Steakhouse.

Clancy mentally face-palmed himself, not wanting to walk in with an actual red mark on his forehead. Morton's was a Chicago-born institution.

"No one does a steak better," Miller said by his side. "And your mom said you'd never eaten here."

"Let's change that."

The server slid a sizzling plate with a massive tomahawk steak on it in front of Clancy, and Miller wished he'd had his camera ready. The doctor's eyes grew round as saucers, then narrowed, brows snapping together above them.

Granted, Clancy had picked the monster steak from the meat cart an hour ago, one of the great vestiges of Morton's, but that had been before the fresh baked onion loaf, the jumbo shrimp cocktail, and the wedge salad smothered in Roquefort dressing. Miller had no idea where Clancy was putting it all in that trim tight body, and by the inquisitive look on his face, Clancy was trying to solve the same problem. He'd tackle it and succeed, no doubt.

Miller's filet mignon was a pebble in comparison, but he didn't have to think too hard on how to attack it. He picked up his fork and steak knife, about to cut into it, when the sommelier appeared beside their corner booth. White towel over his arm, the sharply suited man held a wine bottle in one hand and a corkscrew in the other.

He shifted the bottle to a cradle hold and presented it to Miller. The bottle's plain white label with simple black and green lettering was nothing fancy, but the wine inside was complex and special, Miller's favorite. "2004 Ridge Monte Bello," the somm said.

Across the table, Clancy's silverware clattered to the plate. Not that he noticed, clapping gleefully as he was.

The somm smiled. "Have you had this wine before, sir?"

"Clancy, please," he said. "And no. This one is new to me, but I know it's Miller's favorite."

The somm looked back to Miller for approval, and at his nod, began slicing through the foil around the bottle's neck. "You'll be tasting, Chef?"

"You want to do the honors?" Miller offered Clancy.

Color flooded Clancy's cheeks, making him look all the

more stunning in his black turtleneck and houndstooth sport coat. "Sure, if you think..." His words faded into a shy smile.

"I think you'll know well enough," Miller said with a wink. And honestly, he had little worries, given the storage standards at an establishment like this.

The somm poured a splash into Clancy's glass. "It's a Bordeaux-style blend. One of the best we have domestically. It's very special," the somm said, though by the way he was checking Clancy out, he was thinking more along the lines of how special his guest was. Miller couldn't argue. Clancy tasted the wine and his eyelids fluttered closed, a smile turning up both corners of his mouth.

"You like?" the somm asked.

Clancy opened his eyes, his pupils large, the green irises dark. "I do."

The way the somm asked his question, the way Clancy responded to it, their exchange could have been about the wine or the somm. The latter prospect sent a jagged bolt of jealousy ripping through Miller. Did the somm not even consider that he and Clancy might have been on a date? Is that not what this looked like?

But it wasn't a date, regardless of whether Miller might have wanted it to be. Circumstances what they were, if Clancy wanted to flirt with the admittedly cute sommelier, a man closer to his own age and without a death sentence hanging over his head, Miller had no cause to stop him. Hell, he should be encouraging Clancy to go for it.

The somm filled their glasses and placed the bottle and cork on the silver coaster on the table. "Chef, Clancy"—his dark-eyed gaze lingered on the good doctor—"if you need anything else, please let me or your server know." The somm departed with a furtive last glance at Clancy.

Miller picked up his glass and held it under his nose. "I bet he slips you his number before the night's over."

Clancy's bewildered stare made him laugh out loud. "What?"

"He was flirting with you, or did you miss that?" Miller sipped his wine. Almost as delicious as Clancy's helpless flailing.

He jutted his big knife at the huge hunk of sizzling meat. "There was steak." Then at the glasses. "And wine. I..." He dropped his fist to the table, still holding the knife. "I kind of failed to notice."

Clancy's admission went a long way toward mending the earlier tear of jealousy. Miller picked up his own knife and fork again and cut his steak into manageable pieces. The pain meds were doing their job, none of the earlier courses bothering his throat, but he couldn't be too careful. "It really has been that long, huh?" he asked.

"Yeah, it has. Stinky cheese date in med school might have been the last proper one I went on," Clancy answered. He paused to pop a bite of steak into his mouth and chew, and the look of pure pleasure on his face did wicked things to Miller's body under the table. "Forget dating during residency."

"Well, you should have time again, going into private practice. Or is the somm not your type?"

Clancy fumbled his knife, and even in Morton's low lights, his face flamed bright pink.

"Fuck, Clancy, I'm sorry," he said, voice lowered. "I assumed from our conversation the other night you were out."

"I am. Your assumption there was right. But as far as guys go, he's not my type."

Intrigued, Miller put down his knife and fork and reached for his wine again. "What is your type?"

Clancy was near-on lobster red, and his eyes bounced all over the place. "I like guys who are bigger." His eyes flickered to Miller, then zoomed away again. "Bears," he mumbled low.

Jealousy left the building, replaced by something far more dangerous. Miller reverted to safer topics. "What do you think of it here?" he asked, gesturing at their surroundings.

Clancy let out a huge breath and they both laughed, tension deflating. Once his color returned to normal, he met Miller's gaze and smiled. "The speakeasy vibe—" he lowered his voice "—or is that leftover mobster?—is super cool."

"It's definitely a place with character, a voice, that's been a successful brand for decades now. Others try to replicate it, but this is the original."

"And it's not old and stuffy or cold and ultramodern. It's elegant—white tablecloths, chandeliers, fine china—but in a warm, welcoming way." He scooted around on the tucked leather booth. "It's comfortable. Like I could sit here and nurse my wine all night."

"That's exactly what I used to do. Whenever I'd come into town, I'd get here toward the end of service and enjoy a beer or wine with an onion roll and whatever cut of steak the kitchen had left." He gestured with his knife to Clancy's tomahawk. "That one done to your liking?"

"It's perfect. Simple like you said, but cooked to order and the flavor of the beef really shines."

"The maître d'hôtel butter is the key." Miller pointed at the extra dish of it he'd asked the kitchen to bring out. He knifed off another pat and dropped it on the end of the steak Clancy hadn't reached yet. Then, what the hell, added another to his own steak. After his scare in Wyoming, Miller would be damned if he didn't enjoy all his favorites one last time. Wasn't that the point of this tour, at least for him?

"Again, super simple," he said. "Chopped parsley, a squeeze of lemon juice, salt and pepper. Mix, roll, chill. It's one of the first things I learned to make. Sloan made me keep a log of it in the fridge."

Clancy took another bite and nodded his agreement. After he chewed and swallowed, he set his silverware down in favor of more wine. By the furrow of his brow, perhaps he was recalculating where the remaining half steak was going to fit. "Can I ask you something, about assumptions I made, and something you said the other night in Jackson Hole?"

Or not. Miller could guess where this was headed. He'd stepped right into it; set it up even, with his comment about Sloan tonight and his hazy altitude-induced ramblings. He still wasn't one hundred percent sold on telling someone he'd only just met about the most complicated relationship in his life, but they had a week and a half to go still. An explanation would be required at some point. No sense continuing to beat around the bush.

"Me and Sloan," he ventured. "You're trying to square that with me saying I'm gay the other night?"

Clancy nodded. "Did you mean bi? I know not everyone's comfortable claiming that label, and I'm not judging—"

"I'm gay, Clancy."

Adorably confused, Clancy clutched his wineglass stem with both hands and stared into the dark red liquid like it held all the answers.

But that was Miller, not the wine. "Sloan's my best friend," he explained. "She has been since we were teens and I found her in the town park, bruised and beaten by her new stepdad."

Clancy threw up a hand. "Whoa, whoa, whoa, HIPAA-training activated! Should you be telling me this?"

Miller appreciated the caution, but it was unnecessary in this case. "It's fine. She's on the pro bono committee at her firm and does a ton of volunteer work with battered spouses and children. She'll tell her story to anyone who will listen because, as she says, it's evidence that happy endings are out there for survivors."

And she'd survived a hell of a lot. He'd been seventeen, Sloan fifteen, when he'd found her both crying and spitting mad that rainy, muggy spring night. He knew who she was, they were in the same county high school, but two grades apart, they didn't run in the same circles. Still, he'd sat on the swing farthest from hers, company if she wanted it, protection if whomever had done that to the tiny, beautiful girl came back. Several hours later, she'd moved to the swing next to his and told him everything. His life had changed forever, for the better.

He took another long swallow of wine, washing away the memories of that night. "I promised her I'd do whatever I had to to protect her, which a year later turned out to be marrying her so we could leave town. I had to get her out of that house and away from him."

"How'd your family take that?"

"They scraped together every penny we had, which wasn't much for a brick layer and teacher with four kids, but they did what they could. They understood. Ma had had Sloan in her English class for two years. She'd seen the change before and after her mother remarried."

A hand slid across the table, grasping his forearm. Miller glanced up and immediately understood why the man across from him had become a doctor. Sincerity and compassion poured out of his eyes.

"I'm sorry, Miller."

He slid his arm out from under Clancy's hand and picked up his silverware again. "Don't be. We had an incredible life."

"Why do you make it sound like it's ending?"

Miller almost choked on the piece of steak he'd just swallowed. The truth of his condition was more than he'd intended to share. That was not information for public consumption, especially not for Clancy, who was here to enjoy himself, not care for a patient. One night of that was more than enough.

"Between you and Sloan," Clancy added, and Miller's

panic receded, slightly. The good doctor was sincere and compassionate but also smart and perceptive.

"She found the love of her life," Miller answered. "The business partner of our other best friend, ironically."

"Ouch," he said, features pinched.

"It's not so bad. Tyler's a good man, and she's happy. That's all I've ever wanted for her."

"And you haven't found yours yet?"

Miller popped in his last bite of steak and looked across the table at Clancy, who'd tilted his head slightly.

"My what?" Miller asked.

"The love of your life."

Miller couldn't hold his gaze, turning his focus to the bustling dining room instead. Anywhere but at the possibilities he couldn't consider.

"Have you not had a relationship in twenty years?" Clancy asked.

The misread of his reaction made it easier to respond. "I've had partners, so had she, but nothing serious. Neither of us had ever found anyone we liked being around more than each other."

"Until Tyler."

Miller nodded.

"You also mentioned a cannoli the other night?"

Miller didn't hold back his laugh this time. "They're expecting. The baby was conceived when we were all in Italy at a conference a few months back."

Clancy laughed with him, then sobered. "So you're getting a divorce? That's why you talk like it's ending?

Why she lives in San Francisco and you're selling the house?"

Miller's hand shook where it lay over the base of his wineglass, two fingers parted on either side. Even though it was December, he could still see the tan line where his wedding band used to be. "I signed the papers before we left."

A hand slid over his, pale and long-fingered. "I'm sorry," Clancy whispered, his voice as warm as his hand.

"Nothing to be sorry for. I'm happy for her." So very happy, but that part of his life ending was still a blow. Two of three.

Clancy squeezed his hand, thumb running along the side of his. "I'm sure you are. You only want the best for your best friend. But that doesn't make it hurt any less, does it?"

No, but his hand on Miller's did, more than it should.

With Miller out at meetings Thursday morning, Clancy had scheduled a call with the benefit organizers. They'd been going back and forth all week over email and he'd wanted to put voices to signature blocks. He'd also wanted to drill down on how he could be most helpful. The call had gone so well Clancy was practically vibrating afterward, truly excited for the first time to get back to work soon. Or at least to this aspect of it.

The organizers were looking to him for a list of local

physicians to invite, those practicing in clinical oncology and in reconstructive surgery. Clancy had jotted down names as they'd talked, including his oncology and plastics attendings. But the part that had really excited Clancy was the prospect of reaching out to survivors too, inviting them to attend and share their stories. He hadn't stopped thinking about the possibilities in the hour since the call. About the amazing, brave patients who'd shaped his life the past decade.

The single mom who worked two day jobs and put herself through law school at night so she could provide for her kids. Clancy had met her the first day of his oncology rotation. Earlier this fall, she'd been featured on the local news, helping to cut the ribbon for a new affordable housing project in LA.

The athlete who'd taken up writing as a way to pass the time during chemo treatments that kept her confined to a chair. Clancy would sneak off between rounds to sit and listen to her spin tales. She'd recently sent him her latest published novel. There'd been a Post-It note marking the cameo appearance by sexy Doctor Rhodes who looked absolutely nothing like Clancy. He'd laughed about it for days.

The double mastectomy patient who'd cried when she'd put on her favorite dress again after her reconstructive surgery, and it had fit.

The patient Clancy wanted there most, however, wouldn't be. She'd lost her battle, but he'd found her family's contact information. He just had to figure out how not to tell them she was the reason he'd gone into plastics, why he was going into private practice with his dad. He hoped like hell they wouldn't be disappointed.

That none of his former patients would be.

His phone rang, his dad's picture filling the screen. Clancy didn't want to disappoint him either.

He brought the phone to his ear and traffic noise blasted his eardrum—morning rush hour in LA—and he kicked down the phone's volume. "Hey, Dad," he said, increasing the volume of his own voice. "What's for breakfast this morning?"

His dad was an avid food truck fan, often hitting more than one on his way into the office. "One-stop shopping this morning. Mexican coffee and an egg and chorizo burrito."

Clancy's stomach grumbled, reminding him that he had to leave the hotel room soon and brave the falling snow if he wanted to hit the rest of his to-eat list today.

"How's the trip going?" Alan asked. "You haven't updated me. Tell me where and what you've eaten since we talked."

Thus began a twenty-minute play-by-play, peppered with *oohs, ahhs* and jealous curses from Alan, as Clancy raved about Jackson Hole and Morton's. He tried guessing future stops—New York had to be on the list. Not Per Se, though, as they'd hit TFL already. Maybe Le Bernardin, but after the picnic and their last two stops, Clancy guessed something funkier, more low-key, like Momofuku, or a farm-to-table place like Blue Hill. Alan wouldn't give him any clues. Judging by the changing background noises, Clancy's guessing carried his father off the sidewalk, up the stairs, and into the office. Lots of *good mornings* from what sounded like a packed waiting room. The practice's receptionist, Andrea, confirmed as much, telling Alan he had three patients waiting already.

A door whooshed and the waiting room noise faded. "I can't wait for you to start here, son. We desperately need the backup."

"That's a good problem to have," Clancy said, even as his stomach sank.

No matter what he'd told Miller, he couldn't change his career path at this late date. He couldn't throw away five years of residency and disrupt his father's practice. Scenarios ran through his head. His dad, furious and left in the lurch. His dad, sad and disappointed. His dad, smiling and encouraging him to go for his dreams. He dismissed the first one right away. Not his dad. The second Alan would probably feel, but he'd never let Clancy see it, just like he'd never let Miranda see it when she'd left. He'd only show Clancy the third, and he'd mean it too. But could Clancy live with himself knowing he'd caused the second?

"It'll be good to have you here," his dad said, the words and smile in his voice only driving home the point harder.

"I'm looking forward to it." Clancy hoped the half of him that was excited—that loved the idea of working with his dad and that couldn't wait to do more work for the benefit—was enough to cover up the doubting half.

In any event, Alan didn't have time to question it, Andrea hurrying him off the line and to his appointments. "I'll call you on Christmas! Love you!"

"Love you too, Dad!"

Clancy ended the call, his earlier upbeat mood now as gray as the sky outside. Food. Food would make him feel better, or at least stop his stomach from grumbling.

Bundled up, he headed for Portillo's first and grabbed a hot beef sandwich, the peppers and gravy chasing away the winter chill that had penetrated his multiple layers of clothing. Old Man Winter won again, however, after a stroll down the Magnificent Mile. It was worth it to see the famous street and bridges decked out for the holidays. When he could no longer feel the end of his nose, he ducked into a hip, little sushi bar with an art deco feel. Sushi was another can't miss for him in Chicago, the fish always top-notch, something that had surprised him the first time he'd visited. Hot tea and an excellent sashimi plate later, he was warm enough to head back to the hotel. He decided on The Aviary for dinner—great cocktails and his sort-of-Alinea fix—but he needed to change into something nicer than jeans and a Shark Week tee.

If Miller was back from his meetings, Clancy would invite him to join. Last night still weighed on Clancy's mind. While they'd gotten on with dinner after the heavier turn, thanks in no small part to a sinful chocolate lava cake, Clancy had tossed and turned all night, unable to get Miller's lonely, defeated voice out of his head. There was no evidence Sloan's friendship would waver, marriage or not, but it was still a major change in Miller's life. An unknown he hadn't thought about for twenty-plus years. He needed a friend, especially now. The holidays could make anyone lonely, even in a room full of people. Clancy had seen it time and again during his rotations, the hospital beds more full and their losses more numerous between Thanksgiving and New Year's.

Clancy wanted to be a friend to Miller. Not because he was a famous chef and they had a love of food in common. Not because he was hot in the burly way that was totally Clancy's type. But because Miller was a good man. What he'd done for Sloan was remarkable, as was the patience and kindness he'd shown to him so far. Miller was teaching him more about food every day, sharing his time and knowledge, and filling a friend void that Clancy suffered too, having let so many relationships wither due to school and work. Yes, Clancy's parents had financed the tour, but Miller never made it about that. So if Clancy wanted to invite his new friend out for a drink, or go grab a pizza...

Hmm, pizza.

He was so caught up in his daydream about cornmeal-dusted deep-dish crust covered in mozzarella, Italian sausage, pepperoni and tomato sauce, that he was halfway across the hotel lobby when Miller appeared in front of him.

"Hey, Doc, didn't hear me call from the bar?" He nodded to the corner of the lobby bar where a half drunk Negroni set in front of an empty stool.

"Sorry 'bout that." Clancy pushed back his hoodie. "Was daydreaming about dinner."

"Yeah? What's on the menu?" Miller strolled back to the bar, and Clancy followed, admiring his ass in another pair of snug jeans, Clancy's eyes drawn right to it by the two-seam back flap of Miller's checkered sport coat.

"Hot beef sandwich?" Miller guessed, then he guzzled the rest of his drink.

Clancy righted his gaze just in time. "Had that for lunch. And some sushi. I was thinking The Aviary for dinner, but then I thought of pizza."

"And it was all over?"

"All over. Last thing on my list."

"Mind if I join you?"

Clancy smiled. "I was hoping you'd be back so I could invite you."

"Sounds like a plan." Miller pulled a twenty out of his wallet and tucked it under his glass. "Just need to go up and grab my overcoat."

And bonus, Clancy didn't have to change now. "How were your meetings?" he asked, as they rode the elevator up.

"Good," Miller answered distractedly, texting someone on his phone.

"Restaurant related?"

He pocketed the phone. "Trying to get a scoop out of me, Dr. Rhodes?"

Clancy shrugged. "What if I am?"

Miller laughed but didn't answer, asking instead, "Where's your favorite place for Chicago pizza?"

"I'm a traditionalist. Lou Malnati's." Since his mother had moved to Chicago, he'd spent each trip working down the best-pizza-in-Chicago list. He kept coming back to Malnati's.

"That the place with the super buttery crust?"

"They actually trademarked *Buttercrust.*" He rambled

on about his favorite pizza place all the way down the hotel's long hallway. He paused to inhale as they turned the corner toward their suite, and Miller jumped in.

"You know," he said, "your mom didn't have to put us up in all the fanciest places and suites. This had to cost a mint."

Clancy had wondered how long it'd take Miller to remark on their lodgings, especially after he'd learned about Miller's upbringing. But there was a good explanation for the premium hotels on this trip. "Easier to get bookings," he told Miller. "Higher-end places hold the top suites for celebrities and for concierge companies like Mom's. And this time of year, the cheap rooms are sold out."

"I guess that makes sense." Miller beat him to the door and pulled out his key card.

Clancy put a hand on his arm. "I think you need this vacation as much as I do, but if the lodgings or the plane make you uncomfortable, tell me. We'll make other arrangements."

Miller's eyes locked with his, held, and that spark of heat flared again between them. Standing this close, Clancy could almost feel the warmth of it. Could swear there was a growl in Miller's "Thanks, Doc," before he stepped back, swiped his card, and pushed the door open.

Clancy didn't have a chance to reply, to try and snatch the moment back, because he was too busy trying to lift his jaw off the floor.

Christmas had exploded all over their suite. A decorated Christmas tree stood in the corner nook between the windows overlooking Navy Pier. Lights and garlands were strung over the fireplace mantel and along the window ledges. And on the sectional that had been separated and positioned on either side of the tree lounged his grinning mother and his smug-faced stepfather.

He sucked in a startled breath and smelled pizza, not pine. Following his nose, he spotted two huge boxes from Lou Malnati's on the dining table. He whipped his head back around, looking first to Miller, then to Miranda and Robert. "What's going on?"

Unfolding her legs, Miranda stood, crossed the living area, and folded him in her arms. "Merry Christmas, darling."

Clancy hugged his mother back, confused but glad for this chance he didn't think he'd get. "Christmas isn't for another four days."

"We're headed out of the country tomorrow," Robert said. "And since you were here in Chicago, I couldn't deprive your mother of her family Christmas."

"Thank you," Miranda said to Miller, "for letting us crash your tour."

"No trouble at all," he said with a smile.

Rather than get lost in those attractive laugh lines around his eyes, Clancy hugged his mother again. He drew back a moment later and put on an air of mock anger. "How come we never went to Morton's?"

She led him by the arm to the table. "I take it you enjoyed?" she said, as they loaded paper plates up with pizza slices.

"It was awesome. I had a monster steak, and it came on

a sizzling platter." He dropped his plate on the table and demonstrated a bigger one with his hands. "And the place was super cool. Below ground, dark wood, and leather booths, like a speakeasy but with killer steaks."

Miller leaned in around him and grabbed a slice of pie. "Don't forget the cute somm who gave you his number on the way out."

Miranda's eyes sparkled. "I want to hear everything."

Clancy had actually tossed the somm's card this afternoon. He wasn't kidding; the somm wasn't his type. But he had to indulge his mother, giving her all the details as they ate pizza and drank champagne. An hour later, he and Miranda were on their second bottle while Miller and Robert were sipping scotch on the balcony outside.

His mother canted to the side, reached behind the tree, and righted herself with a flat rectangular box in hand.

"Mom, you didn't have to."

She laid the present, wrapped in silver paper and a glittery bow, in Clancy's lap and ruffled his hair. "It's Christmas."

"You already helped make this amazing trip happen."

She flung an arm around his shoulders and squeezed. "You deserved it."

He kissed her on the cheek. "You're such a sap, Charlotte."

"Oh, come on, I'm totally Samantha."

Proving her point, she refilled their glasses while he ripped into the package, getting glitter everywhere. He tossed the box top aside and folded back the tissue paper. Inside was a large leather scrapbook with an embossed design on the front—a fork, spoon, and knife arranged like a fleur-de-lis. "What is this?"

"Open it up and see."

He lifted the book out and let the rest of the box fall to the floor. Placing the leather binder on his knees, he opened the cover, flipped the blank title page, and found a French Laundry menu attached to the next one. Wait, not just *any* menu. *Their* menu, from last weekend. He ran his hand down the page, a snapshot of each dish flashing through his mind. He flipped the page and there on the next one was a handwritten list of all their Oxbow Market picnic goodies—meats, cheeses, breads, accompaniments, and the wines—on letterhead Clancy recognized as Miller's old restaurant. When had he done this? Before they'd left Napa? He turned the page again and found a printed menu of their room service meal from Jackson Hole on one side and their lunch menu on the other.

"How?" he gasped.

"I have my ways." She tilted her head toward the patio, confirming Miller's participation in the conspiracy. Before he could consider what that meant, what Miller realized this trip meant to him, Miranda ran a finger down the stacked page edges. "There's room here for each menu from the trip."

"This is amazing." He set the book on the coffee table and wrapped her in another giant hug. "Thank you, for everything."

She grabbed their glasses, handed one to him, and clinked the rims. "You deserve the best."

He killed another glassful before going to retrieve their

Morton's menu from his room, along with the gifts he'd bought Miranda and Robert. She was still cackling about the matching plaid snuggies as Clancy slipped the Morton's menu into the fourth spot in the binder. He flipped the page. Blank, of course. "You want to tell me where I'm going next?"

"Nope." Miranda shook her head. "Not risking the Thatcher-Sykes wrath."

Reminded of Sloan, and his and Miller's conversation, Clancy sank back into the couch. "You were right," he said low. "They're recently divorced. Miller's heartbroken."

Her green eyes flickered to the patio and back. "That's not the impression I got on calls with either of them."

"It's complicated. He's happy for her and also not in love with her."

"Because he's gay?"

He startled mid-sip of a fresh glass. Champagne bubbles were always going up his nose when his mother was around.

"One, all that plaid." She grinned as she snuggled down in her own new tartan. "Two, you don't see the way he looks at you?"

Clancy ducked his chin, though why he was trying to hide his blush from his mother, he didn't know. "I hardly know him, Mom."

She patted his cheek. "Don't lie to yourself, or me, darling."

He gulped back the rest of his drink, then fiddled with the stem, twirling the empty glass as he spilled the beans to the only person he could talk to about this. "Even if there was something there, I don't know where he'll be now, with his restaurant closed and the most important relationship in his life changing. And I'm going to be in LA working for Dad." He slouched against her side, head resting on her shoulder, as he stared out at the balcony.

"Since when are you afraid of anything?" She dropped a kiss on his head. "Look at all you've accomplished so young. No fear. Doesn't run in our blood. If you like him, take a shot at something more." She patted the binder. "If it doesn't work out, so be it. You had this trip. You always will."

His stomach fluttered at the thought, at the possibility. The tour was supposed to be about the food, not the chef. But his attraction to Miller wasn't about the chef; it was about the man. That wasn't breaking the rules, was it?

Chapter Six

NEW ORLEANS

"Rise and shine, Doc."

The deep, rumbly voice of Clancy's dreams was accompanied by a hand on his shoulder, gently shaking him awake. Then a far less gentle shake tried to hurl him off his makeshift bed.

"Easy, I got you."

Clancy blinked open his eyes to a very blurry Miller crouched in front of him. "Turbulence." Miller held Clancy in place with one hand and passed him his glasses with the other. "We're descending."

Clancy slipped on his rims and his world came back into view. "We're here?"

Miller nodded and shuffled back across the aisle to his seat, buckling in. The grooves around his eyes were deep, his smile wider than Clancy had seen it yet on this trip. With the sun streaming in through the plane's windows, Miller appeared way too fresh and attractive for having been awake at the ass crack of dawn to catch their flight out. After a night spent tossing and turning, Clancy had conked out as soon as they'd hit cruising altitude.

But not Miller, it seemed. He was wide awake and eager for this next stop. Clancy could see it in his bright eyes; this destination was special. Not that the others hadn't been. Clancy had pieced that together sometime around the second pat of hand-rolled butter at Morton's. Miller had picked these spots not just to give his tour companion a good show. They meant something to him too, and there was something extra about this one. Because Miller in his easy rider jeans, a Jazz Fest T-shirt, and a lavender plaid blazer that was making its first appearance, together with that wide grin, was fucking *extra*.

And Clancy was fucking doomed.

Wait!

Clancy righted himself with a start, gaze darting from Miller's T-shirt, to the purple jacket, to the swampy lowlands out the window. Which were getting closer by the second. He buckled his seat belt, then checked the time on his phone. A little over two hours had passed since take-off. He did the calculations in his head; it all added up. "Please tell me this stop is New Orleans."

Miller's smile grew impossibly wider. "Excited much?"

Clancy crossed his fingers and his toes. "Just to be clear, that's a yes?"

"Yes, Dr. Rhodes, we are in New Orleans."

The cinched-tight seat belt was the only thing keeping him from bouncing in his seat. "Where are we going? Commander's Palace? Brennan's? Cochon?" Or maybe something simpler yet equally raved about. "Camellia Grill."

"Have you been here?"

"No, but I've watched every food show ever filmed here."

Miller laughed until it was drowned out by the skid of tires and the roar of the engines, the plane touching down. When the ambient noise returned to normal, Clancy asked, "So, is it one of those places?"

"None of the above."

No problem. He had at least fifty other places on his NOLA list. But there was one thing that was a must. "Fine, but you are not bringing me to New Orleans and depriving me of beignets and chicory coffee." As soon as the words were out, Clancy regretted how demanding they sounded. And how couple-y.

Miller, however, breezed right over them, seemingly still amused. "Oh, so now it's not just your popcorn obsession? It's coffee too. And you want beignets with it?"

"I'm a doctor. I survive on coffee, so when I can have the good stuff, yeah, I want it. And who doesn't love powdered doughnuts?"

Miller rolled his eyes, and it was the most attractive thing he'd done to date. "Do not let one of the NOLA natives hear you call them that."

Clancy mimed zipping his lips, as they rose and began gathering their things.

"I'm going to count how many beignets you eat before we leave tomorrow morning," Miller teased.

Clancy tapped his chin with a finger. "Just one meal, then?"

"Well, two, technically, as I planned to grab muffuletta sandwiches on the way to the hotel, if that's okay with you?"

"More than. And dinner tonight?"

The cabin door swung open, and they started down the steps to the tarmac.

"We're meeting a friend of mine," Miller said.

"Another chef?"

Miller threw a wicked grin over his shoulder. "Thinking of cheating on me?"

Clancy missed a step and would've taken them both down if not for Miller's arm around his waist. He ignored how good that felt and the rising blush that set his cheeks on fire. The heat didn't recede until Miller released him on the tarmac.

"Well, it is Greg Valteau, so I won't hold that reaction against you."

Thank fuck they were on solid ground, or else Clancy would've missed another step. "Holy shit, the head chef at Dram? Wait, we're going to Dram?" A gastropub that boasted one of the country's largest whiskey collections, Dram had won a slew of best new restaurant awards this year. Clancy was so excited he didn't even bitch about it being humid here in December.

"I didn't say that," Miller replied, as they approached the waiting town car.

Clancy thrust out his bottom lip, dreams of Pappy Van

Winkle tastings and Drambuie-soaked pork ribs floating away in the damp air.

"Aww, don't give me that face, Doc." Miller opened the town car door for him, while the valet loaded their luggage into the trunk. "I promise what I have in store won't disappoint."

Clancy spun in the doorway. "Maybe you ought to get me a beignet first."

Miller pushed him into the car, laughing. "Where does it all go?"

On the edge of New Orleans's French Quarter, Port of Call wasn't flashy from the outside. An older building with gray siding, dark storm shutters, unmarked awnings, and a weathered wood sign over its entrance. The inside wasn't flashy either. Woven ropes below an exposed ceiling, wood-paneled walls, a big wooden bar, and seating areas with basic wooden tables. It reminded Miller of a hulled-out ship, which, given the name and location, only a few blocks from the river, he supposed was the point. But Port of Call wasn't a seafood joint. A server set a monster burger and baked potato in front of Miller, both covered with freshly grated cheese, and he forgot all about ships.

Now this was something to look at.

Across from him, Greg was tucking a napkin in his shirt collar, preparing to get down and dirty, and beside Greg, Clancy had already picked up his burger and had on his how-do-I-attack-this face.

"I know it's not Brennan's or Commander's Palace," Miller said.

Clancy didn't take his eyes off the burger. "No complaints here."

"Don't overthink it," Greg said, dark eyes twinkling. "Just go for it."

Clancy nodded and did just that. Grilled mushrooms escaped out the back, cheese from the sides, and grease down Clancy's chin. Laughing, Miller snagged one of the extra napkins the server had wisely left behind and reached across the table. He stopped a few inches short of his intended target, caught in the laser beam of his friend's stare, no longer mirthful but sharpened with curiosity.

"Here, Doc." Miller handed the napkin to Clancy instead.

Already on the scent, Greg shifted in his chair toward Clancy. "Not the New Orleans stop you were expecting?"

"Well, no, but holy shit, this is the best burger I've ever had." Clancy paused to wipe his chin, then took another bite and had to repeat the whole hilarious process over again. He looked blissfully happy—not quite Oh-God-Truffles happy but pretty damn close.

"That's why we're here," Miller said. "No one does burgers better."

He'd said the same about the service and creativity at TFL, O'Banon's simple yet unique spin on goat cheese, the view in Jackson Hole, and the butter and steaks at Morton's. And he'd say the same again before the tour was over. It was part of the reason why he'd picked these places. He wasn't leaving this planet without visiting and tasting the best, one last time. And barring that incident in Wyoming, he was fairly certain he'd make it through the next week. He'd felt back to normal in Chicago and great this morning, excited to revisit Port of Call and bring Clancy here, especially after his comment about loving a good burger. Miller had also been excited to visit his best friend, though Greg seemed to be on Team Clancy at the moment.

"You are taking him for beignets too, right?"

Miller dropped his fork from where he'd been scooping up a bite of baked potato. "For fuck's sake."

"What?" Greg grinned. "You can't deprive a NOLA virgin of Café Du Monde."

"Oh, I know." Miller pointed his fork at Clancy. "He had on a Mario Kart T-shirt and corduroy blazer this morning. You notice the jacket's gone and it's now a God-awful Dodgers shirt."

"Casualties of the powdered sugar war." Clancy smiled around a mouthful of burger. "And I could have put on the Lakers shirt."

"I will leave your perky ass on the tarmac."

"Keep your promise of more beignets tomorrow, and I promise to keep the Kershaw jersey buried in my suitcase."

"I see it, I will burn it."

Someone cleared their throat, and Miller was reminded that he and Clancy weren't alone. Greg's dark eyes were now both curious and highly amused. Consistent with his shit-eating grin.

Fuck.

Greg had always had a thing for cop shows, fancying himself an amateur sleuth. When they'd worked together, it'd been Greg's favorite game to peek into the dining room and speculate about their guests. What did they do for a living? What would they order? What was their drink of choice? Who would they go home with? Miller could practically see the guesses and questions swirling in his friend's head about Clancy.

Thankfully, Clancy's curiosity beat his to the punch. "How long have you two known each other?"

"Almost twenty years," Greg answered.

"We washed dishes together," Miller said, "in New York."

"Who worked their way up the line faster?" Clancy asked.

"First place we worked wasn't so formal."

"But at the next"—Greg jutted a thumb at Miller—"this one was on sauté in less than a month, then up to roundsman a month later."

"Meanwhile, Mr. Culinary School there couldn't get his hollandaise to stop breaking."

Greg held his arms out wide in a come-at-me gesture. Miller flicked a mushroom at him, and they dissolved into laughter. "We all have our demons," Greg said once the hilarity subsided. "Which is why that particular one of mine is nowhere on my menu. Fuck eggs Benedict." That set off another round of laughter, and the story of how Greg screwed up an entire brunch service his first week in their second kitchen. "The sous-chef made me stay there until three in the morning until I got one to work."

"Where were you?" Clancy asked Miller.

"Down the street at the pub where Sloan worked."

"Where we all used to work," Greg said. "I had to hobble back to our apartment that night with a tipsy fool on each arm."

"Your fault, dude."

"You guys all lived together?" Clancy asked.

Greg nodded. "Shared an apartment with him and Sloan in Harlem until I got the chance to move back here and chef at Commander's Palace."

Clancy's mouth rounded into an O and Miller could see the fanboy wheels spinning. He pumped the brakes, though, asking instead, "You're from New Orleans originally?"

Greg smiled proudly. "Born and bred."

Greg's absolute devotion to his hometown was one of the things Miller loved most about his friend. After Katrina had hit, Greg had been a mess. Stuck in New York, fifteen hundred miles away from his family and his beloved city. Granted he'd been safe, and working in a kitchen most rising chefs would kill to cook in, but every day away from his hurting hometown wore on his Cajun soul. When he'd gotten the offer to chef at Commander's Palace, it had been a no-brainer. It'd left Miller and Sloan stretched for the rent, but they'd been the ones to talk Greg into taking the job. Sloan had flexed her law school mock trial skills, and Greg, like Miller often did, folded under her logic. Like Miller had done buying this purple plaid jacket, a nod to

Greg's alma mater's school colors. For the grin it'd won from Greg when they'd arrived, it was worth it. Miller hadn't gone to college—he didn't have any college sports allegiances—so he could pull for Greg's LSU Tigers. He sure as hell wasn't wearing the black and gold for Greg's favorite professional team.

"So then, what are your favorite places to eat here?" Clancy asked Greg.

There was the foodie fanboy. Miller couldn't help but smile.

A good fifteen minutes passed, Greg going on about his favorites and Clancy excitedly asking follow-up questions. Miller flagged down the server for another round of drinks and finished his potato. He moved on to his burger next, cutting it into bite-sized pieces his throat could handle.

"You too good now to pick up a burger and eat it with your hands?" Greg said.

Miller flicked him his eyes, and a middle finger. "Fuck off, Valteau." The dig from Greg didn't bother Miller half as much as a certain someone's bushy brows snapping together. "Do not tell him where we worked in New York," Miller said to Greg, hoping to distract his travel companion.

"Oh!" Clancy bounced in his seat. "So New York is on the menu."

Mission accomplished. "Of course it is," Miller said. Because also, no-brainer.

Clancy whipped his phone out of his pocket. "I can Google and see where you two crossed paths."

"Those sorts of first jobs are not on our Wiki pages."

"Only the big ones," Greg said. "Michelin stars, big openings, clos—" He cut himself off and darted guilty eyes toward Miller, who waved him off.

Of the past year's hits, losing the restaurant was, relatively, the least painful. And it'd worked out for the best; he would have had to close it anyway. "It's fine, Greg. You were the one who walked me through the closing process after all."

Clancy glanced back and forth between them. "You've closed a restaurant before?" he asked Greg.

"Three of 'em. I worked at Commander's for a few years before striking out on my own. Plenty of physical spaces were open after Katrina, but they were open for a reason. It took more than a few years for this town to bounce back." He looked again at Miller, voice and eyes earnest. "You'll bounce back too."

A piece of food lodged in Miller's throat. He forced it down and focused instead on the meld of flavors in the burger. Beef, cheese, mushrooms, and a buttered bun. Nothing fancy, just simple, good ingredients, perfectly cooked. This stop—this trip—was a lesson in where he'd misstepped at his previous restaurant. There was a reason his staff meals always won raves, and not just because it was free food. If he were to open a new concept, he could already see how he might rectify his mistakes.

No, he cut off his own thought. *No use going there.*

Miller ate while Clancy peppered Greg with more questions. It wasn't until the server cleared their plates and they'd ordered another round of drinks that Greg, smiling wide, leaned forward and put his forearms on the table.

Now what was he up to? Miller prayed for an embarrassing story and not Greg Valteau, amateur detective.

He got neither.

"There's something I've been meaning to ask you," Greg said. "Since you'll have the time off now, and since I know you'll stand up for Sloan at the wedding, I was wondering if you'd stand up as my best person too."

Ice water gushed through Miller's veins. There was such sincerity, such happiness and hope, in his best friend's eyes, and yet darkness fast encroached on Miller's periphery, closing in on what was left of his ever-shortening life.

"Wait, you're marrying Sloan?" Clancy said. "I thought she was marrying some guy named Tyler."

Greg aimed a raised brow at Miller. "He knows?"

Miller just nodded, still trying to figure out how to let his friend down easy without spilling the whole truth of the matter, to Greg or Clancy.

"Tyler is my business partner," Greg answered Clancy. "I introduced them."

"And you're getting married too? At the same time?"

Greg smiled wide. "To my beverage director, Tony. We're planning a double wedding." He shifted his attention back to Miller. "I've been pestering Sloan to go ahead and ask you to be our best person, but she keeps putting me off. A win for me, as I got to ask you in person now."

A win. Miller bit back a bitter laugh.

Fuck, now he wished Sloan had told Greg the real reason she hadn't asked him yet—that Miller might not make it to summer. But Miller had insisted she not, hoping he'd never have to tell Greg. He was being a shitty friend to both of them, leaving Greg out of the loop and leaving Sloan to explain why, but Miller didn't have it in him to confront Greg's inevitable anger and equally inevitable tears. He couldn't bear to listen to another friend try to convince him to fight, to give up everything he was for a slim chance of survival and a life full of question marks. He couldn't put the thought of a tasteless life into the mind of the best, most talented chef Miller knew. He wouldn't curse Greg with that nightmare, or himself with the pity that would no doubt shine from Greg's beautiful eyes knowing someone he loved was living that hell. Greg had too big a heart for that; it'd tear him up from the inside out. Miller would rather curse himself to the ass-kicking Greg would eventually give him in the ever-after.

"I told her it was perfunctory, of course," Greg carried on. "But we're getting down to the wire on details, and we need to—"

"No," Miller forced out.

"No?" Clancy squawked in surprise.

Greg, however, rolled with it. "Look, I know this may be tough for you, with Sloan moving on, and maybe you're mad I introduced her to Tyler."

Patently false. Miller couldn't be happier for Sloan, but given the circumstances, it was an understandable assumption, for an outsider. Which Greg was not. "That's not it, and you know me better than that."

Greg's face fell, confronted with the truth. Greg had lived and worked with them—had partied and gone out to the clubs with Miller—he knew the score where it stood with Miller's sexuality and with Miller's relationship with

Sloan as well as anyone. He was grasping at straws, trying to explain Sloan's behavior and Miller's refusal. Trying not to be hurt or take it personally. Miller wished he could tell him that's what he was trying to save him from, but all he could do was stand and grab his blazer off the back of the chair. He fished the trip card out of his wallet and tossed it on the table. "I have to go."

Greg shot to his feet, blocking his exit. "Miller, what the fuck is going on?"

"Look, I'll go," Clancy said, starting to stand. "You guys can talk."

"No." Miller waved him back down. "Stay and finish your drink." He turned to Greg. "Take him to The Rum House for some of that colossal key lime pie."

"Miller, I don't understand." Hand on his arm, Greg looked at him with tears glistening in his dark, soulful eyes. Greg wore his heart on his sleeve, always out there for the world to see, with absolutely no shame. "You're my best friend. I'm sorry if I did something to upset you, but please—"

"Never be sorry for being in love and for being happy. None of you, you hear me." Miller cupped his friend's beautiful tear-streaked face, brushing away the wetness with his thumbs. Miller admired that openness, loved him all the harder for it. "Thank you, for always being there for me. For bringing all that is you into my life. I couldn't have asked for a better friend." He leaned forward and lowered his voice for Greg's ears only. "I'm sorry I can't be a better friend for you now. That I won't be there to see you get all the love and happiness you deserve." He dropped a kiss on

Greg's forehead then turned, bolting from the restaurant exit before either man could see the pain and regret in his own eyes.

One would think a big, bearded guy in a purple blazer would not be difficult to find. Except that Clancy had found a half dozen already, and none of them were the one he was looking for. Friday night in the French Quarter, a week before LSU played in a bowl game, and it was a sea of purple battling waves of red and green, an equal abundance of holiday dressed revelers out in the streets.

And in the bars too, which Clancy also had to battle to get into. Bouncers reveled in hassling him, because, according to almost everyone, no way was he thirty years old. Eventually they'd let him in, but not without some teasing and cajoling.

"Precocious," one said.

"Fake," another pronounced about his driver's license and UCLA Med ID.

Clancy was sure he'd appreciate his baby-face genetics when he was fifty and looked thirty-five, like his ageless mother, but fuck this shit when he actually needed to get in and out of those bars quickly and find *his* purple-suited giant.

Something was seriously wrong with Miller. They hadn't known each other long, but Clancy wouldn't hesitate to say one of Miller's defining characteristics was his loyalty, not to mention his complete and utter devotion to

Sloan. He suspected Greg was a close second on Miller's priority ladder. But Miller wouldn't be their best person? He'd miss seeing the two most important people in his life get married? At a wedding event that was clearly one of the biggest events to happen among their group of friends?

Clancy wanted to ask why. On top of a list of other questions that were filling his brain. Why did Miller cut all his food into tiny portions? Clancy had noticed it tonight and at Morton's. A new development, per Greg. Why the pain and nausea meds? Had to be internal, because there were no visible muscular or skeletal issues. Had Miller really been suffering altitude sickness in Jackson Hole or had it been something else? Why was Miller selling the house, especially if he'd have more time now? Why the fatalistic look in his eyes or the bleakness in his voice that made Clancy's heart clench every time the dark clouds rolled in? Why even this tour? Full of all of Miller's favorites, like a last—

Clancy violently pushed his slipping glasses up his nose, as if the motion could cut off his racing mind. He realized what he was doing. Running diagnostics. But fuck, it was his job. It was what he'd spent the last decade learning how and training to do. No more than Miller could turn off being a chef, analyzing every flavor profile, Clancy couldn't turn off being a doctor, especially not when running through the streets and bars of New Orleans felt an awful lot like his trauma rotation. He suspected his quick diagnostic assessment was correct, or at least close to some version of it, but Miller hadn't disclosed any health conditions to him. Why would he?

Who was he to Miller but a meal ticket and travel companion?

A friend.

Clancy had committed himself to that much in Jackson Hole, and again in Chicago, and he had no reason to turn his back on that commitment or on Miller. Not when Miller seemed to desperately need one; if only Clancy could find him. Because as his friend, even if he'd bite his tongue and not ask his questions, Clancy had to make sure Miller was safe and not puking in some corner or about to pass out like he'd been in Wyoming.

In and out of another bar with no sign of him, Clancy texted Greg an update. They'd traded numbers outside Port of Call before heading in opposite directions around the French Quarter, promising text updates. A reply came right back. No sign of Miller on Greg's side of the Quarter either.

"Fuck." On to the next bar, then.

Clancy pocketed his phone and jogged across the street to one that looked like the Alamo from the outside. He waited in line to get in, and mercifully, once he reached the front, the bouncer didn't haggle with him. Inside, the space was long and narrow—a blues band playing on the stage at the far end, a big open area in front of the stage packed with dancers, and in the back, where Clancy had walked in, a bar and a smattering of high-top pub tables. Clancy scanned the stage and crowd. No sign of Miller or his purple jacket. He turned his attention to the bar next, and finally he could breathe, unencumbered. At the far end, a familiar form sat hunched over a cocktail glass.

Miller's coat was gone, his tattoos on display, his hair was run through, the curls coming loose, and his eyes were closed, lashes fluttering as he sipped his drink and swayed to the music.

Clancy shot Greg a text, letting him know he'd found Miller and that he'd text again when they were safely back at the hotel. He sensed Miller didn't need or want another confrontation with his friend tonight; he certainly hadn't wanted the first one at all. And if peace was what Miller needed, Clancy would try to give it to him. He wove his way through the crowd toward Miller's end of the bar and claimed the stool that opened up next to him.

The bartender picked up the previous patron's tip and asked, "What'll it be?"

"Whatever he's having."

Miller's eyes popped open, and he swung his face toward Clancy. "What are you—"

Clancy cut him off, not giving Miller the chance to tell him to leave. "What did I just order?" Miller's cocktail tonight was reddish-brown; not his usual Campari-red Negroni.

"Vieux Carré."

Clancy scrunched his nose in a look that had drawn a laugh from Miller before. "English that up for me."

He didn't get a laugh, but Miller did release a big breath, easing some of the tension in the air around them. Miller propped an elbow on the bar and began ticking off ingredients on his fingers. "Rye whiskey, cognac, sweet vermouth, Benedictine, and both bitters."

"So, pure alcohol?"

The bartender set the cocktail down in front of him. "Pretty much."

Clancy sniffed and reared back, nostrils stinging. He was supposed to pour that down his gullet? At least his reluctance drew the laugh out of Miller he'd been after. Clancy bumped his shoulder. "Good to hear that."

"I don't want to—"

"Why this drink?" Clancy asked, determined to hold on to the easier mood, to hold on to Miller here with him. "From what I've seen, you're a Negroni guy. Why the changeup?"

Miller held his gaze, probably assessing if there was an ulterior motive in Clancy's question. Clancy didn't look away.

After a moment, Miller broke the stare down and sipped his drink. Clancy was afraid he'd lost him, but then Miller lowered his glass and swirled its contents. "The French translation is literally, 'French Quarter.' It was created here in New Orleans, and it's as much New Orleans in a glass as a Hurricane, maybe more so. It's a melting pot of flavors—the spiciness of the rye, the sweetness of the vermouth, the herbal notes of the Benedictine, the fermented fruits of the cognac, and the bite of the bitters. Like all good New Orleans creations, it's a mix of things, a flavor meld that's rich and decadent, and if you can find it barrel-aged, all the better."

Clancy took a cautious swallow, digging into the complexity of the drink and detecting all the flavors Miller mentioned. "You can't order these at home?"

"You can, but you order it here"—he rapped the bar with

his knuckles—"in New Orleans, because you can always get it made with Sazerac. The distillery releases limited barrels out of state. Most bars where we are just use whatever rye whiskey they have in the well, unless you specifically ask for Sazerac."

Clancy held his glass out for a clink, then took another sip, the meld of flavors in the drink growing on him. "And Port of Call?" Clancy raised his voice to be heard over the band's increasing volume. "We didn't get to have our usual conversation. I know we're yelling, but the night feels incomplete without it."

Miller scooted his stool closer. "It's the way they make the burger. It used to be a steak place, but they got famous for grinding the meat—steak quality—and making burgers out of it. And they don't smash the patty or gussy it up much. Grilled mushrooms and freshly shredded sharp cheddar. Add in the loaded baked potato as a side, as opposed to the usual fries, and it's original, simple, and delicious. They don't try to do too much."

"Do a few things really well."

"Exactly, like these guys." Miller jutted a thumb toward the stage. "Four instruments, classic R & B, and pretty damn good, albeit loud."

"What are you really good at?" Clancy asked. "In the kitchen."

Miller's laugh was bitter, stealing the heat Clancy was enjoying, from the cocktail and Miller's nearness. "I don't even know." Miller threw back the rest of his drink in one go. "If you asked me that question a year ago, I would've known the answer, or thought I had. Now..."

Clancy shifted closer. "Surely some things haven't changed. Name one thing, then I'll tell you one."

Miller contemplated his giant ice cube. "Fairly certain I can still out-sauce anyone in the kitchen."

"Greg sure thought so."

Miller's frame tensed, and Clancy immediately regretted the mention. Before he could apologize, Miller asked, "And you? I'm sure it's some medical marvel."

Sure, those were up there, no doubt. Well, not marvel level yet, but he was really good at what he did. But talk of medicine, of cancer especially, wouldn't salvage this night. No, Clancy had something else in mind. Something that would work out the awkward tension around them and make them both forget the gray clouds, at least for a little while. Something he'd become very good at living in WeHo since undergrad. While he'd steered clear of relationships, Clancy hadn't been a monk. There was always at least one guy in the crowd who loved a twink who could shake his ass. And Clancy was fairly certain he knew who that guy was tonight.

Clancy downed the rest of his drink, a mischievous glint in his eyes that Miller hadn't seen there before. He liked it way too much. Combined with the flush working its way up Clancy's long, slender neck, and the smirk hitching up one corner of his mouth, the whole package was sexy as hell. He slid off his stool toward Miller, putting himself right between Miller's spread knees. Miller could feel the heat radiating off him.

"I'll show you," Clancy whispered hotly before slipping out of Miller's reach.

"Doc," Miller called after him, mortified that his voice sounded so strangled. "Where are you going?"

"To do what I'm really good at." He threw a devilish grin over his shoulder and shook his ass.

Fuck me.

The torture worsened as Clancy hit the dance floor. If Miller was Clancy's type, Clancy was his. No question. The attraction that had sparked at first sight, that had simmered all week long, was swiftly heating to a boil. Miller couldn't tear his gaze away from the long lithe limbs, tight tone body, and firm round ass, moving perfectly in time with the music. LA boy had moves, like he felt the music in his soul. Color continued to rise on Clancy's cheeks, the tip ends of his hair dampened with sweat, and through three songs, his eyes didn't stray from Miller's. The black-rimmed glasses he repeatedly had to adjust put just enough nerd on the picture to make Clancy as endearing as he was sexy.

Miller wasn't the only person noticing. Clancy attracted attention from multiple directions, including from a man in a red velour jacket and matching Santa hat. An inch or so shorter than Miller, he had wide shoulders, a barrel chest, and thighs that strained the seams of his jeans. Big and built, Clancy's type, and moving closer to dance with him, instead of around him.

Seventies Santa laid a hand on Clancy's hip, and the

connection between Miller and Clancy snapped, the latter's attention drawn to the interloper. Miller was off his stool the next instant. If he thought too hard on it, he'd reverse course and walk out the door instead of onto the dance floor. Let Clancy pursue things with the attractive man who was clearly interested in him. Who wouldn't be? And why shouldn't it be Santa? It sure as hell shouldn't be Miller, who had a death sentence hanging over his head.

He had no business making any sort of claim on Clancy. No business getting more involved with him, even if only for the week they had left together. No business shoving his body between Santa's and Clancy's, knocking Santa's hands off him, and grasping Clancy's hips. No business, when Clancy grinned and stepped forward, coasting his hands over Clancy's hips and splaying his fingers across the curve of that perfect ass.

Santa ceased to exist, Clancy's attention totally on him.

"Dancing," Miller shouted over the music. "Wouldn't have figured."

Clancy leaned forward, speaking right into Miller's ear. "Did you miss the part where I like dick and live in WeHo?"

Laughter bubbled out of Miller, and Clancy's goofy smile made him impossibly sexier. That body, those moves, and still the irrepressible brightness. Miller stepped closer, swiping back Clancy's damp hair and letting his fingers drift slowly through it. "Fuck, you're stunning."

Smile wide, Clancy draped his arms over Miller's

shoulders and brought their bodies into brushing contact. "Dance with me, Chef."

Miller didn't even care about the slip, not when it was uttered in that low, sexy voice, seducing him into movement.

Song after song, they swayed and writhed in sync, their bodies like magnets inching closer and closer. Miller couldn't say how many songs it was before his forehead fell against Clancy's and the last bit of distance between their bodies vanished. The instinct was there to close the distance between their mouths too, but almost as strong was the profound relief rushing through Miller. He'd needed this release, needed to let go and forget about everything except moving his body in time with the gorgeous man in his arms. Clancy had known that, had recognized it while they'd sat at the bar, and had made it happen. He'd been exactly what and who Miller needed tonight.

"Thank you," Miller whispered.

"You're welcome." Clancy's warm breath tickled his lips. "But this is ninety-five percent selfish on my part."

"It's one hundred percent selfish on mine."

Clancy looked up with dilated eyes, only a thin ring of dark green visible. He licked his lips, and if he hadn't spoken, Miller would have claimed them. "I'm more than okay with that."

Unhooking his arms from behind Miller's neck, Clancy ran his hands over Miller's shoulders and down his arms, tracing the ink. They traveled back up, then down his chest, fingers curling in Miller's T-shirt. Clancy dragged them backward until his back hit the wall. Miller tried to slam on the brakes, not wanting to crush Clancy, not wanting to eat him alive in public, but Clancy kept hauling him forward. Cheek to cheek, chest to chest, Clancy slid a knee between Miller's legs and pressed his thigh up against Miller's straining cock. Clancy canted his hips, revealing his own need, and Miller couldn't stop himself from rocking forward. He shoved a hand between the wall and Clancy's ass and grabbed a handful of cheek, holding Clancy and his dick tight to him, chasing after this feeling. Heat, relief, life, desire, all driving him higher. He snuck his other hand under the hem of Clancy's shirt, dragging his fingertips through the sweat at the small of his back. A shiver raced through Clancy, and Miller thrust his hips again. He couldn't remember the last time he'd been this turned on, had felt so wanted while also wanting so much.

Clancy nipped his earlobe. "Be selfish a little longer." He dragged his lips along the line of Miller's beard and over his cheek, angling toward his mouth.

Miller wanted to taste him, more than he'd ever wanted to taste anything. Wanted to taste the hot, flushed skin behind Clancy's ear, the sweat from his back that slicked Miller's fingers, and the softly curving lips that had tempted Miller every time they'd closed around a damn fork. He wanted to know how the bitter, spicy sweetness of the Vieux Carré mixed with Clancy's own unique flavor.

But then Clancy skirted a hand up, over the knot in Miller's throat, and reality came crashing back down. No bigger than an acorn, the tumor might as well have been a fucking boulder, crushing him under its weight. Miller couldn't have a taste of Clancy. If he did, he wouldn't be able to walk away from this—from him—at the end of next week. It'd be like the truffles; one taste and he'd be addicted for life. The life Clancy promised and Miller couldn't have.

Miller ripped himself out of Clancy's arms. "I'm going back to the hotel," he said, avoiding those too expressive eyes and what would no doubt be a hurricane of lust-filled confusion. "I'll see you in the morning."

Chapter Seven

Clancy was left in the dust again, a heaving, turned-on mess, and after the roller coaster of a day already, he didn't have it in him to search the French Quarter's streets again for Miller. He'd said he was going back to the hotel. Clancy would check there first. Sure enough, when Clancy made it back to their suite, Miller's bedroom door was closed and a shadow moved in the light visible under the door. A light that went out a moment later.

Texting Greg as he retreated to his own room, Clancy closed the door and fell back against it, pocketing his phone and wiping a hand down his face. A million thoughts, regrets, and questions raced through his head. None of which he could do anything about with Miller shutting him out. He could go over there, knock on his door until he answered, and demand some answers, but Clancy hadn't done that earlier at the club and he wouldn't do that now. Miller had enough to deal with. Clancy had gone too far already, he'd overstepped, and he couldn't blame the cocktail either. After that huge burger and baked potato, the alcohol hadn't even made him tipsy. All he'd aimed to do was make Miller feel better, make him forget, and he had for a few minutes.

Until his fingers had run over the unmistakable lump on his neck.

Confirming Clancy's diagnosis.

Cancer.

And Miller was bound and determined not to talk about it.

His determination didn't waver the next morning either. Clancy woke to coffee and beignets but no Miller. He'd left a note saying he'd gone to breakfast with Greg. Clancy hoped Miller would talk to his friend and tell him the truth. Even if he didn't, hopefully they'd make peace.

Not in the cards, judging by Miller's sour mood when he returned minutes before they were scheduled to catch their car to the airport. Both rides, on land and in air, were silent affairs. Miller kept his sunglasses on and his earphones in whenever they were alone, as if they were strangers, farther from friends than when they'd begun the tour. And since Miller couldn't exactly get away from him, given said tour, Clancy respected his need for privacy. It was none of Clancy's business, even if he wanted it to be. As a doctor. As a friend. As—

No. Clancy shook off the thoughts, leaving them in New Orleans. Not carrying them with him as they deplaned in Boston, not with him as they diverted to a rental car counter instead of a town car, not with him as they drove out of Logan. And not with him over the next ninety minutes as they drove away from Boston, including through three massive roundabouts during which Clancy closed his eyes and tried not to lose his collective shit. Clearly he carried the thoughts with him. What else was he supposed to think about during those harrowing minutes in the circles of doom?

By the time they were on the ferry to Martha's Vineyard, all of Clancy's thoughts and words were fighting to get out. He watched through the windshield as Miller stood by the ferry's rail, a lone figure seemingly oblivious to the blowing snow flurries as he stared straight ahead.

To the island where they would be stuck together for the weekend.

Fuck. Clancy had to say something or else this was going to be the most awkward Christmas Eve weekend ever.

He tossed his empty coffee cup aside, grabbed his scarf from the back seat, wrapped it around his neck, zipped up his hoodie, and buttoned his coat over everything. Bundled as well as an LA boy could be, he shoved open the car door, took one step out, and had to cling to the door to avoid wiping out. Steadying himself, he carefully made his way to the rail where Miller stood. And just as carefully, he approached the conversation, starting with something easy. "Thank you for the coffee and beignets this morning."

"I promised you," Miller answered flatly, not giving him a glance.

Careful and easy took a flying leap off the side of the boat. "Do you still want to be here?" The next second, Clancy registered how that question could be taken, beyond just this trip, and he wanted to jump over the rail himself. "On this trip," he clarified. "Because if you're just here because you promised, we can call it off. You can keep the money—"

"It's not about the money."

"Fine, but Miller..." He leaned a hip and hand against the rail, trying to get Miller to look his way, to no avail. "If this trip is making you miserable, if you don't want to be around me, if you—"

Miller's hand over his silenced the rest of Clancy's words. "I want to continue, and I don't want to do it alone."

"But do you want to do it with me?"

Miller finally gave Clancy his eyes, and they were red-rimmed and bloodshot. Clancy sucked in a sharp breath, fearing the worst.

"Yes," Miller said softly.

Clancy didn't hide his huge exhale, and Miller's answering smile was worth it. The world steadied below Clancy's feet even as the boat rocked over the waves. He drew his hand back and shoved both of them into his coat pockets. "Where are we going, then? On Martha's Vineyard?"

Miller glanced back out over the water, toward the island that was growing nearer. "The first place I chef'ed."

"I thought that was in New York with Greg."

He shook his head, a strange mix of pain and longing streaking across his face. "When Sloan and I left home, we came here first. A friend of Ma's ran a B and B in Edgartown. It was the summer season and she needed the extra help. She rented us a dingy little basement apartment for cheap, Sloan cleaned and helped manage the inn, and I was the on-site handyman and landscaper. But I still needed to get out and make some extra cash."

"So you found a restaurant to work in?"

"The kitchens in New York and San Francisco might have refined my skills, but Oscar M'Raihi gave them to me."

"I can't wait to meet him."

A trilling ringtone pierced the quiet, and Miller dug his phone out of his pocket. A video call request from Sloan lit the screen. Miller hit Accept and held the phone out so both he and Clancy were visible. "Hey, babe," Miller said. "What's up?"

She looked to be in her office, elbows on her desk, eyes closed as she pinched the bridge of her nose. "We've got a problem."

"What's going on?"

The shiver that ran through Miller could have been from the cold, but that's not how Miller sounded. He knew Sloan well enough to sense something was wrong, to be worried. Clancy stepped closer, taking a bit of his weight.

When Sloan opened her eyes, they were as tortured as Miller's, like she'd been crying too, but Clancy didn't think they'd spoken earlier today. Miller's escalating distress confirmed as much. Whatever this was, it was news to Miller too. Clancy eased an arm around Miller's waist and Miller didn't shake it off.

"Sloan, talk to me," he said. "Is it—"

"I'm fine, so's the cannoli and Tyler. I'm calling about the next stop on your tour." She swallowed hard. "I got a call from Noelle. The restaurant's closed."

"Who's Noelle?" Clancy asked.

"Oscar's daughter." Miller gave Clancy more of his weight, but he didn't take his fearful eyes off Sloan. "Why's it closed?"

"I'm sorry, baby. Oscar had a heart attack. He's gone."

Clancy caught the phone just before Miller lost it over the rail, then he caught Miller.

Mortality could fuck right off.

Miller didn't need another reminder of it. He had a knot in his throat that wouldn't let him forget it every time he fucking swallowed, and now, the person and place he'd looked forward to visiting most on this tour were gone. He'd skipped right over denial—Sloan's face was all the confirmation he needed—and gone straight to anger, all the rage he'd banked since getting his own diagnosis roaring back. He shot out an arm and swept it across the hotel room's marble vanity. Plastic bottles and industrial strength glass hit the carpeted floor with a muffled thump. Wholly unsatisfying, as was the string of "fucks" Miller let loose.

But it was enough to draw Clancy's attention, his fist pounding on the connecting door between their adjacent rooms. "Miller, open up!"

"I'm fine," he hollered.

"Bullshit! Open the door, so I can make sure you're not hurt."

Miller laughed, the bitter, unhinged cackle making his own ears ache.

"Miller! Let me in!"

Clancy had done enough already. Holding up his weight when the news had taken Miller's legs out from under him. Then navigating across the island to Edgartown and getting them checked in to the hotel. Miller had shown Clancy more than he'd intended.

"Enjoy the night off, Doc."

The knocking quieted, and a second later, Miller's phone rang. He stepped to the bedside table, checking it. Sloan, again. He didn't answer, again. Once the ringing stopped, there were another few seconds of silence in which Miller considered breaking it with the vase on the fireplace mantel, but before he could grab hold of it, the banging restarted, this time on the glass door to the patio his and Clancy's rooms shared.

Clancy stood outside in his jeans and T-shirt. "Open the door, Miller!"

"I'm fine, Doc, see." He held his arms out wide.

Clancy did the same, as if to say, *I'm not going anywhere*, but the blinking neon message, from his visible shivering and rising goosebumps was, *It's cold as fuck out here*. Yet still the other man didn't move, just kept getting colder and more soaked by the falling snow.

"Fuck." Miller stalked across the room, opened the

door, and yanked Clancy inside by the front of his shirt. "Get in here."

He went to close the door, but Clancy's ice-cold hand on his arm stopped him. "No, leave it open. I want to smell the snow and hear the waves."

"It's freezing, Clancy."

He squeezed gently. "Please. This is my first time on the Atlantic, and I miss the sound of the waves."

Miller released the door. "Fine but sit here." He dragged one of the armchairs over in front of the gas fireplace, pushed Clancy down into it, and flicked on the blaze. "I'll be right back." He hustled to the bathroom, grabbed a towel, snatched the plush robe out of the closet, and returned to Clancy, thrusting the lot of items at him. "Dry off and wrap up."

"I'm supposed to be checking on you," Clancy said through chattering teeth.

"I'm fine, seriously." He dragged the other chair over for himself. "Get yourself warm."

Clancy finished wiping down, tossed the towel aside, and wrapped up in the robe. He tucked all his limbs in the chair and under a woolen blanket. "It's cold as balls out there."

"It's winter." Miller gestured outside. "In Massachusetts."

Clancy yanked the robe tighter around him. "From LA. Even counting my trips to Chicago, I do not have the constitution for this much snow in a week."

The bark of laughter surprised Miller, though after a week with Clancy, it shouldn't have. His ability to deflate whatever balloon of tension was weighing Miller down was an unexpected gift on this trip.

As was his unfailing compassion. "I'm sorry about your mentor."

"Thank you." He patted Clancy's knee, then slid back in his own chair. "He would have been eighty-two next year. I don't know why I'm surprised."

"Doesn't make it suck less. I lost patients that were north of a hundred and while I knew they'd lived good, long lives, it didn't make losing them any easier."

"How'd you do it?" It sounded like utter hell to Miller. He was having enough trouble dealing with his own impending death, and now Oscar's too. He couldn't imagine dealing with it for a living. Going to work every day knowing you could lose someone. Not for him.

"I'd focus on making it easier for them to move on."

Was that what he was doing for Miller? He was making it easier in some respects, like making him laugh, but the thought of moving on wasn't getting any easier. And wasn't that what this trip was about? Revisiting all his favorite places—his favorite tastes—so he could move on, having had his last suppers. Yet moving on felt harder than ever.

"Tell me about him," Clancy said softly.

Miller stood and walked over to the open door, leaning on the jamb and looking toward the waterfront where Oscar's was located.

Was.

He fought to get words out around the lump in his throat, this one of a different sort than the physical one that was always there now. "He was quiet, calm, and patient. He taught me how to make a sauce and not break it." He smiled, remembering all the nights he'd then tried to teach Greg. His smile dimmed, however, as he recalled round two of the argument they'd had that morning. He'd left his friend on no better terms than he had the night before. A cold gust of wind pushed him farther into the past. "But for all his calm, Oscar was also energized about his food and the diner's experience. It was his own little world, and he wanted people to visit and enjoy it."

"Sounds like a great chef to learn from and work under."

"The best I had." Miller turned from the door and reclaimed his chair, scooting it closer to the fire. "A kitchen is like any other workplace. The mood and tone of a place is set at the top by the head chef. If he's a screamer, and there are some seriously loud screamers in the culinary world, everyone, from the line cooks to the servers, are on eggshells. The diners notice."

"So the opposite is better?"

"Not necessarily." He threw his feet up on the ottoman Clancy was using and snatched a corner of his blanket to cover his own feet. "If the chef is too calm, too quiet, you run the risk of boring your staff and dining room. Granted, there are some people who want that experience, but personally, I like a lively dining room. I want everyone, from the diners to the dishwashers, excited and happy to be there."

"That's why we were coming here?"

"In part." He shifted his gaze before Clancy could

discern the entire truth. That Miller couldn't get to the end without visiting his beginnings, one last time.

Clancy knocked his foot under the blanket. "What's going to happen to his restaurant?"

A thought flitted through the back of Miller's mind and he shut it right down, not allowing himself to give voice or further thought to it. That wasn't moving on; not the way he had to.

"His daughter will decide."

"Is she a chef?"

He shook his head. "She worked in finance, in Boston, until she retired and moved to Phoenix, though her son and his family still live in Cambridge. She was out here with her son when Oscar had his heart attack. Not the holiday any of them wanted, but at least they were together."

Clancy's brow furrowed, gaze unseeing as he contemplated. "Hmm."

Miller chuckled. "What problem are you trying to figure out now?"

"All the restaurant stuff is still there?"

"As far as I know, yeah. He only passed earlier this week. They've been more worried about cancelling reservations and making funeral arrangements."

Noelle had been trying to reach him, but she only had the restaurant number, which was now disconnected. When she couldn't reach him, she'd left a voicemail for Sloan. The funeral would be after the holidays, in France where Oscar wanted his ashes scattered. Sloan was already booking their flights. Part of Miller recoiled at the idea—he had his own impending death to deal with; no extra funerals, please—but he owed it to his mentor, assuming Miller was healthy enough to make the trip. Which assumed he survived this one, his confidence almost as shaky now as it had been in Jackson Hole. Not to mention the roadblocks that kept cropping up.

Clancy, though, had a work-around. "Call her," he said. "See if we can use the space tomorrow night."

"For what?

"Christmas Eve dinner." Clancy leaned forward, gaze focused and alight. "Cook for us. Show me what Oscar taught you."

Miller liked that idea, far more than he should.

They met Noelle outside a local bakery the next morning. Miller walked into the older woman's open arms, and Clancy, not wanting to intrude, squeezed Miller's biceps and continued inside to peruse the pastry cases. They joined him a few minutes later, both red-eyed but also smiling.

"Noelle's going to let us use the restaurant tonight," Miller said.

"Utilities are on until the end of the month," she said. "You should be set."

Clancy gave her a hug too, whispering, "Thank you for helping to make this miracle happen."

She squeezed him tightly. "It's what my father would've wanted."

They shared a quick breakfast of croissants and coffee with Noelle, then gave her a lift to the ferry terminal so she could return to her family in Boston. From there, the rest of the day was a blur. They hit three different markets, Clancy feeling like he was a game show contestant, grabbing items off shelves as Miller shouted out his list. They were moving so fast, only a half day available before shops started closing early, that Clancy couldn't guess exactly what Miller was planning for dinner, only that clams, steak, and a lot of butter, bacon, and cheese were involved. No complaints from him.

They circled back to the bakery midday, and Miller exited with a mystery box of he wouldn't tell Clancy what. As Miller played Tetris with the loaded rental car, Clancy spotted a general store still open across the street. Christmas decorations, with a SALE sign, hung in the front window.

"I'll be back in five!" He crossed the street before Miller could shout back an objection or ask what he was up to. When he returned in ten, Miller met him by the car with a carrier bag bearing the logo of the neighboring wine store. It was a tight fit—wine bag on Clancy's lap, a bag of goodies he wouldn't let Miller see in between his feet—but Clancy smiled the entire five-minute ride to the waterfront restaurant. It was an immaculately kept three-story New England colonial—cedar shaker shingles weathered gray, as was the custom, with bright white trim around the roof and windows. Not a single shingle was broken or cracked and the windows and trim were as clean as could be.

"If the inside is anything like the outside."

"Oscar bought the building in the eighties," Miller said, as he unlocked the service door. "He was meticulous about keeping it up." He disappeared inside and returned a moment later with a rolling service cart. "Oscar was hell on the first-floor retail tenants, inspecting their spaces regularly, but he held himself to the same standard with his residence on the third and with the restaurant."

"On the second floor?" Clancy asked, as they loaded up the cart.

"Yep." Miller smiled over his shoulder. "Wait until you see the view."

Cart full, they rolled it directly into a service elevator, squeezed in behind it, and rode up to the second floor. Clancy stepped out of the cab and froze.

"Doc, you gotta move."

"Can't." He was too busy staring out the bay windows that lined the dining room's exterior walls, giving every table a spectacular view of Nantucket Sound. "How the hell wasn't this your favorite view?"

Miller chuckled behind him. "Help me get these groceries put up and you can stare out the windows all afternoon. I've got work to do."

And so did Clancy, the bags of decorations that wouldn't fit on the cart dangling off his arms. Snapping out of it, he dropped them on the big stone hearth that separated the dining room from the kitchen, shrugged out of his coat and scarf, tossing them on top, and helped Miller ferry the rest of the bags into the kitchen.

The cook-space wasn't huge but it looked plenty roomy for a head chef and several other line cooks, definitely big enough for Miller to maneuver around in tonight. Clancy would have investigated further, except Miller's hands landed on his shoulders and turned him around. "Out you go."

"I can help prep."

"Every meal on this tour has been a surprise. This one won't be different."

Miller sent him on his way with a smile and smack to his ass that made Clancy blush and grin, a little turned on and a lot pleased at Miller's uplifted mood. Maybe this idea would work. And he needed to do his part as well.

Three hours later, Clancy stepped back and observed the results of his labor. Not too bad for drugstore decorations. What had looked like a ghost of a restaurant with a spectacular view just a few hours ago, now glowed with warmth from the roaring fire in the hearth, the twinkling lights strung overhead, and the tall taper candles arranged in the middle of the solo round table in the center of the space. He'd covered the table with a white tablecloth, put garland around the center table candles, and set plates on either side, a red plaid napkin, frosted pinecone and small ball of mistletoe in each. The Christmas transformation was completed with a larger ball of mistletoe hanging from an exposed ceiling beam by the center window and garland on all the ledges.

Sometimes it paid to be the son of a woman who'd made her career as a hostess, first in their home, then arranging homes away for people worldwide.

Satisfied, Clancy dug his last purchase out of the bag, pulled it on over his T-shirt, readjusted his glasses, and wandered back toward the kitchen. He was about to tease Miller on taking too long, the wafting aromas killing him, but Clancy was struck speechless at the sight on the other side of the pass-through.

Miller looked *happy*. The first time this entire trip. Sure, he'd enjoyed himself, Clancy had made him smile and laugh, but there'd always been a slump to his shoulders, a shadow in his eyes, a gray cloud hanging over his head, even on the crowded dance floor in New Orleans. But here, he looked happy and at home. In a chef's coat, sleeves rolled up and tattooed forearms bared, he moved around the familiar kitchen humming to the nineties rock on the radio and tasting something out of a huge stock pot. He was as warm and vibrant as the fire that crackled in the hearth.

Clancy's fascination with him wasn't because he was a foodie and Miller was a chef. He'd put all that away the first night, focusing on the food and the tour, and thinking of Miller as a person first, a chef second. But seeing him like this, it was impossible to separate the two, much less Miller from the tour. Like you couldn't take the doctor out of Clancy, there was no taking the chef out of Miller. Not when it made him this happy. Deep lines around his sparkling blue eyes, his smile bright in its chestnut beard, and his face red with color, with life, that had been missing thus far. Miller had called him stunning the other night, but he had it the other way around. Miller was the one who was stunning.

Clancy's crush went nuclear.

"Why's it always Pearl Jam?"

Miller glanced over his shoulder and almost dropped his tasting spoon into the soup pot. Clancy stood leaning against the kitchen side of the stone hearth, trying to be casually suave, but the plaid knit sweater with the crocheted dancing gingerbread man was the farthest from suave ever created.

"Please, God," Miller said. "Tell me there's not one of those for me."

"No." Clancy sulked. "They didn't come in giant."

"Thank fuck." He nodded at the fire. "You know, you can put both of us out of our misery and make it go away."

Green eyes wide, Clancy clutched at the front of his sweater in exaggerated horror. "Are you threatening Gingy?"

Miller struggled for air between his guffaws. "Gingy?"

Clancy smirked. "I sense a *Shrek* marathon in your future." He pushed off the hearth and walked the length of the prep table toward the fridge at the other end of the space. "And you didn't answer my question."

Miller barely beat him there, throwing out a hand, palm to the stainless steel. "Tell me what you want, and I'll get it out."

Clancy looked like he wanted to argue, but decided against it, instead vaulting onto the closest clean edge of the prep table. Miller bit his tongue, silencing the "Off!" on the tip end of it. He'd never let that fly in a professional kitchen, not even after hours. The prep table was sacred, the final place a plate was inspected by him and the expeditor before it was handed off to the server and then on to the diner. But this wasn't a professional kitchen tonight. It was just him and Clancy sharing Christmas Eve dinner.

"Hey." Clancy nudged his hip with his foot. "This okay?" he asked, as if sensing his raised hackles.

Miller pressed his leg down by the shin. "Just keep your feet and legs clear so I can move about." He opened the fridge enough to poke his head in without giving Clancy an eye to what he was preparing. "Now, what did you want? I need to get back to cooking our dinner."

"Bubbly, if you got it."

"Of course I got it." Noticing Doc had a thing for champagne, Miller had grabbed a bottle at the store and put it in the back of the fridge with two glasses to chill. He presented the Bollinger to Clancy, as the somm had done the Monte Bello the other night. "This do you?"

Green eyes lit with delight. "More than. You know what else would?"

"What's that?"

"An answer to my question."

Miller handed the glasses to Clancy and peeled off the foil from around the bottle's neck. "Persistent thing, aren't you?"

Clancy shrugged. "Doctor."

Miller tossed the foil into the trash, yanked the dishtowel off his shoulder, and used it to twist the cork free, the *pop* and *hiss* two of the most satisfying sounds to his ears. Much like the music. "It's what I grew up on."

"Nothing is that simple with you."

"Oh, is that right?" Miller said, as he filled the glasses.

"Every stop on this trip has had special meaning to you. What does this music mean to you?"

Miller set the bottle on the prep table next to Clancy's hip. "You're too fucking perceptive."

"Again, doctor." He circled one of the glasses in front of his face, gesturing at himself, and he held the other out to Miller.

Miller sipped as he moved up and down the line, checking on his dishes roasting in the ovens, stirring the soup and sauces, venting the pressure cooker. Everything was right on schedule. He leaned against the counter opposite Clancy. "We didn't have much money growing up. We couldn't afford concerts, especially since most of them were up in Charlotte and we were four hours away on the coast. But after our first summer season here, Sloan and I had saved up enough to go see Pearl Jam play at the amphitheater in Mansfield."

"Were you always a fan?"

He shook his head. "They were on the radio all the time back then, but I wasn't really into music. Not like Sloan was, and Pearl Jam was her favorite. She was obsessed with them, and it was her birthday."

"Some present."

"To this day, her favorite." He took another sip, remembering that late August day. It was hot, humid, and packed. He'd never seen anything like it, and the perma-grin on Sloan's face that entire night, hell the entire week before and after, had been worth every lock he'd fixed, every hedge he'd trimmed, and every dish he'd washed that summer. "Once I saw them in concert, I got it."

"Got what? I've never seen them."

"To watch someone do what they truly love, in this case music, and to actually see and hear them feel the music and words in every bone of their bodies, it was incredible. They were the music."

Almost like Clancy had been on the dance floor in New Orleans, his body swaying in time to the R & B, bringing Miller's along with it, whether Miller had wanted to or not. But he had, so very much, and he'd be lying if he said he hadn't since thought about dancing close with him again.

He'd also thought about Dr. Rhodes. Like Pearl Jam onstage, and Clancy on the dance floor, Miller could only imagine Clancy's brilliance in full doctor mode. He'd seen tiny glimpses of it already. In Wyoming, when Miller's body was hurting, then across the table from him in Chicago and beside him on the ferry, when his heart was hurting too. Clancy knew how to care for people. It's what he did best.

"Like you here in the kitchen," Clancy said, reflecting his thoughts. "You're practically glowing."

"I'm hot and sweaty."

Clancy swiveled his empty glass. "Po-ta-to, po-tah-to."

Miller chuckled. "Fine, you're right. These are the first dishes I learned, and while they're nothing fancy, I do love them."

"There's no price tag on love."

Miller glanced away, downing the rest of his champagne, the sentiment hitting harder than expected. He'd thought so many things were priceless but now... Now, he knew what price was too high for even love. He wouldn't—*couldn't*—ask his loved ones—Sloan, Greg, his family—to pay it, especially not when he didn't have the emotional or physical capital himself.

The tap of the bottle on the rim of his glass drew Miller back from the darkness.

"More?" Clancy asked.

"Yeah, please." He waited for Clancy to fill both glasses, then took another long swallow, ignoring the darkness in favor of dissecting the flavors of his favorite champagne. With each bubble that burst on his tongue, fresh brioche mixed with hints of spice and pear, and a lingering nuttiness rounded out the mellow finish. Mellow, plus Sloan's favorite song on the kitchen speakers, brought to mind a question that had been nagging Miller for a while. He didn't want to consider why the question or answer mattered, telling himself he was just curious. "Why don't you blink when I mention Sloan?" Why was Clancy so mellow about it?

"She's obviously the most important person in your life."

He stated it so matter-of-factly, without the least bit of judgment or resentment, that Miller would have stumbled had he not been braced on the counter. "Not everyone gets that. Past *friends* have felt threatened."

"I'm guessing your past *friends* didn't have my parents."

Ignoring the implication Clancy had clearly picked up on, Miller gestured for him to go on.

"It's different from you and Sloan in that my parents were in love once, high school sweethearts, but they grew up and apart, fell out of love. It happens, but it doesn't mean they don't still love each other. And they still have me and other things in common. Mom and Dad share a wine collection, and she and Robert stay with Dad whenever they're in LA. Mom and Dad are still tight, they talk at least once a week, and Robert is cool with that. Why would I expect you and Sloan to be any different?"

Why would he, given those family dynamics? And that's what it was, refreshingly dynamic. "Not everyone has that experience or is as enlightened."

"I know I'm lucky. I've had friends whose parents can't stand to be in the same state as each other." He took another swallow of his drink, then set the glass aside. "Plus you're gay, so nothing's happening there with Sloan."

"I could be bi."

"But you're not. You said you're gay, not my place to question how you define your sexuality. If you were bi, I still don't see the problem. Men and women can be friends." He spread his hands wide, like his eyes. "Shocker."

Miller hung his head, laughing. Oh, how many times had he heard the opposite. "I repeat, not everyone is as enlightened."

A foot entered his periphery and nudged his knee. "I'd like to try and make an enlightened guess as to what's on the menu tonight, if I'm allowed?"

Miller smiled, grateful for the return to a safer topic and questioning again why he'd led them down the other potentially awkward path. "Okay, Doc, what's cooking? See if you can sniff it out."

Bounding off the counter, Clancy scrunched up his nose in an exaggerated sniff, then hilariously had to save his glasses from falling off. After a second, his face morphed—eyebrows climbing, eyes widening, mouth rounding into an O—as if he'd discovered a secret. "Clams and steak."

Miller threw the cork at him. "You know that from the grocery store, goofball."

Clancy snatched the cork out of the air, laughing, but then his brow furrowed, doctor-face on, as he sniffed more seriously. He strolled up and down the line, pausing over the stock pot and using a hand to waft the escaping steam toward him. "Seeing as we're in New England, I'm guessing clam chowder."

"Okay, genius, what's in the oven?" Miller scooted over, blocking Clancy mid-bend, and blocking the oven door window. "Nuh-uh-uh, no peeking."

"Hardball, much," Clancy grumbled, squinting with one eye closed. "Well, that"—he pointed at the saucepan on the stovetop—"is béchamel, and I'm guessing the steak you bought at the store is in the oven, and by the smell"—he inhaled again—"a wine sauce, maybe Madeira."

"Good nose." Miller hip checked him out from in front of stove, so he could check again on the simmering soup and sauces. "And dessert?"

Genuine shock crossed Clancy's face. "You do dessert?"

"Sloan has the sweet tooth of a twelve-year-old. If I didn't feed her dessert at every opportunity, she'd have murdered me years ago."

"Can she be my best friend too?" Clancy threw a smile over his shoulder, as he ambled back down the line, toward the pastry station at the far end of the space, away from the hearth and ovens. He ran a finger along the cutting board and stuck it in his mouth, tasting. "Flour, cream, and...Earl Grey tea?"

Miller checked again on his pots, stirring sauces to hide his blush. Clancy probably didn't intend for that maneuver to be erotic, but Miller's body had other ideas.

"And something with chocolate." Clancy held up a baking chocolate wrapper from the trash can, grin cheeky.

"Fucking cheat."

Clancy sidled back to his side. "You gonna tell me if I'm right?"

Miller held him in suspense a few extra seconds. "Nope."

Clancy shoved his chest, laughing. "Now who's the fucking cheat?"

"I'm the chef. My kitchen." He tried not to think about how right that sounded, or how right it felt to have Clancy in it with him.

"Save the chowder!"

At least that's what Clancy guessed was in the covered ceramic bowls on the silver serving tray that wobbled precariously on Miller's hand. He'd walked around the hearth, into the dining room, and rocked to an abrupt halt, seemingly forgetting about the tray, which had Newton's first law of motion on its side. For a second, Clancy was afraid he might have to dive across the table and ruin all his hard work, but at his shout, Miller's latent serving skills kicked in and he corrected, saving not just the soup but the entire tray.

"I wasn't expecting this." Miller's eyes roamed around the dining room as he approached the table. A wide smile bloomed on his face, teeth gleaming in his beard. "It looks amazing." He unloaded the tray—tossing the balls of mistletoe at Clancy with a laugh and a blush—and took another look around. His eyes, twinkling with merriment and the white lights overhead, caught on the mistletoe by the window and his blush deepened.

"I didn't mean to be presumptuous," Clancy said, about the mistletoe and the decorations, generally. "I just wanted to make the place look festive."

Miller lowered himself across the table. "You succeeded." His gaze met Clancy's and the heat in those blues was turned up to at least an eight on the stove-top dial. "It's lovely," he said, voice gravelly, sounding like he meant more than just the decorations.

Make that a nine.

Clancy was grateful for the table and napkin covering his lap. "Thank you," he said softly, his own cheeks heating.

Their gazes held another beat before Miller reached across the table and palmed the silver dome atop the bowl in front of Clancy. "Let's see if my efforts in the kitchen can live up to your efforts out here." He lifted the cover and the smell alone was enough to answer, *Yes!*

The taste of the soup—Clancy had guessed correctly, clam chowder—pushed the answer to a resounding *YES!* It was rich and hearty, with enough pepper and herbs to balance out the sweet cream and briny clams. Like a whiff of the sea on the cold winter breeze, chased away by warm comfort that trickled out from Clancy's stomach all the way to his fingers and toes.

"This is so much better than the stuff I eat between rounds."

Miller glared. "I thought we agreed never to speak of such heresy again."

"Residents can't be choosey, though the explosion of food trucks parked in the hospital lots has been a godsend."

"One of the best food trends to come out of LA."

"You think so?" Clancy scooped out his bowl with the light and fluffy bread Miller had picked up at the bakery. "Dad and I agree wholeheartedly, but I'd be curious to know what restaurant chefs think of them."

"I can't speak for all brick-and-mortar chefs, but I think they're brilliant. Physical restaurants are expensive. Rent, servers, supplies, marketing, and so on. You bleed more money than you can ever imagine, especially up front. Food trucks aren't cheap, but they're cheaper. The advertising is on the side of your truck, literally, and social media gets the word out. You can serve more people per minute than a restaurant, it's more appealing to the younger, on-the-go crowd, and the menu is usually limited. The successful ones don't try to do too much. And it takes real skill to do the work in such a tight area. The folks who run them, who cook in them, are no less a 'chef' than I am. Hell, they're probably more so."

"You've thought about it?" Clancy asked, then worried he'd stepped in it when Miller rose.

But Miller had merely stood to clear their plates, stacking the bowls and silverware, then loading them onto the tray to take to the kitchen. "Not really. Those fine dining expectations we talked about." He disappeared behind the hearth, but his booming voice carried on the conversation. "And those trucks aren't really built for a guy my size."

"I've seen some massive trucks," Clancy said, raising his voice so Miller could hear him as well. "I bet you could fit." He topped off their glasses with the white burgundy Miller had poured for the soup course and the next mystery dish he wouldn't reveal. "What concept would you do?" he asked, as Miller reappeared. Balanced on his left hand was a sterling silver tray carrying fresh silverware and two square charger plates with individual-sized casserole dishes on top.

Aromas of béchamel and ham ticked Clancy's nose, making his mouth water, but Miller held the tray high and out of view, laying out the utensils first. "Truck's not for me." He gestured around them. "I love the vibe of a dining room too much."

It was empty but for them tonight, but Clancy hadn't

missed how Miller had repeatedly and fondly surveyed the dining room, as if he could imagine it full of diners.

"And there are dishes I love to cook, like this one"—he set a plate in front of Clancy—"that would not work out of a food truck."

Clancy stared at the cheesy baked goodness and thanked all that was holy. And unholy, because it was equally possible that's where this deliciousness had come from.

Miller laughed. "I didn't think your Oh-God-Truffles face could be beat, but there we have it."

"I'm sorry. I was working my way through the pantheons and thanking all the gods."

"You just have to thank some old French farmer for this one."

Clancy picked up his fork and knife and poked through the cheesy top layer. More of the rich aroma wafted up and he bent over his plate, inhaling deep. When his eyeballs righted, he cut deeper through the layers and stalled in surprise. "Wait, is that some type of lettuce?"

"Welcome to my idea of a salad course," Miller said with a wink.

It was the best "salad" Clancy had ever had, though the endive had lost all of its nutritional value, wrapped as it was in ham, coated with béchamel, and baked under a layer of freshly grated Swiss cheese.

After savoring the last bite, Clancy rested back in his chair and patted his belly. "I don't think that salad is on anyone's diet."

"You liked it?"

"Loved it."

Their gazes caught and locked. Miller's blue eyes, reflecting the flickering candlelight, flecks of gold on fire, without the cloud of darkness swirling in them, were lovely. He still had that glow about him, brighter now as he enjoyed the dishes he loved, here in this place he loved. Miller broke the staredown first. "Well, if you loved this one," he said, standing, "let's see what you think of the next dish."

Clancy loved the next one too, of course. The beef Wellington Miller served as the main, with its rare tenderloin center and Madeira mushroom gravy was umami personified, but before things got too dark and earthy, the light-as-air pastry the beef was wrapped in delivered just the right amount of texture and sweetness. The bitter wintergreens on the side, together with a smoky, rich French Bordeaux to drink, rounded out the course and palate.

By the time they reached dessert, and Miller strolled out of the kitchen with the silver tray of goodness, as Clancy had come to think of it, Clancy was primed and ready. And when he tasted the chocolate soufflé with Earl Grey crème anglaise, it was beyond semi-orgasmic. Hell, beyond orgasmic. It was a night full of hot-sweaty-blow-your-mind-sex, in a baking ramekin and gravy boat. He eyed the latter, debating whether to turn it up and drink the remaining crème anglaise right from the boat.

Miller followed his gaze, accurately reading his intent. "I will think less of you."

"I'm not sure I care right now." The sauce was calling

his name, loudly. But he didn't want to be rude. How else to tackle the problem? A moat! He scooped another spoonful of soufflé into the middle of his dessert bowl and drowned it in sauce until the fluffy chocolate cake floated. "There." He spread his hands over the dish. "Problem solved." He loaded his spoon with a tiny bite of cake and as much sauce as he could manage without making a mess.

"First time I tried the profiteroles at Bouchon," Miller said, "I almost tipped the gravy boat to drink the rest of the Valrhona chocolate."

"Then who the fuck are you to judge?"

Those deep, attractive lines appeared at the corners of Miller's eyes. He reached across the table and snuck a fingertip into Clancy's moat.

Clancy knocked his knuckle with his spoon. "I will defend my castle."

They both busted up laughing, louder even when Miller built a castle and moat of his own. They eventually stopped giggling long enough to finish the soufflé and sauce, and Miller loaded their empty dishes onto the tray, taking them back to the kitchen.

Clancy, needing a stretch and some extra room for his digesting food, stood and wandered over to the window, loving the reflection of the harbor on the dark, inky water. He could only imagine what it was like here during high season, when the docks and boat slips would be packed. In off-season, there were people walking along the docks still —locals, some seasonal travelers—but the overall sense of the place was unhurried and peaceful. A vacation town on vacation. In any event, he bet Oscar's had been packed year-round, the location prime and the homey food enjoyed by locals and tourists alike.

"Madeira?" Miller, chef-coat undone over his T-shirt and jeans, strode his way with a squat bottle, its details hand painted on, and two tulip-shaped glasses in hand.

His ease and confidence were so sexy Clancy had to stop himself from lunging. "Sure," Clancy managed, hoping his voice didn't sound as strangled as his dick felt in his jeans. Miller filled the glasses and handed one to him. He sipped the nutty, sweet-tasting wine and stared back out the window, looking away from the too-attractive man at his side. "Greg was right," he said, aiming for distraction. "The sauces were amazing."

"And the rest of the food?"

"Even more so."

"Good." Miller turned and rested back against the window ledge. "The least I could do for the amazing job you did out here."

Tearing his gaze from the water, Clancy mirrored Miller's position, taking in the space and his Santa's helper handiwork again. "The place has great bones. I can only imagine the vibe was as comforting as the food, when it had a full dining room and bustling kitchen."

"It's my favorite place I've chef'ed. My favorite place to cook."

"I know." Clancy set his glass down and shifted, hip against the ledge. He raised a hand, tracing the laugh lines that had tempted him all week. "It's all over your face, Miller." The warmth, the peace, the sense of home.

Home. Comfort. Here.

An arena full of stadium lights blasted on in Clancy's head. "Why don't you do this, then?"

"Pardon?"

"The fine dining concept didn't work for you. So try this." Clancy waved a hand toward the dining room. "This is what you love. It's clear as day here." He cupped the side of Miller's face. "Do this. Cook what you love. And do it here."

Miller set his glass aside and circled Clancy's wrist, drawing the hand away from his face. "It's not that easy."

Clancy, though, was on a roll, ideas and visions spiraling. "It'd be amazing, Miller. Comfort food is all the rage, and you can put a classier finish on it. But only if you want to. And you'll have investors lining up. You don't have to conform to the fine dining expectations."

"Oh, that's rich."

The harsh snap of Miller's voice drew Clancy up short, making him blink. A gray shadow had fallen over the man who'd previously been alight with warmth.

"Shit, Miller, I'm sorry."

But now Miller was on a roll, dropping Clancy's hand and stepping away, the storm clouds gathering. "You're standing here telling me to go against expectations, and what are you doing with your life? With your future?"

What was that about needing more room for food? Because suddenly Clancy's stomach was on the floor.

Miller kept right on landing hits. "You're going into your father's plastic surgery practice like the good little son, and it's not what you want at all, is it, Dr. Rhodes?" The words and glare were as cold as the biting wind outside. "To spend the rest of your life nipping and tucking Hollywood's richest?"

Clancy cast his gaze back out at the ocean and struggled for the words he'd never said to anyone, much less himself.

Before he could summon them, Miller snatched his glass and downed the rest of his wine. His voice was close, his breath hot with anger when he spoke again. "Don't tell me how to live what's left of my life when you can't admit what you really want out of yours."

Chapter Eight

NEW YORK CITY

Miller cursed himself, and Sloan, for planning this trip in December. Granted, there wasn't another option, not with the ticking time bomb in his body, but right now, he'd much rather be hiding in a corner on the SeaStreak Ferry or in a random cab on the train, than stuck in a car all day with the man who was making him question all his decisions.

Once they'd hit the mainland, it should have been a five-hour drive to New York, but between intermittent snowfall and Christmas Day traffic, they were way past the five-hour mark when they hit the tunnel into Manhattan. They'd both made attempts at polite conversation, but every effort had fallen flat. Miller regretted how he'd acted last night, how he'd snapped at Clancy and what he'd said, but figuring out how to apologize without opening the door to a conversation he didn't want to have was challenging. And the pall of regret and awkwardness was stifling their usual easy rhythm. Making matters worse, Miller had had to pay closer attention to the road. He'd insisted on flying into Boston versus Martha's Vineyard on Saturday so Toby and their pilot could more easily depart again. Ditto the driver. He was unwilling to have them miss Christmas Day with friends or family on their account. They'd meet back up with both tomorrow, assuming Miller got himself and Clancy to the hotel in one piece. He did, barely, and by the time they got there, Miller was wound so tight he had to pry his fingers off the steering wheel. At least tonight's "meal" wasn't at a set time. He could crash for a few hours, get some distance from Clancy, and get his goddamn head out of the clouds where it had been spinning all last night and today, coming up with concepts, branding, and menus for a revived Oscar's.

Which he wouldn't be around to open.

And even if he got treatment—which he also cursed himself for considering—if he lost his sense of taste, then what the fuck good would all his planning do? He wasn't putting out food he couldn't taste. His balls weren't big enough for that, especially after the failure of his first solo venture. The chance of success—at defeating his cancer or opening a new restaurant—was in the single digit percentages, at best.

Pointless.

Hopeless.

No matter how strongly the idea he'd first had and ignored, until Clancy so eagerly brought it up again, had taken root.

Just like the man himself, like the attraction that kept

driving Miller closer to that smile, to that laugh, to that joy that brightened everything.

All Miller had to offer was death and darkness.

More pointless.

More hopeless.

Lacking the energy or patience to fight the crowd at the reception desk, Miller let Clancy handle check-in while he hung back, skirting around the edge of the packed hotel lobby to the entrance of the attached restaurant. It was popular, well known, and busy with holiday revelers. He'd hoped for that kind of traffic at his place, had counted on it being located in a hotel, but it'd never materialized. Maybe Clancy was right. The hotel was upscale and the same had been expected of the restaurant. Was it that obvious Miller's heart wasn't in it? Or was it that the wine country dining scene was already so saturated with places like it? Both? His name had drawn crowds early, but the buzz wore off, and with it, the crowds.

What was it about this place that worked? The open kitchen, the lively vibe? Something about it spoke to the part of Miller that had worked for ten years in New York. By contrast, nothing about his old restaurant, except the hidden farm table and the employees he loved, spoke to him. Not the space, not the concept, not the food. And if it didn't speak to him, how could it speak to diners? There was no story there. No life. Fitting.

"Are we having dinner here?" Clancy asked, reappearing at his side.

"No, but close by and much more laid-back."

"As long as there's gelatinous cranberry sauce on the menu."

Miller spun, horror-stricken. "Did we not learn our lesson about food heresy?"

A wide grin split Clancy's face. "That's the most expressive I've seen you all day."

And smile gone, as Miller was reminded of his terrible mood. Clancy tried to hide his own disappointment by shoving a room key in Miller's hand. "Room's ready."

Miller couldn't get an apology in as they dodged guests and bellhops across the lobby, nor did he want to speak it in the packed-to-capacity elevator. They were in the hallway, on the way to their suite, before he finally managed to grab Clancy's arm. "Doc, I need to apologize."

"For?"

"My shitty mood. On Christmas Day, no less."

"I'm the one who overstepped last night. It's my fault." Avoiding his gaze, Clancy shook himself loose, took the last few steps to their door, and swiped his card in front of the electronic lock.

Miller put his hand on the knob, preventing him from opening it. "But I didn't have to snap like that." He lightly clasped Clancy's chin and tilted his face up, forcing his gaze. "Or throw your own life decisions back in your face. I overstepped too. I'm sorry."

"You were just so happy. I liked seeing you like that." He cast his earnest green gaze aside again. "And then my mouth got ahead of my brain."

"It's okay." Miller pushed Clancy's glasses up his nose. "I wish Oscar's was the answer, but it's not."

"What is?"

There wasn't one, simple as that. But rather than bringing the mood down further, Miller said, "Right now, rest."

He pushed into the room and halted, Clancy stumbling into his back.

"What's wrong?" Clancy poked his head around Miller's shoulder. "Hmm, that's not right." He stepped back, swinging the door partially closed to check the room number. Yep, it matched the room number written on the paper holder in Miller's hand. Clancy squeezed in next to him, the both of them considering their "suite." While the room was luxurious with top-of-the-line furnishings, as Miller had come to expect and had held his tongue over the last two stops, it was exactly that. A room. Not a suite. There was a sofa in a tiny seating area, a desk, and a bed. As in one. One room, one bed.

Clancy checked the door to their left. Bathroom.

Miller checked the one to the right. Connection to the other bedroom, through which he heard the squeal of small children.

"There must have been a mix-up." Clancy crossed the room and picked up the phone on the desk. "I'll call down."

There was a knock on the door behind them, and Miller dealt with the very harried valet, who didn't give him an option of not taking their bags, Clancy's escalating argument with the front desk be damned.

"We seem to have very different definitions of *suite*," Clancy said into the phone.

Miller tuned it out, knowing what the conclusion would be. It was Christmas week in New York City; there were no more rooms. He stared out the window onto Central Park, the light dusting of snow giving it a magical quality in the setting sun. At least the view was good.

Clancy slammed down the phone. "There was some sort of mix-up," he said, hands on his hips. "This is technically a suite, and there's a sofa bed."

"In case you haven't noticed, Doc, I'm six-three. I haven't fit on a sofa bed since I was in high school."

"I'll call Mom," he said, digging out his cell phone. "See if she can find us something else."

Miller closed his hand over Clancy's. "One, don't interrupt her and Robert on vacation. Two, it's Christmas Day in New York City. We're not going to find anything else, definitely not anything this nice."

Clancy glanced helplessly around. "I can sleep on the sofa."

"Don't be ridiculous."

His gaze whipped back to Miller, eyes wide. "What are you saying?"

Shit, what was he saying?

A stray thought of Clancy only being a couple inches shorter than him, no better suited for a sofa bed, had been why he'd suggested it, wasn't it? Not because those green eyes looking up at him were darkening. Not because there was color rising on those winter pale cheeks. Not because the desire to taste those full, curved lips had only gotten worse since Friday night. Not because Clancy had played a starring role in all those daydreams of reopening Oscar's that had been plaguing Miller since last night.

Before Miller could sort an answer out of his mess of feelings, another knock sounded against the door.

"I told them I'd call back down," Clancy said, brow furrowed.

Miller crossed the room ahead of him and opened the door.

Sloan's smiling face greeted him. "Merry Christmas, baby."

Another person appeared at her side, his dark brown eyes full of mischief. "Is it time to party yet?" Greg said with a wink. "Because we need to party."

Miller waited for the door to close behind Clancy, who, rest assured, would get nowhere with the front desk, before he rounded on his two best friends. "What are you doing here?"

"Wasn't gonna miss the annual reunion at Eli O's," Greg replied.

Sloan unwound her scarf, ginger curls tumbling loose, and tossed the plaid cashmere onto the bed with her coat. "And I've spent every Christmas with you for almost twenty-five years." Stepping to Miller's side, she wrapped her arms round his waist and smiled up at him. "Did you honestly think I wouldn't spend this one with you too?"

He kissed the top of her head. The sentiment tugged at his heartstrings, but as much as he appreciated it, as much as he hated to admit seeing her here was the best Christmas present he could have hoped for, he couldn't be that selfish with her time anymore. "What about Tyler?"

"He's here too, out on Long Island with his family."

"And Tony?"

"Also with them," Greg answered. "Wedding planning." At Tyler's family's Hamptons house where the double wedding would be held next summer, after Sloan had the baby, after Miller would probably be gone.

By the narrowing of Greg's eyes, he'd followed the direction of Miller's thoughts. "Which is the other reason I'm here," he said. "You should have told me."

"You told him?" Miller said to Sloan.

"How else was I supposed to explain my lack of surprise that you refused to be our best person?"

Miller ripped out of her arms. "It wasn't your place to tell him."

"Bullshit!" She stepped forward and rose on her toes, getting as close to in-his-face as possible. "He's a part of this family too, and how would he, or I, or hell, Miller, your family back home that you haven't told yet either, feel when you drop dead and we didn't get a chance to say a proper goodbye."

The gut punch robbed Miller of his words.

But not Greg, who pushed off the windowsill and came to their side. "Or convince you what an idiot you're being."

"I've heard it all from her already."

"And all of a sudden you've decided not to listen to

her?" He thumped the back of Miller's head. "Have you lost your goddamn mind? She's always right."

"This isn't her decision," Miller barked back.

"Isn't it? She's your—"

Miller held up a hand. "Not anymore."

Greg slapped it away, bringing them nose to nose. "I was going to say best friend. And family. Like I am. We're not letting you go that easily."

Sloan slid in between them, hands on Miller's chest, voice far too much like the fifteen-year-old he'd found in the town park almost twenty-five years ago. "I'm sorry, baby, but not telling him has been killing me. Trying to plan this wedding and thinking about you not being there with us..."

A tear streaked down her cheek, and Miller yanked her into his arms. He could never stand to see her cry, at fifteen or almost forty. "You're going to have a beautiful wedding." He looked over her head at Greg. "Both of you."

Sloan glared up at him, the lawyer fighting back. "It'd be more beautiful if you were there too."

Holding his course was harder with each tear she shed. He never wanted to bring her pain, but this was better for all of them. It'd save them more pain in the end. He dropped another kiss on her crown before retreating to the windows, staring out at the wintery park again.

"Why, Miller?" Greg asked behind him. "Explain it to me."

In the glass, he caught the reflection of Greg's hard dark eyes. "Of all people, I shouldn't have to explain it to you."

Greg crossed his arms, not giving an inch. "Well, you do."

"We're chefs." Miller turned and rested back on the ledge, facing him. "Our lives revolve around taste—perfecting seasoning, pairings, entire menus. How much salt to add? Does it need acid? Where's the perfect balance of sweet and savory? If I lose the ability to taste, to do those things that are essential to my daily life, both for work and my soul, which is highly likely with the course of chemo I need, not to mention radiation and possible surgery, then what the hell am I supposed to do with myself? Who the fuck am I?"

"None of that may come to pass," Greg argued. "And even if it does, you're not the first chef to have cancer or to lose their taste buds. We've seen others do it and succeed. You've got twenty years of sense memory to fall back on. Losing your taste buds doesn't mean you don't know how to run a restaurant or kitchen."

He pushed away from the window, hands flailing. "Like the one I just ran into the ground?"

Greg clasped his shoulders and gave him a hard shake. "One bad venture, Miller. I've had three. Your past accomplishments aren't erased by that one failure or this disease, and neither is the person you are out of the kitchen. To me, to Sloan, to the rest of your family." His eyes flickered to the door and back. "To Clancy."

Miller shrugged him off. "Don't bring him into this."

"But isn't he? I know what I saw in New Orleans."

Sloan, sitting on the edge of the bed near Miller, patted

his ass. Her eyes were still wet but knowing. "Something you want to tell me, honey?"

"Don't look so smug, dear," he said, lowering himself next to her.

She brushed her long curls out of the way and snuggled up to him. "If he's what convinces you to live, then I'll be smug all I want."

"Why are you so stubborn?" Miller grumbled.

"Why are *you* so stubborn?" she parried back.

Greg rolled his eyes. "Why did I ever get mixed up with you two?"

"Because you love us too," Sloan said with a grin.

"I do." He claimed the spot on Miller's other side. "And I'm not ready to lose you."

"Greg," Miller forced out of his own tightening throat. "I don't want either of you to see me like that, to have to spend your time—"

"Our choice." His friend's hard brown eyes had turned soft and pleading. "Don't give up on us, Miller, and I promise, we won't give up on you."

Someone cleared their throat on the other side of the room. Miller whipped his head around, looking over Sloan's carrot-top, to find Clancy in the entry way, his shoulders slumped and arms dangling at his side. Resigned.

Had he heard their conversation? Or was his reaction about the room?

"Let me guess, no other rooms," Miller said, venturing on the latter.

"None."

"We'll make it work," he said to Clancy.

Greg bumped his shoulder. "If this night goes as it usually does, you'll both be too drunk to care at the end of it."

"Where exactly are we going?" Clancy asked.

Miller smiled. "Where it began for the three of us."

"Well, well, well, look what Old Saint Nick dropped on my doorstep."

The voice bellowed. *Bellowed.* No other word for it, booming over the crowd noise in the small, packed pub.

Clancy stepped out from behind Miller, expecting to find another man Miller's size. He wasn't expecting an elf. Or rather, a short, rail-thin older man with weathered skin, dark eyes, and a smattering of salt-and-pepper hair peeking out from under an elf's hat.

"Eli!" Miller shouted back. "How old's that costume by now?"

The man dressed as an elf, Eli, cut through the crowd and greeted Miller with open arms. "Come smell it and tell me."

Miller made a token effort to wave off the impending hug, but judging by his wide smile, and how tightly he wrapped the older man in his arms, he didn't care much about the stinky costume. He practically swallowed Eli, whose arms barely reached around Miller's chest.

"You're too skinny, Sykes," Eli conversely determined. "Fire a double shepherd," he shouted toward the kitchen, before giving hugs to Greg and Sloan. "And you two, of course. My three musketeers."

"Four this year," Miller said, dragging Clancy forward. "Eli, this is Clancy Rhodes."

Eli raised a brow. "Your..."

"A friend spending the holidays with us."

Clancy's stomach didn't exactly flutter, more like a wonky somersault, both confused and pleased. *Friend* was more than he deserved after butting his nose in where he had no business, but *friend* wasn't half as much as he really wanted.

Eli didn't give him more than a moment to obsess over it. "Elliott O'Connor," he said, hauling Clancy into a hug. "Do you know what you've gotten yourself into, kid?" He pulled back and cut his eyes to Miller, Sloan, and Greg. "Double, double, toil and trouble there nearly tore this place apart."

"We did no such thing," Sloan said.

A chorus of "Bullshit" rang out from the crowd.

None of Clancy's friends argued. "You three worked here? This is the pub you mentioned before?"

Greg nodded as he collected their coats and scarves and hung them on one of the hooks by the door. "Everyone here tonight is an Eli O's alum."

"It's a Christmas tradition." Eli wagged a finger at Miller, Sloan, and Greg. "That they started."

"So who's gonna tell me that story?" Clancy asked.

Miller pointed at Sloan. "She's the mastermind. She tells it best." He cleared them a spot at the bar and pulled a stool out for Sloan.

Clancy claimed the one next to her, assuming Miller would take the one on his other side. When he moved the opposite direction instead, Clancy shot out a hand and grabbed his wrist. "Hey, where are you going?"

Miller flipped his hand over, squeezing Clancy's, and Clancy's stomach fluttered more than somersaulted this time. And again when Miller smiled, fondly like he had last night, before it'd all gone to shit. "I'm gonna go eat."

Greg rejoined them and slung an arm over Miller's shoulders. "Did someone say eat?"

Miller squeezed Clancy's hand once more, pecked Sloan's cheek, then headed toward the kitchen with Greg.

"Save us some," Sloan called after them.

Miller returned, "Yes, dear," to the crowd's laughing amusement.

Half-turned around on his barstool already, Clancy surveyed the pub. It was bigger than he'd first judged. Long and narrow toward the front, where they sat at the bar, but beyond the other end of the bar, and the spiral staircase that led upstairs, the space opened up considerably. Tables filled half the space, a pool table and dart lanes the other. The mezzanine level above, visible through the metal balcony rail, held more tables and dart lanes.

Clancy twisted back around to look at the bar. It was old and well-worn with too many chips and carvings to count. The other side had all the usual bar stuff as far as Clancy could tell, but he didn't spend too long looking, his attention drawn instead to the antique mirror over the back bar. It was plastered with pictures, more than a few of them of Miller, Sloan, and Greg. Toes hooked through the stool rail, Clancy leaned forward to get a better look.

Until his view was abruptly cut off. "Well, hello there, handsome."

Clancy shifted back, considering the bartender who'd rested his forearms on the bar top directly across from him. He was cute, thirty-five or so, with jet black hair and black eyes to match. Given his features and short height, Clancy guessed a relation of Eli's.

"Ever the flirt, Pattycakes," Sloan said.

"You keep bringing in these beautiful boys, gorgeous. What am I to do?"

Sloan threw an arm out in front of Clancy. "This one's taken, Patrick."

And Patrick wasn't really his type.

Wait, what? He was *taken?*

Before he could ask Sloan what she was on about, Patrick stuck out his bottom lip in a cute, full pout. "There went my Christmas present."

"Bring us two Negroni, and I'll leave you a big tip for a present."

"A water," Clancy cut in. "And a Jameson, neat."

Patrick grinned. "Miller called ahead and warned me." He leaned over the bar and kissed her cheek. "Congrats, babe. If anyone deserves it, it's you."

She patted his cheek, smiling sweetly. "Thanks, Patrick."

"I'm still not making you that Negroni."

"I just want a taste."

"Nope!" Patrick laughed all the way to the other end of the bar.

"You know you can't have alcohol, right?" Clancy said, doing his doctorly duty.

"Oh, I know, and I wouldn't. But as the former bartender of the bunch, I have to give them a hard time."

"You used to tend bar?"

"Yep, they cooked, and I waited tables until I was old enough to get behind the bar. Never looked back."

Patrick returned with their drinks, made sure they were all set, then scurried off to fill more orders.

"You know," Clancy said, voice lowered, "when I texted you an SOS last night, I didn't mean you had to rush here." After he'd so royally overstepped, and sensing the tour was going to go from awkward to worse, he'd texted the person who knew Miller best, begging for an intervention.

Sloan smirked. "I was already on my way."

"Of course you were." Clancy rolled his eyes, and Sloan sputtered around a sip of water. Clancy laughed and handed her a napkin. "But seriously, thank you for coming."

"I wanted to be here with him." She balled up the napkin and tossed it over the bar into a back bar bin. "We do this every year, and Greg and I were already out on Long Island. I was just trying to give you and Miller some space."

"I don't think space is what he needs right now. That's why I suggested you bring Greg too."

Miller needed the people who were most important to

him, and he needed to be reminded how much he meant to them.

"I realized that too," Sloan said. "Greg filled me in on what happened in New Orleans."

Clancy stared into his whiskey. "I didn't want that to be their last meeting."

"You know what's going on, then?"

He touched his throat in the same place he'd felt the lump in Miller's Friday night. "He's got cancer."

"Advanced stage."

"Fuck." Clancy threw his whiskey back in one go. There was no other appropriate response. Well, besides covering his face with his hands and having a good cry, but that was the last thing Sloan needed, on the verge of tears herself. It wasn't late stage, but advanced was hardly better. He knew the statistics, and remembered his patients, those who'd survived and those who hadn't, those who'd be at the benefit in a few months and those who wouldn't. Depending on the exact size and location of Miller's tumor and how far it had spread, he could have less than a twenty-five-percent survival chance.

Don't tell me how to live what's left of my life, Miller had said last night.

What's left.

The thought he'd had and dismissed in New Orleans came roaring back. "He doesn't want to get treatment," Clancy put together. "That's what this is all about. A tour of last suppers?"

She blinked back tears and took a long drink of her water. "A side effect of the recommended treatment is loss of taste. And if they need to do surgery, he could lose part of his tongue and throat."

"Fuck his taste buds," Clancy cursed low. "And we can reconstruct the rest. If he doesn't get treatment, he'll lose his life."

"If he can't be a chef, if he can't taste, he thinks that's as bad as being dead, maybe worse."

Noise erupted from the far end of the bar. Miller had emerged from the kitchen carrying a giant tray of food and wearing a huge grin. Everyone around him was cheering and smiling too. He was the center of everything, in a kitchen of one or a pub of fifty. And not just because he was a chef, but because that sort of life, that sort of warmth, bleeding out of him in his smile, his eyes, and the laugh lines around them, drew people in. How could it not?

"There's so much more to him, to his life," Clancy murmured.

"I know that," Sloan said, "and the more people who can help Miller see that the better." She curled a hand around his arm. "I don't want to lose him."

With Miller moving closer to the center of his world too, Clancy didn't want to lose him either.

Miller stood by the upstairs balcony rail, nursing his bottle of Gravity Stout and taking in the packed pub. There wasn't much to distinguish this Eli O's Christmas party from the last one. The bar had a few hundred more carvings in it, the dartboards a few thousand more pinpricks, and there were more gray hairs on guests' heads and less hairs on Eli's, but all in all, it was the same homey Irish pub and the same loud, rowdy party Miller had started twenty years ago and attended every year since.

And yet everything about it this year felt different.

As hard as he tried to smile and be the circus ring-leader everyone expected, Miller stood apart from it, watching from the outside, even as he'd physically stood right in the middle of the crowd. He was the one who'd put himself on the perimeter, mentally and emotionally, after the hard sell Sloan and Greg had lobbed at him. It was getting harder to stick to his decision, but as much as his friends thought—or more accurately, hoped—it would all turn out okay, promised that they wouldn't leave his side through treatment and recovery, Miller couldn't ask them to do that. He couldn't ask Sloan to give up the precious time she would otherwise devote to the cannoli, to Tyler, to becoming an equity partner at the firm. He couldn't ask Greg to give up time at Dram or to look at him without pity when Miller couldn't taste anything or had to eat through a tube. He couldn't ask his family to worry about him, not when his parents were ready to retire comfortably and not when each of his sisters had successful jobs and kids to raise. His family was finally—*finally*—in a good place, and he would not bring them down. And he couldn't ask Clancy to take a chance on a guy he'd only known a week.

Wasn't that just the kicker? His parachute, in the form of a sexy, green-eyed doctor, had arrived after he was already speeding too fast toward the water.

"Thank you for bringing me here."

Speaking of the mixed blessing.

Clancy approached, glass of whiskey in hand.

"Good food, yeah?" Miller said.

"Can't complain about shepherd's pie, bangers and mash, colcannon, and boxty on a cold night like this."

"What'd you like about it?"

He seemed to consider a moment. "I can taste the history of this place, of Eli's family, in it."

Miller felt the same. This place was home for Eli's family, and for a time, had been home for Miller's found family too.

"It's also great for soaking up this," Clancy added with a tip of his glass. "Though I was promised a night of drunken debauchery."

Miller leaned his forearms on the rail and pointed at his two best friends. "They're behind the bar now. Party's just getting started."

Sloan flipped two bottles at once, deftly catching them, spouts down, and poured the booze directly into a shaker. The crowd cheered.

"So she really did tend bar here," Clancy said, hip to the rail next to Miller. "She told me she did, but I didn't totally believe her until now."

"Best bartender Eli ever had." He raised a single finger to his lips. "Don't tell Patrick."

Clancy mimed zipping his lips and throwing away the key. As usual, they didn't stay closed more than a minute. "How long were you all here, together?"

"Me and Greg, just a couple of years before we moved on to other kitchens, but Sloan stayed. She put herself through CUNY undergrad and Columbia Law." Miller glanced back at his friends, remembering fondly how Sloan would get home from classes, wrangle him and Greg out of their beds, shove extra-large coffee mugs in their hands, then drag them here every night, never a minute late. She never slowed down. Still didn't, even pregnant. She'd make a great mom. No sleep necessary.

Clancy drifted from his side to a nearby table. "You all love it here."

"This was home, and the energy..." Miller gestured at the bar crowd below and the dart players behind them. "Oscar's was a great place to learn the fundamentals, and Martha's Vineyard a good place to get our feet under us, but this was our first time really out on our own."

"If you loved it here, why'd you leave?"

Miller claimed the chair beside him. "First Greg and I went to work in other kitchens in the City, and then after Katrina, Greg left. With his hometown hurting, he couldn't stand to be away. When I hit thirty, Sloan got it into her head that we should 'settle down' and start living like grown-ups."

"Sounded to me like you two had been doing that since you were teens."

"Po-ta-to, po-tah-to," he tossed back at Clancy.

He grinned. "So you decided to move across the country to the second most expensive city in the US?"

Miller pointed his bottle at him. "Okay, Mr. Never Left Home."

Wincing, Clancy rolled his empty glass between his palms. "Touché."

"I'm sorry, that wasn't fair."

"But no less true." Clancy rested back in his chair and crossed one leg over the other. "I envy you that, having been all these places."

"California was the right move. I love this, but it's tiring after a while. And the kitchens are different too."

"More screamers?"

As if on cue, one of the groups behind them shouted, as did Eli, calling an order into the kitchen to fire more bangers. Miller chuckled. "More like everyone's a screamer here. I got the opportunity to chef and improve my craft somewhere new, and Sloan was ready for sun."

"How'd she handle that first summer in San Francisco?"

Miller dropped his head back and groaned, remembering that first Fog City summer full of rants and tears. "I have never made so much pastry dough in my fucking life."

Clancy's bright laughter brought him back upright.

"That said, she appreciated the difference between firm offices. She'd still be an associate here, if not already burned out, and she'd be fighting a very entrenched old boys' club. She still has to work her ass off in California—the Bay Area is its own special kind of rat race—but she's already a junior partner and she gets to wear jeans to the office. It worked out for us."

"Would you come back here and chef?"

Miller glanced out over the balcony again. Would he, yes. Could he, no.

Clancy quietly cursed. "Shit, I apparently can't not overstep."

Miller looked back and Clancy had hung his head, his glasses sliding down his nose. Miller reached across the table and pushed them back up. "You're a doctor, kind of your job. I know you mean well, but my future isn't here." It wasn't anywhere. Not here, not with Greg, Sloan, or Clancy, no matter how much he might want that to be true.

Clancy closed a hand over his, holding it to Clancy's cheek where it'd drifted, Miller unable to resist the present. "Your future is wherever you want it to be."

But it wasn't really, even if he wanted it to be right here with this man.

"Hey!" came Greg's shout from below. "No long faces." Miller tore his gaze from Clancy to find his friend standing on the end of the bar top closest to them. "And why aren't you drunk yet?" He shouted over his shoulder at Sloan. "Negroni for your boy, another whiskey for his."

"How about a Vieux Carré instead?" Clancy said, long face long gone. "Made with Sazerac, please."

His smile chased away Miller's long face too. "Make it two."

Greg clapped merrily, as both Eli and Sloan swatted at him to get down. "Let the debauchery begin!"

Miller laughed. "Here we go!"

After several bumbling attempts, Clancy finally got his Eli O's menu tucked into the leather binder. He nestled the book back in his luggage, then plopped down onto the end of the hotel bed, bouncing. He planted his hands in the mattress, pushed up, and bounced again, giggling.

A stern-faced bear glared back at him. "This is a five-star hotel, Doc, not a bounce house."

Clancy threw his scarf at him. Or rather, he tried, but the damn wool wouldn't detach from his hand.

The angry bear transformed into an unbearably handsome man. And why did he have to stand so close and smell so damn good? Wanting more, Clancy flailed and made it extra hard for Miller to help get his scarf and overcoat off.

"You know," Clancy started, loud, and cringed at his lingering bar volume.

The bar, where he'd lost count of how many cocktails he'd tossed back. Enough for him to climb on top of the bar and dance with Greg, wailing out the lyrics to Pearl Jam songs. Dancing and singing for Miller, who swayed behind the bar with Sloan, but whose eyes never strayed from Clancy, tracking his every move. The attention had only driven Clancy higher. Spinning faster.

Spinning ideas he wasn't supposed to have.

Spinning, spinning, spinning.

Miller finally freed him of his outerwear and threw it, with his own, on the sofa. "You know what, Doc?"

Oh, he'd spun right away from his earlier thought, which he couldn't remember anymore. He closed his eyes and fell back on the bed. "I'm kind of glad for the smaller room now. Not so much of it to spin."

A tug on one foot, then the other, and Clancy's shoes were off, his toes freed too. The better to curl when another strong waft of bourbon, sweat, and kitchen flopped onto the bed beside him. "I told you not to try and out-drink an Irishman," Miller said, head propped in his hand, looking down at him.

"I'm Irish!" Clancy waved a hand at his green eyes and managed to knock his glasses askew.

Miller's answering smile was crooked, half out of focus, and no less gorgeous. "Did you grow up in an Irish pub like Patrick?"

"Point taken." Clancy aimed an index finger at the bridge of his nose, trying and failing to right his glasses. "But I dance better than him."

Miller removed the pestering glasses altogether. Much better idea. He reached behind him and put them on the table, then turned back, resuming his model pose. "I won't argue you that. The leprechaun's got two left feet."

"Did you and Sloan dance at your wedding like you did tonight?"

"No, we got married at the courthouse. We left for Boston that same afternoon. And 'Black' wouldn't have been my song of choice."

The lyrics flitted through Clancy's mind, all too fitting as he thought about them now. "Would it be now? Is that how you feel?"

"About Sloan? No." Miller tilted toward him, fingers weaving through his hair like they had on the dance floor in NOLA.

Clancy couldn't see his expression. Everything was a blur, inside and out.

Things got more confusing when Miller levered up

and removed his shirt. Not confusing. Hot, everything was hot. Sparks raced up and down Clancy's spine, through his blood and along his skin.

Skin. Inked skin.

Miller stretched back out beside him, tattoos on full display. Clancy scooted closer and before he could stop himself, traced his fingertips over the dark lines, feeling more than seeing the abstract designs. "Did you get these here?"

"Some of them."

"Is it Māori?"

"Not exactly. More like a recipe buried in abstract line work."

Clancy whipped up his gaze. "A recipe?" Miller nodded, and Clancy returned to squinting at the design on his left arm. "I don't see it."

Miller chuckled, the warm breath and warmer sound sending another riot of sparks through Clancy. "Because you're blind and drunk."

And inherently curious. Doctor, duh. He reached out, tangled his fingers with Miller's, and brought their joined hands to his opposite arm. "Show me."

Miller inhaled sharply. Clancy cursed and retreated —*shit*, he'd overstepped again, thinking and wanting things he wasn't supposed to—but then Miller, hand still in his, drew him back in. "Close your eyes," he whispered hoarsely.

Clancy snapped his eyelids shut, willing to do anything to prolong this closeness. Miller guided his hand back against his skin and began tracing what Clancy recognized as shorthand. When he finished spelling out the last ingredient, Clancy opened his eyes and smiled. "Oscar's béchamel sauce?"

Miller flattened their hands over the tattoo, like a benediction. "Yeah," he said, voice hoarser still.

Clancy looked up. Something wet glimmered on Miller's face. Before Clancy could reach a hand up and feel for himself, Miller switched one hand for the other in his and began tracing the tattoo on his right arm. Clancy tried to put it together but couldn't make the pieces fit. "Some sort of dessert." Butter, sugar, eggs, flour, and other baking staples. "But I don't remember anything like it."

"Because we haven't had it." Miller rubbed the spot between Clancy's eyes, and Clancy relaxed his brow, closing his eyes under the soft caress. "It's my mother's chess pie recipe."

Pie sounded good. Warm like the body he was resting against. Comforting like the smell of the kitchen. Clancy buried his face in Miller's shoulder and inhaled. "Will you make it for me sometime?" he mumbled, the cocoon lulling him closer and closer to sleep.

Lips brushed his forehead and big, strong arms closed around him. "I don't know if I'll have time."

Clancy ignored the flitting thought of ticking clocks and nuzzled closer, nose under Miller's chin. "Want more time with you." Wetness from above made his nose twitch, but he ignored it too. "I really want to kiss you, but I'm about three seconds from passing out. Will you hold a three second kiss against me?"

The kiss lasted a respectable ten.

Ten seconds of gentle lips moving against his. Of the spicy sweet trace of cocktails, tinged with fresh salt. Of the fleeting promise of home on Miller's breath and in his touch.

Ten seconds. More than a brief touch, but not nearly enough.

Miller pulled away first and tucked Clancy's head under his chin, dropping another kiss on his forehead. "I'm glad you're here with me."

Clancy curled his fingers around Miller's right arm, around the recipe he'd yet to taste. "Please," he murmured, clinging to the promise of it and holding on to the man who was becoming the center of his world.

For as fuzzy as he'd been when he fell asleep, Clancy woke completely clearheaded. He startled at first—at the heavy arm over his waist, the furnace blazing against his back, and the gentle breaths ruffling the hairs at the nape of his neck. But the next second he remembered where he was, who he was with, and the kiss they'd shared last night.

His chest ached. It wasn't enough.

One night wrapped in each other's arms. One barely there kiss, even though that brief, gentle touch had been the best kiss of Clancy's life. One trip together, experiencing something they loved in common.

Clancy wanted more nights, days, and years to get to know Miller. The picture was as clear as day in his head. Of Miller in an open kitchen, the center of a lively restaurant, featuring the simple dishes he loved best. Of Clancy strolling in at the end of his day, teasing, kissing, guessing dishes and ingredients. Of tasting the pie that's recipe was inked on the arm Clancy still had his hand curled around. Of Sloan and Greg visiting with their families, Uncle Miller their favorite, Clancy a distant second. Wouldn't bother Clancy one damn bit. Miller was the center of their world, and he wanted him alive and happy.

Not dead.

Clancy wouldn't let that happen. The world would not be a better place without Miller Sykes. He had to do everything—anything—to make sure that bleak future didn't come to pass.

It was time to call an audible and shatter some expectations.

Chapter Nine

Miller woke feeling more rested than he had in days. More rested than he usually did after an hour flight, that was for sure. Retrieving his phone from the seat pocket, he flipped it over in his hand and did a double-take at the time. He hadn't just been asleep for the sixty minutes it took to fly from New York to DC, where they were supposed to dine tonight at a funky seafood spot in Georgetown. Being stuck in the land of Dungeness crab, Miller wasn't leaving the East Coast, for possibly the last time, without some Maryland blue crab.

But according to his phone, he'd slept for over four hours. And they were still in the air; descending, judging by the pop of pressure in his ears. He glanced out the airplane window and squinted, blinded by the bright sun. Once the spots in his vision faded, he looked out again, hand over his eyes to reduce the glare. He took in the unexpected landscape, his brow lifting until it tickled his fingers. They hadn't been circling DC for three hours.

Below were hills of green grass and brown brush, dissected by freeways ten lanes wide, packed with slow-moving traffic. He touched the window. Cool, but not East Coast winter cold.

He popped out his earbuds and glanced across the aisle to where Clancy was staring out his window. "What's going on, Doc? Where are we?"

The smile he turned on Miller was almost as blinding as the sunlight. He tilted his head toward his window. "Come see for yourself."

Miller unlatched his seat belt just as they hit a bump of turbulence, and the seat belt light dinged on a split-second later.

"Hurry up." Clancy used his foot to spin the chair across from him outward, toward Miller. "I'm not going to tell."

Miller quickstepped across the aisle and fell into the offered seat. He rebuckled, rotated, and looked out the window. Palm trees, high sandy cliffs, and the ocean, stretching as far as Miller could see.

"We're back on the West Coast?"

Clancy nodded. "OC, technically."

Orange County. Well, that explained the view, on both sides of the plane. But... "Why?"

"You've shown me so many places that are special to you. I wanted to show you a place that's special to me." His smile softened, full of that same sweet eagerness that had first appeared in Napa. "I hope you don't mind."

Miller's stomach tightened. The warmer stopover sounded delightful, maybe even more delightful than the crab he'd miss, but he couldn't help feeling like there was more to this than Clancy was letting on. Things had spiraled the last few days—the blow-up with Greg in New Orleans, the unintentionally romantic Christmas Eve gone awry in Martha's Vineyard, Sloan and Greg's surprise visit, then last night with Clancy, after Eli O's.

"I know it's an extra back-and-forth before the last stop," Clancy said, interrupting Miller's thoughts before they reached the place they'd gone all morning, and in his dreams too. "But as much as you like a good view, I think this will be worth it. And I promise you'll still get your blue crab."

"You knew where the next stop was?"

"A little birdie told me," he said with a wink. He reached across the space between them and lightly grasped Miller's right arm. "Please."

Clancy's long, slim fingers bisected his mother's chess pie recipe, and Miller's thoughts picked right back up where they'd left off. Remembering how those fingers had traced his tattoos last night and ratcheted up Miller's building need for him. How they'd clenched around his arm when Miller had brought their lips together, unable to resist the cresting need any longer. It hadn't been the crushing kiss he'd anticipated, but it was all the more perfect for its sweetness, for the hint of flavor. If he'd tasted more, he'd be even more of a wreck than he already was, second-guessing all his decisions.

Thanks to the drinks, he'd fallen asleep shortly after Clancy, the ongoing debate in his head silent for a few hours until the alarm had woken him to an empty bed.

Clancy had left a note on the table—*At brunch downstairs with Sloan and Greg.* Miller had missed waking with Clancy in his arms, but the remembered heat of his hand on his arm had lingered. Now the heat was real, Clancy's hand there again, and against his better judgment, Miller wanted to keep it there.

He laid a hand over Clancy's. "All right, Doc, show me what you got."

What Clancy had was quite possibly the best view of the Pacific Ocean Miller had ever seen. Standing on the balcony of their corner suite at the Ritz-Carlton Laguna Nigel, Miller watched as the sun slowly descended over the water toward the far-off horizon. The hotel sat high atop a cliff, the waves crashing with a thunderous *boom* on the beach below. In the gazebo on the cliff's edge, Clancy chatted with a suited older gentleman while servers bustled around them, setting up a space heater in one corner, a champagne bucket in the other, and a dinner table in the middle. Miller had no idea what they'd be eating—he'd held himself back from looking at the in-room dining brochure—but regardless of the cuisine, the view and the company would be spectacular. The relatively balmy sixty-degree weather was icing on the cake. If someone had told Miller he'd be dining *al fresco* on this tour, he would have laughed, but it felt right. Something else he wouldn't have wanted to miss, one last time.

He was just rolling up his dress sleeves when a sommelier approached the gazebo. Recognizable by his sharp suit, the tray of drinkables he balanced, and the white towel over his arm, the somm handed Clancy a cocktail glass first, a Negroni judging by the color. Clancy placed it on the table, turned back around, and at seeing the bottle the somm presented, Clancy burst out laughing, some joke between them that Miller couldn't hear.

Didn't matter. Miller's chest ached all the same, Clancy's laughter like a warm blanket full of hidden knives. Was it luck or a curse that'd brought this wonderful man to him now, when he had so little time left?

As if sensing the attention, Clancy shifted his gaze toward their balcony. His sparkling green eyes locked on Miller, and he smiled, wide and bright.

Miller had his answer. He was the luckiest man alive, at least for tonight.

Same as he'd had no business stepping onto the dance floor in New Orleans, he had no business stepping off the balcony and cutting across the lawn to the gazebo. No business accepting the invitation in Clancy's eyes or his offered hand at the bottom step of the gazebo. But Miller was as powerless to stop himself as the waves crashing against the beach below. One more memory. One more night to enjoy an amazing meal with this amazing view and an amazing man. He prayed Clancy would forgive him afterward, and if he didn't, well, his reserved seat in hell would be worth it.

Miller snagged the last ring of fried calamari off the plate in the center of the table and popped it into his mouth, humming contently. Clancy agreed. If more people's first experience with calamari were like this—juicy, tender, and lightly seasoned—versus an overdone brick or a soggy fried rubber band, then maybe more people would love the delicacy as much as he did.

Miller washed his bite down with champagne and relaxed back in his chair, making room for the servers to clear away their appetizer plates. "Why here?" he asked, turning the familiar question around on Clancy.

Clancy was surprised he'd waited this long. Through the amuse-bouche of yuzu chawanmushi, through the seafood appetizers of swordfish dip, fresh oysters, tuna ceviche, calamari, and the Maryland blue crab Clancy had requested special, and through cocktails and half a bottle of champagne. The light conversation over the small plates had been easy; what Clancy needed to say would not be. While he'd hoped to get a bit farther into the meal before going there, he hadn't expected to make it this far.

He chickened out and stalled some more. "The view isn't enough?" He gestured with his glass out at the ocean. The dark water rippled under the night sky, reflecting the moon and stars and the lights of the hotel and nearby residences. A thousand little points of brightness.

"I don't think you hijacked our trip for A-plus calamari and a view." His gaze swung from the ocean to Clancy, eyes darkening, and when he spoke again, his voice was low and rumbly. "No matter how spectacular."

A tingle raced up Clancy's spine, heat hit his cheeks, and the fluttering kicked up in his belly. He sipped more champagne, pretending the alcohol was the reason for his blush. Any excuse to hold on to this feeling longer. The one where Miller flirted with him and still enjoyed sharing his company.

"Spill it, Doc."

He set his glass on the table and stared out at the ocean again. "Worst day I ever had, this is where I ended up."

"Clancy." Miller's voice was gentle, as was the hand he laid atop his. "Given that look on your face, I hate to think you drove down here from LA after a day like that."

Clancy couldn't help but laugh, recalling his flailing that afternoon. "I didn't drive. I called Mom, who was in town." She'd been a complete Miranda when he'd needed it most. "I told her I needed to escape and that I didn't care where the plane took me. LAX to John Wayne was the first flight plan she could get cleared."

"That can't be more than ten minutes in the air."

"About right. Thirty, gate to gate. By the time I got to one airport and left the other, I could have driven the distance faster, but I was in no shape to get behind a wheel."

"What happened?"

Clancy flipped his hand, palm to palm, and wound their fingers together. For the comfort. And to keep hold of Miller.

"Fourth year of med school, I lost a patient on my oncology rotation."

As expected, Miller tried to yank free his hand, but Clancy held tight.

"What's this about?" Miller's eyes were no longer dark with desire or warm with concern. They burned bright with betrayal. He'd figured out this was a setup.

Withstanding the icy glare, Clancy would be damned if he let Miller go without saying his piece. He'd been nervous before about starting this conversation, but now that he had, Clancy was determined, and desperate, to see it through to the finish.

And was stalled by a pair of servers who approached with the next course. Fucking karma. Clancy kept his cool, holding Miller's hand and making polite conversation with the servers as they described his achiote salmon and Miller's chipotle miso black cod. The very California fusion of Asian and Mexican flavors was another reason he'd brought Miller here. The mix of cultures on their plates reflected one of the things Clancy loved most about his hometown.

As soon as the servers retreated, Miller forcibly freed his hand. "Did Sloan tell you?"

"No, I figured out." He jutted a thumb at himself. "Doctor, remember?"

"Oh, I remember." Miller tossed his linen napkin on the table, pushed back his chair, and stood.

Clancy grasped his wrist. "Please, just let me finish my story, and then if you want to leave, I won't stop you." He inched his hand higher, thumb tracing the edge of the recipe tattooed on his arm.

Something in Miller seemed to give. Not all the way— an ocean of wariness swirled in his blue eyes—but he gave a jerky nod and sat back down.

Thank the fucking Lord.

He picked up his fork and knife and began cutting his

food into small bites. That'd been one of the first clues. "Go on," he ordered gruffly.

"There was a car waiting for me at the airport, and it brought me here. I sat in this gazebo, nursing a bottle of Veuve—" Clancy gestured at the bottle with the same yellow label in the ice bucket "—and cursing God, Allah, Buddha, and every other deity I could remember, for taking my patient's life. Julie was a forty-year-old mother of three, an elementary school teacher who had half her life still in front of her. But every mention of her future came with an asterisk. She'd tested positive for BRCA, the breast cancer gene, in her twenties and had already survived one round in her thirties. Her body couldn't withstand it a second time."

Miller's jutting Adam's apple worked overtime. "Clancy, you don't have to—"

Clancy held up a hand, took a few bites of his food, and downed a long swallow of liquid courage. "Eventually Manny, the hotel manager who was out here earlier, got me back to my room and in front of the fire pit with a pack of s'mores. That night, I called my dad and said I'd go into practice with him, and the next day I withdrew my oncology residency applications."

"Who could blame you?" Miller said. "Who'd want to go through that every day?"

Clancy shrugged, helpless in the face of the truth. "Me." His conscience and his heart couldn't fight it any longer. "It was the wrong decision."

Sterling silverware clattered as Miller laid his down on the gold-rimmed plate. "I don't understand."

"I sat by Julie's bedside every day that last week, once she was admitted to hospice. I did what I could to make her comfortable. I hope that I made the end of her life a bit better for her and her family. And at the moment she died, I was in the OR, helping to remove a tumor from another patient."

"But you still lost your patient."

"I did. I still do, volunteering on the oncology ward. And I will lose more when I make it official."

"What are you saying?"

"You were right. I don't want to join my dad's practice. Face-lifts aren't enough, and while reconstructive surgery may keep me close, it's not close enough for me. I want to practice oncology. I want to see Julie's family at the benefit in a few months and tell them what a difference she made in my life, for the better. I want to help people live, and for those who can't, make the end more peaceful for them."

Miller cast his eyes down at his plate, but not before fear, pain, and sadness streaked through them. And resignation. God, the resignation was enough to bring down a mountain.

Unless Clancy could stop the landslide. "I don't want you to be one of the latter, Miller. I want to help you live, if you'll let me."

Miller poked at his food. Anything to avoid Clancy's eyes and words. But with his first bite, they couldn't be avoided, the cod like a machete on its way down his throat, the knot of fear that had lodged there making it even more painful than the usual tumor-caused razor blades. He forced the fish down with a gulp of water.

"Can you promise me, if I get treatment, that a year from now I'll be able to taste this?" He waved a hand at his plate of lovely food, the flavors on his tongue bright despite the pain that came with swallowing.

"No, I can't even promise you you'll live."

Simple, honest, no bullshit. Miller should appreciate that, but all he could do was regard the ocean with a cold, bitter laugh.

Metal scraped against stone tiles, Clancy pushing back his chair, and a moment later, he crouched in front of Miller, hand on his right arm. "What I can promise is that I will be there for you every step of the way. So will Sloan, Greg, your family, and the rest of the people who love you. And we won't love you any less if you can't taste this food a year from now."

Miller's heart galloped, running from fear, from fate, and from one two letter word in Clancy's promise. "We?" The breathy single syllable was barely audible over the waves, but it was loud enough to bring a soft smile to Clancy's face.

He moved closer, between Miller's spread knees, and lifted a hand to his cheek. Heat radiated from his gentle touch, far too tempting, just like his words. "You're amazing, Miller Sykes. And not just because you're a fantastic chef. Your loyalty, your heart, your smile." His thumb teased the lines at the corners of his eyes, then drifted down to the corner of his mouth, before skating his bottom lip. "Those are the things I'm falling for. Not your taste buds."

Miller knew he should keep running, right off the gazebo's cliff, but that enticing warmth, those softly curving lips, those green eyes so full of emotion drew him into Clancy's arms and into the kiss that had tempted him from the very first night he'd laid eyes on Clancy Rhodes.

It wasn't a gentle brush like last night's kiss. Miller wanted to taste, all of it, at least one time. Hands lifting to frame Clancy's cheeks, he tilted his head, angling for better access, tongue sweeping inside Clancy's inviting mouth. Miller groaned as flavor hit him like a crashing wave, pulling him under and tossing him about. The nuttiness of the champagne, the heat of the achiote peppers, the salt and butter dichotomy of the salmon and squid, the lingering acid of the ceviche and chawanmushi. And underlying all those flavors, Clancy. A taste like no other. Bright and full of hope.

The promise of a flavorful life he couldn't have.

Miller ripped his mouth away. That was why he'd held himself back. Why he had to walk away right this second. That taste, this man, didn't—couldn't—belong to him. "I'm sorry," he said. "But I don't want to live in a world where I can't taste that ever again." He dropped his hands and stood. "I'm glad I got to know you, Clancy Rhodes, but this is the end of our tour."

Clancy rocketed to his feet and grabbed his wrist. "Miller, don't."

Using his wrist in Clancy's hand, Miller tugged him closer and used his other hand to push the black-rimmed glasses up Clancy's tear-slicked nose. "You'll be an amazing oncologist. You made the end of my life more beautiful than I could have ever imagined. Thank you for that." He pressed a kiss to Clancy's cheek, tasting his brightness one last time, before he turned and stepped into the dark.

Hands full, Clancy clicked on the balcony fire pit with his toe and sank into one of the patio chairs. He tucked the s'mores kit in his lap while he peeled the foil off the champagne bottle that'd been waiting for them in the room. A celebratory dessert Clancy had hoped to share with Miller. Instead, he'd lost another patient today. No, not a patient. The man he was falling in love with.

No use bullshitting about that either. Like his mother said, he had no talent for it. He'd suspected it was love when he'd woken up in the wee hours of the morning, wrapped in Miller's arms. Had known it when he'd gone to his knees in front of Miller in the gazebo and pleaded for him to live. Had felt the crushing weight of it when Miller, after giving him the best kiss of his life, gave him an equally heartbreaking one goodbye.

But he hadn't been able to bullshit himself or Miller any longer. About what he wanted, out of a career or out of life, including Miller. At least he'd made a decision on the former and that decision wouldn't change, regardless of losing Miller. If Clancy could save someone else the pain he felt right now by giving their loved ones hope, or by giving them peace, then his own pain, this trip, falling in love with Miller Sykes, would be worth it.

Clancy wrenched the cork free, brought the bottle to his lips, and tipped it up, guzzling, despite the bubbles burning his nostrils.

Ten days.

Ten days for his world to be turned upside down, to be sucked into the vortex that was Miller Sykes, and to be spun out of the tornado here, of all places, on the new worst day of his life.

Fitting.

He took another slug from the bottle, then turned his attention to the box in his lap. He untied the brown ribbon and slid out the courtesy card from the resort. His vision blurred and he swiped his fingertips under the edge of his glasses, wiping away the wetness. As much as he appreciated the mix of flavors in their dinner dishes, this was what he'd most wanted to share with Miller. A simple dessert yet one of the most satisfying, one you couldn't help but smile over. How could anyone be sad when eating s'mores? He laughed at his own illogical question, the evidence to the contrary streaking down his face. Or were his emotions the illogical thing here?

Logic was hard, s'mores were easy.

He unpacked the kit onto the fire pit's granite ledge—skewers, graham crackers, vanilla marshmallows, and chocolate from one of the factories up in San Francisco. He toasted a marshmallow and smushed it with a piece of chocolate between two crackers. He felt slightly better after eating it. He took his time with the second, longer still for the third. By the time he reached the last one an hour later, the realization that Miller wasn't coming back had set in.

Clancy thought to get up and check his phone, but he didn't want to read the text from Miller saying he'd have the valet come get his bags. He'd said the tour was over. Delaying the inevitable wouldn't change the outcome. Clancy took another swallow from the bottle, skewered the last marshmallow, and extended it over the gas flames.

The electronic door lock clicked behind him.

He bobbled the skewer, almost dropping it onto the fire. Getting hold of it and himself, he laid the skewer and sandwich pieces on the granite ledge and rotated in his chair. "Miller?"

"Yeah, Doc." Miller stepped into the room, through the shadows cast by the single lamp, half in and half out of life. He dropped his shoes on the floor, emptied his pockets onto the glass dining table, and walked around the end of the Murphy bed that housekeeping had pulled down and made. He raked a hand through his windswept hair and a visible shiver ran through him. It was warmer here than on the East Coast, but it'd cooled after sundown. If Miller had walked on the beach, it would have been especially chilly down there, away from the heaters and fire.

Fire.

"Shit." Clancy whipped back around and found his last marshmallow a gooey blackened mess. "Fuck."

He was about to toss it into the fire when Miller's hand closed around his wrist.

"Wait." He slid into the other chair. "It's not a total lost cause."

Hope propelled Clancy's heart into his throat, choking off his words. Miller took the skewer, blew on the marshmallow a few times, then carefully peeled away the blackened char, flicking the carbon off his fingers and into the flames. The soft middle of the marshmallow spread over the remaining chocolate and cracker in Miller's other hand. He used his finger to spread the marshmallow around a bit more, added the other cracker on top, then held the extra gooey sandwich out to Clancy for a bite.

Leaning forward, Clancy closed his eyes and tried not to think about his lips and tongue skating over Miller's fingers. About the taste of Miller that wasn't there for the first three sandwiches. About lingering longer with his lips on Miller's skin.

Fail on all counts.

He opened his eyes, feeling ten degrees warmer and hard as a rock in his jeans. He heated and hardened more as Miller, eyes locked on him, ate the other half of the s'mores and licked his fingers clean.

"What is this?" Clancy managed, voice cracking like a teenager's. He cleared his throat and tried again. "I didn't think you were coming back."

"I made myself a promise."

Hope swelled. "About getting treatment? Did you change your mind?" Miller shook his head, and Clancy's hope nose-dived, along with his stomach. "But—"

"I promised myself one more night. That I'd live in this

moment with you. I can't promise you tomorrow, Clancy. Just tonight. Is that enough?"

"No."

Miller's face and voice fell. "I understand." He stood and turned to leave.

Clancy shot to his feet, blocking his retreat. "No, you don't understand. I've spent the last ten days with you and it's not enough. One more night with you will never be enough." He stepped closer and laid his hands on Miller's broad chest, sliding them up and around either side of Miller's neck. When Miller flinched, Clancy held on tighter, ignoring the lump under his palm. "But I'll take it. I'll take one more night with you, and hope you change your mind about tomorrow and beyond."

"Clancy—"

He swallowed whatever Miller was going to say in a crushing kiss, sealing their mouths together. No more promises, no more protests, no more caveats. Whether this turned out to be their first or last time together, Clancy was going to make love to the man who'd opened his eyes and stolen his heart.

Logic and self-preservation had urged Miller to go by the front desk and ask for another room, preferably on the other side of the moon from the man who was making him question everything. But every step had led him back to Clancy, to the stunning man he'd spent the past ten days with. The man who was laid out on crisp white sheets beneath him, bared and flushed, back arched and writhing, as Miller licked and kissed all over his lean, trim body.

Tasting.

His chocolatey sweet lips and delectable mouth that kept Miller coming back for more. Obsessing over the inviting warmth in each kiss.

The tang of sea spray and smoke that had gathered behind Clancy's ears and at the base of his throat. The essence of coastal California on the LA boy who'd brought Miller here to experience it with him.

The fresh scent and tart taste of lemon verbena soap that tickled Miller's nose and tongue as he sucked one then the other of Clancy's nipples. Bright, so very bright, just like the man himself.

Clancy shuddered, and Miller released him with a parting nip. He buried his face in the wiry patch of hair at the center of Clancy's chest, lapping up every smell, taste, and sensation.

"Oh, God, yes." Clancy's fingers tangled in his hair, holding him there. Denim scraped against Miller's bare sides, Clancy hitching up his legs, and Clancy's erection, straining behind his zipper, rutted against Miller's abdomen. Miller groaned, open-mouthed, into Clancy's chest, as he rocked back, the friction against his own trapped dick almost unbearable.

Clancy tugged on his hair and Miller levered up, bringing their lips back together, feasting on Clancy's mouth. On the traces of nutty champagne, spicy pepper, and tart citrus, on the lingering sweetness of the chocolate and vanilla marshmallows, on the want and need infusing Clancy's taste and stoking his own. Never had Miller wanted someone this badly. It was New Orleans, ratcheted up a thousand.

Clancy hiked his legs higher, like he was trying to climb a rope, and in doing so, dug his ankles into Miller's back and dragged his cock along his torso. Miller soared higher. He coasted a hand over Clancy's hip, over his ass, and down the seam of his jeans, rubbing and cupping him between his legs, teasing the heat and hardness.

"We'll get there," Miller promised.

Clancy shoved his head back into the pillow and groaned. The strangled, needy sound would haunt Miller's wet dreams for eternity, but it wasn't enough to deter him from his mission. He nipped and licked his way down Clancy's arched neck. "I want to taste every inch of you first, while I still can."

Clancy lifted his head and, hand in Miller's hair, yanked his back, demanding his gaze. With his glasses off, Clancy probably couldn't see him well, but Miller sure as fuck could see him. Pupils blown out, lips kiss swollen, cheeks a bright attractive red. His serious-as-a-heart-attack expression, though, dominated the lust. "We've been on this tour together. I want to taste you too."

Voice a whip of demand, there was nothing Miller wouldn't give him. And what Clancy said was true. He'd been with Miller every step of the tour, fully engaged in the food and destinations. He'd thrown himself into the experience one hundred percent, proving that nothing was on his no-no list. Miller couldn't have asked for a better companion. If Clancy wanted to fully immerse himself in this experience too, then the more pleasure for the both of them.

"Okay, Doc." He moved off Clancy so they could strip the rest of the way. It'd been years since he'd done a sixty-nine, but if this was his last time— He shook off the thought, putting away tomorrow and focusing on tonight, living in this moment, with the man he'd spend tonight with, if he couldn't have all the tomorrows with him. He raced to catch up with Clancy, who already had his pants and boxers off. Miller added his to the pile of discarded clothing and shifted to roll onto his back.

Clancy caught him by the shoulder, hauling him front to front again. He nuzzled under Miller's chin and dropped kisses along his jaw. "Want you on top."

Despite most of his blood rushing south, Miller had a tiny amount still left in his head. "I'm too heavy."

"You're not." Clancy inched up and stole a peck on the lips. Miller stole more, carding his fingers through Clancy's thick, soft hair and crushing their mouths together, wanting more than a peck, more than just a second.

Clancy broke for air and rested his forehead against Miller's. "Want you on me, around me." He skated a hand down Miller's spine, over his ass, and tipped him forward, demanding more of his weight and bringing their cocks into rutting contact. "Please," he said with a roll of his hips.

The last bit of Miller's blood raced south to the other head presently in the driver's seat. "Fuck, okay, but stop that if I've got any hope of lasting."

Clancy laughed, and the warm, bright sound and rumble of his body did Miller no favors. Before it was too late, he pushed up onto his hands and knees, swiveled the other direction, and straddled Clancy, knees on either side of his head. He stretched forward, hands roaming down the length of Clancy's body, over the ridges and dips off his abdomen, and along the line of dark hair bisecting his pelvis. Miller fanned out his hands, fingers splayed, and traced the model-worthy hipbones on the way down to lean, strong thighs, which Miller nudged farther apart.

Clancy dug his fingers into Miller's ass cheeks, tilting his ass up, his cock down, and closed his lips over the head, sucking hard. Miller indulged in the hot, wet suction for a moment then pulled up and out, still wanting to savor more of Clancy before losing his mind. Clancy groaned and arched beneath him, cock straining and glistening. Miller wanted to taste it, taste him, but he couldn't skip to the main course without savoring the starters. One quick flick of his tongue over the head, an amuse-bouche, before he skated his nose down Clancy's length and buried his face in the patch of dark hair. Miller inhaled and licked. Freshness gave way to musk, man, and sweat.

Clancy's hands ran up his legs and curled around the front of his thighs. "Fucking tease."

"I'm savoring."

"I'm starving," Clancy replied, then swallowed Miller's cock to the root.

Miller shook, hands slipping off Clancy's thighs and planting in the bed. He curled his fingers in the sheets and struggled to hold himself up, to not thrust into the scorching heat. Clancy wasn't helping, using his hands around his thighs to spread them farther, to bring Miller lower, down on top of him like he'd wanted. Clancy swallowed, throat clenching around his tip, and Miller wobbled, arms going weak. There was no way not to thrust, which only revved Clancy more. A groan danced up Miller's spine and Clancy's cock swelled, demanding attention. Miller welcomed the distraction from his own building pleasure. He took hold of Clancy's erection, hand around the base, and lowered his mouth to the head, sucking it between his lips and teasing the slit with the tip of his tongue. Salty, sweet, smoky, with a touch of that brightness he'd forever associate with Clancy. More perfectly balanced than anything he'd ever tasted. He swirled his tongue around the head, like he had that hunk of bread around the soup bowl in Wyoming. Soaking up all the delicious flavor. Miller hummed with delight. He carefully took Clancy's cock down farther, and Clancy sucked him harder in return. A feedback loop of the very best kind.

Balance restored and rhythm steady, Miller used his free hand to tease Clancy's thigh, loving the ripple of tense muscles beneath his fingertips. He loved it even more when he got a full shudder for teasing Clancy's taint and fondling his balls. Clancy bucked, causing a twinge of pain in Miller's throat, but Clancy quickly corrected. Before Miller could even dwell on it, he was distracted again by Clancy's spit-slick finger teasing his hole. Balance and rhythm faltered, Miller's entire body quaking, as Clancy teased the sensitive nerves around his entrance. Clancy pushed in and Miller gasped, overwhelmed with the sensation of being stretched open.

"Yeah, that's it," he groaned. Giving up any semblance of strength, he stretched out his arms, fingers tangling in the wiry hairs on Clancy's legs, and buried his face at the base of Clancy's cock. He kissed and teased while thrusting into Clancy's mouth in time with those long, talented fingers.

Fingers that found his prostate and nearly sent Miller over the edge. If he didn't stop this now, it was all going to be over, and as stretched out as he was from the main course, he didn't want to miss dessert.

He pulled out and up, and Clancy's mewl almost ruined Miller's plan. Almost had him sinking back down, but his empty ass clenched, reminding him of what he needed. He rotated and had to pause to admire the gorgeous man beneath him. If Clancy had looked delectable before, the affect was ten times more powerful now. Hair mussed, eyes half lidded, cheeks red, and lips glistening. Miller had to taste him again, taste them, and it was better than any kiss they'd shared before. His own flavor added to the addictive mix that was Clancy's. Like the ounce of Campari that turned a martini, a drink Miller couldn't stand, into his favorite Negroni. He drank until his head spun, until Clancy wrapped a hand around their cocks and reminded him of the last course. He tore himself from Clancy's mouth and kissed a path to his ear. "Need you to fuck me," he whispered.

Clancy jolted, stroke faltering, and Miller drew back to find his half-lidded eyes gone wide. Not the first time he'd gotten that reaction, the usual assumption being he was a top. He smiled and kissed his way back down Clancy's neck. "You've already got me half open."

"I wasn't sure."

"I'm versatile but prefer to bottom."

Clancy's smile met his as they kissed again. "Whatever you want, I'm game." He resumed his torturous, wonderful strokes. "But I still want you on top."

"I need to get—"

Clancy flung out an arm toward the side table.

Miller stretched over, yanked open the drawer, and found condoms and lube inside. He dropped the bottle onto the bed and began ripping into the condom packet. "Prepared."

Clancy stilled his motions with a hand on Miller's cheek. "Hopeful."

Tears sprang out of nowhere, stinging the backs of Miller's eyes. He angled his face into Clancy's palm, hiding the wave of emotion that crashed over him. Clancy brushed his thumb over his lips. "Put the condom on me, Miller, and make love to me, please."

Miller blinked back the tears and kissed Clancy's palm. "I can do that." He finished opening the condom and rolled it onto Clancy's dick. Clancy whimpered, back bowing with restraint, and Miller bent over him, kissing his sternum, teasing his nipples, and licking into the hollow of his throat. "Almost there," he said, before snagging the lube and righting himself.

He squirted a generous amount into his hand, tossed the bottle next to the pillow, and rose on his knees, reaching behind himself to finish the prep Clancy had started.

Clancy's gaze burned. "Fuck that's hot." He grabbed the lube, squirting some into his own hand and stroking himself, until he couldn't take it any longer. He shoved his head back into the pillow, keening, "Now, now, now."

More than ready, Miller knee-walked forward, reached behind himself to take hold of Clancy's slick cock, and positioned it at his entrance. He sank down, past the brief burst of pain until all that remained was sated fullness. Miller clenched his ass, feeling every inch of Clancy inside him.

Clancy wrapped a hand around Miller's right arm, over the tattoo, and pulled Miller down on top of him. "Come here." He planted his feet in the mattress, making it easier for Miller to push back on his cock, finding their rhythm as they kissed.

Fuck, it was perfect. Clancy was perfect. Everywhere around him, in him, warm and bright, as if he could push away all the darkness.

As if.

He couldn't. It was too late. Miller found this, found Clancy, too late.

He felt the sting of tears again, the wetness he couldn't hold back, and he sat upright before the tears splashed down on Clancy's face. But his rhythm faltered, too tossed around inside to hide from the outside. Clancy's scrunched-closed eyes popped open. He was up the next second, chest to chest, even as they stayed connected, rocking back into rhythm.

"Hey." He cupped Miller's face, brushing away the tears. "Talk to me."

The love shining out of his eyes made the tears come faster. "Why can't you be mine?" Miller choked out.

Clancy leaned forward, kissing the wetness away. "I am, Miller. You just have to stay with me. Please, stay."

Could he? Would Clancy's brightness be enough to see him through the darkness ahead? Or would Miller only bring him pain? Only set himself up for a harder crash into the water? Would it all turn to black?

Clancy's answering kiss was anything but dark. It was full of fire, of conviction, of promise. As was the sure stroke of his hand around Miller's cock and the firm hold of the other one around his neck. As if he could dissolve the lump there with the sheer force of his love.

As if.

Maybe...

When they came together, there were stars behind Miller's eyes. Bright and stunning.

Clancy woke with a start, instantly alert like he'd been yesterday morning. Except this jolt to consciousness hadn't been peaceful. Something had triggered the part of his brain that'd been conditioned and trained to respond to emergencies. Something that had him reaching for the stethoscope that wasn't around his neck.

Also missing, the man he'd shared his bed with last night.

Retching—hard and painful, punctuated by heaving gasps and a muffled grunt of pain—split the silent night.

Fuck.

Clancy scrambled out of bed, shoved on his glasses, and grabbed his phone off the side table. He raced to the bathroom, skidding to a halt in the doorway. If he hadn't been trained to stay calm in the face of all manner of medical horrors, he would have lost it right then, and every bit of his dinner from the night before too. It wasn't the worst he'd seen, but this was Miller—his skin a sickly shade of pale, his top mop of curls a matted mess, and his lips dappled with bright red blood. His knuckles too, where they were white-knuckling the rim of the toilet bowl.

Fuck. Fuck. Fuck.

Kicking into action, Clancy snatched a hand towel off the vanity, dowsed it in cool water, and dropped to his knees beside Miller. Blue eyes flickered to him, an apology and a plea in them, before another round of vomiting forced Miller back over the bowl.

Clancy held the damp rag to his forehead and threw his other arm around Miller's shoulders, struggling to get a grip on the hot, sweaty skin. Retching this hard would leave Miller sore for days, and Clancy aimed to minimize the violence to his body. But it was the blood that worried him most, more of it coming up with the remnants of Miller's dinner.

Once the heaving subsided, Miller sank back on his haunches. He didn't resist as Clancy pulled him into his arms, cradling him against his chest. Clancy lowered the damp rag from his forehead to his lips, wiping them clean, before tossing the towel into the sink.

Miller pressed his face into the crook of Clancy's neck. Even after the cool cloth, the lingering heat was worrisome. "Didn't mean to wake you."

"We need to get you to the hospital."

Miller shook his head. "It'll pass."

"Who's the doctor here?" He grabbed his phone off the vanity.

"It was you."

"Exactly." He pulled up the dial pad and hit 9-1-1.

Miller closed a hand over his before he could press Send. "It was you." His hazy eyes took too long to focus, whether from the tears or the fever, Clancy wasn't sure, but it only escalated his concern. "When 'Black' was playing," Miller said, "I was thinking about you." Giving up the fight, he sagged against Clancy's shoulder and closed his eyes. "You're so fucking bright." Tears spilled, hot and wet on Clancy's skin. "But not my sky."

Clancy cradled the back of his head and kissed his forehead. "I want it to be yours, Miller."

"Why can't you be mine?"

Those words, uttered during their lovemaking.

Clancy recalled standing on the bar at Eli O's, wailing out the same, Miller's gaze locked on him. It hadn't been about Sloan. It had been about him.

Miller sank heavily against his body, his pulse racing and breath ragged.

"Miller! Miller!" Clancy forced his shaking hand

holding the phone to still and pressed Send. "Stay with me!" he urged Miller, lips to his forehead, praying for a miracle, as the phone rang.

"Love you, Doc."

He was gone before Clancy could say the words back.

Chapter Ten

LOS ANGELES

Miller's senses came back online one at a time, registering his surroundings.

The steady annoying beep that woke him.

A chemical smell that made his nose twitch, and a chemical taste on his tongue that made him want to take a pastry scraper to it. Antiseptic and medicinal, and not in the interesting Laphroaig sort of way.

He had a pretty good idea where he was.

The rough material against his legs and torso confirmed as much. He moved to lift the scratchy gown off his skin, but a sharp pinch to the back of his hand made him wince and drop his hand back to the bed.

Scotch, or better yet a Vieux Carré, would be good right about now. Something to blank his mind and turn his senses back off. Make him forget.

A hand closed over his. Its delicate weight, sure hold, and long nails were as familiar to Miller as his own grip. He knew whose arm that hand was attached to without even opening his eyes. But he did, to his best friend at his hospital bedside.

"Hey, babe," Sloan said, sounding as tired as she looked. Her red hair was pulled into a sloppy topknot, her blue eyes were shadowed by dark circles, and her smile was fleeting at best.

Miller tried to speak and managed a pitiful croak. Everything—lips, tongue, mouth, throat—were dry, like he'd swallowed a whole bag of cotton balls. Fuck, this was worse than a hangover.

Sloan grabbed a paper cup off the nearby tray table and brought the straw in it to his lips. "Slow," she cautioned.

She needn't have. The pain in his throat limited him to only a few sips. It was enough to wet his lips and tongue and make his voice work, albeit hoarsely. "What are you doing here?"

"Where else would I be?"

"Long Island."

She returned the cup to the table and grasped his hand once more. "I was there, two days ago."

His fingers clenched around hers. "Two days ago?"

"You've been out almost thirty-six hours," came a different voice, drawing Miller's attention to the doorway. Dressed in scrubs, a stethoscope hanging around his neck, a badge attached to his shirt pocket, Clancy looked at home. He was a doctor, in the flesh, doing the thing he loved, exactly where he was supposed to be doing it, even if his messy brown hair, pale skin, and slumped shoulders also looked like he'd been awake all thirty-six of the hours Miller had been out.

"It's Thursday?" he asked.

"Midday."

Shit. He turned his head to Sloan, too fast, and winced again. His body ached, all his muscles protesting, even the ones he didn't think he was using. "Southport?" he hissed, as the wave of pain crested.

"I called your mom," she said. "Told her you'd be delayed a few days."

"What else—"

"That's all I told them." She stood and brushed down her slacks and sweater. The deep wrinkles in the fabric hinted at how long she'd been sitting in that chair, as did the silent communication passing between her and Clancy, like they'd grown close enough to develop their own signals. "I'll give you two some time," she said. She stepped to his bedside and laid a hand on his chest, atop the plaid hospital gown someone had found for him. "Listen to what he has to say," she whispered, and the look in her eyes wasn't far removed from the look she'd given him that night decades ago at the park. Desperation, sadness, and no small amount of anger. "Please, Miller, if you ever loved me or the rest of your family, listen." Bending, she pressed her lips to his forehead. "I love you."

Righting herself, she grabbed her purse from beside the chair and crossed to the door. She stopped next to Clancy, rose on her tiptoes, and kissed his cheek. "Make him listen."

Miller chuckled. At least she was an equal opportunity

drill sergeant. He waited for Clancy to close the door behind her before he spoke. "I guess I should be thanking you."

Clancy fell back against the door. "Or cursing me. Near as we can tell, the citrus from our dinner was probably what caused the unhappy gut. Sloan said you had a bout of gastroenteritis a few weeks ago?"

Miller nodded.

"If you hadn't fully recovered, chances were high for a relapse, given your weakened immune system and all the travel and dining out we were doing. Lots of germ exposure. You had a fever, indicating infection, and the citrus accelerated the flare-up in your GI tract, causing the cramps and vomiting."

An upset stomach. Fuck, he'd thought it'd been the end for the second time in two weeks. Because, in truth, he had no idea what the end was supposed to look like. He'd tuned out most of those conversations after his diagnosis, as they'd all ultimately led to talk of treatment.

"I woke up with my stomach in knots, and then when I started throwing up..." He gestured at his throat. "It hurts."

"You tore things up good. I saw the blood and called in an airlift." Clancy pushed off the door and stopped at the end of the bed, hands braced on the rail there. "They've medicated the tissue for pain and infection, but it's only a temporary fix. With the location of the tumor—"

"I can still taste, though. I can taste whatever medicine they gave me."

"If you don't get treatment soon, you won't be tasting anything, much less breathing."

Miller turned his face away, as much as the pain allowed, and cast his gaze out the window.

Air whooshed out of Clancy, then after several heavy steps, out of the cushion of the bedside chair as Clancy took a seat. "You're at UCLA's Cancer Center," he said. "If there's anyone who can save you, it's the team here."

"Can they save my sense of taste too?"

"Maybe, but Miller, right now, this is about saving your life. One battle at a time." Clancy gently grasped his chin and slowly rotated his face back around. "And I meant what I said the other night. I will be with you every step of the way."

That same conviction Miller had tasted in Clancy's kiss now burned in his eyes. But fuck, to never taste that again, to never get another taste of Clancy. "If I lose—"

Clancy's hold tightened. "You will still be Sloan and Greg's best friend. The cannoli's godfather. Son to your parents, brother to your sisters, uncle to your niblings. You will still be you, Miller Sykes." He released his chin and pushed back the curls tickling Miller's forehead. "You'll still be a good man who has a family that loves him and wants him to live. The man I want to live because I'm falling in love with him too."

"I can't ask—"

"You didn't; we're offering. So much of who you are, what you do, is considering and sacrificing for other people. What you did for Sloan, what you do every year for the Eli O's alums, what you do every night for diners. So consider that we want you to live, consider that you are our number one priority right now, and consider that we don't want you to sacrifice yourself." He rested a hand on Miller's cheek, and Miller nuzzled into it, hiding from the stunning man and his beautiful words, Clancy's convictions challenging his own. "But you have to be the one to decide," Clancy said. "How badly do you want to live? Because this will be the fight of your life. But I promise you, Miller, I will do everything in my power to make it worth it. And whether we have one year or fifty together, I also promise to make sure you have peace at the end."

Could he fight that war, not knowing if he could win it? Did he have enough fight left in him? Could he bet on the fifty over the one? With Clancy on his side, the odds were definitely better, but were they good enough? Was the promise of even one year with Clancy and a peaceful end enough? Could there be peace knowing he'd left Clancy and his other loved ones behind? He closed his eyes against the tumbling dilemmas. "I need time to think."

"That's better than a no." Clancy brushed his lips over Miller's cheek. "The oncologist will be in shortly to go over your options. Sloan has your medical power of attorney so she needs to be the one with you. Then when I get back, I'm happy to talk through any of it with you."

He stood and Miller caught his hand, clutching it as tight as his weakened muscles could, desperate to keep him close. "Where are you going?"

"To tell my father I can't join his practice. That my future is here."

"Fuck, Clancy, don't give up your future for me. I might not even have one."

Clancy smiled. "I meant my future as an oncologist, be it at this hospital or one wherever you are."

More of their conversation in the gazebo came flooding back. "Are you sure?" The last thing Miller wanted was for Clancy to make a huge, life-changing decision, just because of him, especially when he was so very far from a sure bet.

Clancy's smile was so confident, so bright, Miller had to close his eyes. "When you were in surgery, I called Julie's family and talked to them about where I'd been, where I was going, and the benefit. I'm more sure than I've ever been, Miller. Thank you for helping me see that." His lips brushed Miller's, a gentle touch like their kiss in New York. The taste of coffee, Clancy, and what could be. "I hope you fight to see that future with me."

In his mind's eye, Miller saw a familiar open kitchen, a big stone hearth, and Clancy standing in front of huge plate glass windows, cup of coffee in hand, the sun shining on Nantucket Sound behind him. For the first time, Miller let himself savor the possibility.

Clancy pushed open the frosted glass doors of his father's medical office, expecting to find a bustling waiting area inside. Instead, it was empty, suspiciously so for a Thursday afternoon. Behind the reception desk, Andrea gave him a beaming smile. "Clancy, good to see you."

"Where is everyone?"

"Your father cancelled his afternoon appointments,

and the other doctors are at a conference today and tomorrow." She stood, grabbed her purse from under the desk, and came out from behind the counter. "Go on back," she said, squeezing his shoulder. "They're waiting for you in his office."

She was gone, door locked behind her, before Clancy could ask who "they" were. More than a little confused, he crossed the waiting room and opened the door to the patient rooms and doctors' offices. On the way to his father's office, he paused in front of the office that would've been his, running his fingers over the brass nameplate. Taking the office down the hall from his dad's had always been expected, and a not small part of Clancy mourned the passing of that expectation. He would have enjoyed practicing with his father, but a bigger part of him knew, deep in his gut, that this wasn't where he belonged, as much as that other part of him wanted to. He hoped his father would forgive him. After all his parents had done for him, the last thing he wanted was to disappoint any of them.

Laughter down the hallway from behind the cracked door of his father's office drew Clancy's attention. Rather familiar laughter, in fact. Closing the distance, he pushed open the door and found his father behind his desk, as expected. The two other people on the sofa were not.

"Mom? Robert?" Clancy said, staring in disbelief at his other two parents. "I thought you were halfway around the world on vacation."

Miranda scooted out from under Robert's arm. "Sloan called. She said you needed us here, so we flew right back."

Because he had needed them, so very much. Because Sloan, someone he hoped to call family in the future, had recognized it, had probably felt the same herself, and had acted to meet that need, for him. And none of them had hesitated. The past thirty-six hours—hell, the past week and a half—finally caught up to Clancy and he couldn't hold back the gut-wrenching sob that broke loose.

His mother was there to catch him. "Oh, darling." She wrapped her arms around him and hugged him tight.

When his legs began to give way, Robert dashed to his other side, and together, they maneuvered him to the couch. The tears continued to flow, everything he'd bottled up for the sake of being strong for Sloan and Miller gushing out. Fear, anger, frustration, hope, love. God, the love that had snuck up on him so fast yet so powerful, and if that love didn't have an outlet, if he lost Miller, which was a very real possibility, he wasn't sure his heart would survive it.

"I'm sorry," his mom said. "When I encouraged you to go for it with him, I didn't know he was sick. I would never wish this pain on either of you."

"Couldn't be helped." Clancy sniffled back tears, trying to get his emotions under control. "Sloan told you?"

"She called from a hospital line. I recognized the number."

His dad appeared before him, holding out a glass of whiskey. "And you showed up here looking wrung out, in scrubs, and wearing an oncology department badge." He straightened his index finger from around the glass and pointed at the visiting doctor badge on Clancy's lapel.

Clancy looked down and flicked his badge. He'd gone from Task A to Task B, with an intermission for crying. Changing clothes was a detail that hadn't once crossed his mind. Besides, the scrubs were a comfortable, everyday occurrence until a month ago. It felt right being back in them.

He took the glass from his father and waved it under his nose, letting the sting clear out his sinuses and burn away his tears. He took a healthy swallow, then rested his elbows on his knees, glass between his palms. "Throat cancer. I'd been piecing it together, and Sloan confirmed it in New York. It was a tour of last suppers, as much for him as for me. All of his favorite places and meals." Clancy threw back the rest of the whiskey, handed the tumbler to his dad, and rubbed the heels of his hands against his tired, stinging eyes.

"Is there a treatment?" Robert asked.

"Yes, though given the cancer's advanced stage, the survival rate isn't high. I got him under my former attending's care, and we developed a treatment plan." He described it in high-level detail, his father nodding along. "She's going over it now with Miller and Sloan. There's a chance to save him, but there's a catch."

"He may lose his sense of taste," his father correctly surmised.

Robert whistled low. "Tough blow for a chef of his caliber."

Clancy sank back into the couch. "That, and a mile-wide sacrificial streak, were why he'd decided not to get treatment."

"Did you convince him otherwise?" his mother said.

"I hope so. I'm falling in love with him." He dropped his head back on the cushion top, laughing at the ceiling, the sound bordering on hysterical. "After only ten days. How is that possible? Maybe I'm delusional at this point."

Miranda hauled him upright by the arm and gave him a very Miranda face. "Now, listen here, Clancy Rhodes. I've loved two men in my life." She waved a finger at his dad and Robert. "I knew, both times, after only one date. One. And I knew, as soon as I saw you and Miller together in Chicago, that you were it for each other. He's head over heels for you too."

His dad laid a hand on his knee. "Just be there for him."

"I can't do that and be here," Clancy said, no longer able to avoid the primary reason he'd come here this afternoon.

Alan's smile was crooked, half knowing, half resigned. "Can't say I'm surprised."

"What?" he gasped.

"You walked in here in your scrubs, strung out and aching for the man you love, but there was also a spark in your eyes that's never there when you talk about plastic surgery. It grew even brighter when you talked about his treatment."

Clancy hung his head, trying to hide that spark that lit just at the mention, not wanting to be disrespectful. "I want to practice oncology," he admitted.

"It won't be an easy road," Alan said. "You're seeing

that up close and personal, at thirty. Thirty more years ahead of you in this career. Are you sure?"

"I'm sure." He lifted his head and met his father's eyes again. "But I don't want to leave the practice in a lurch."

"It's fine, son. We'll manage."

Except that Clancy could see panic in his father's eyes. But he could also see a way around it, as clear as day now where before it'd been tangled up in everything else going on. "Hear me out." Clancy scooted forward to the edge of the cushion and readjusted his glasses. "I can give you six months, maybe twelve. I'm going to have to apply for oncology residencies, and I want to do the benefit still. I'm already in contact with the organizers and potential guests. Let me help you bridge the gap, let me work with you for a little while. I'd like that chance. And if Miller seeks treatment here—"

"When he gets treatment here," Miranda interjected.

"When he gets treatment here," Clancy started again, going with her hope, "then I can be here for you both, at least temporarily."

"That would help, tremendously," Alan said, letting out a relieved breath. "And I'd like the chance to work with you too, if only for a little while."

Clancy reached for his hand. "I'm sorry if I disappointed you."

"Disappoint me?" Alan squeezed his hand. "Impossible, Clancy. Sure, I'm disappointed I won't get to work with you for very long, but *you* have not disappointed me. Everything you've achieved, the man you've become, the fact you want to tackle one of medicine's greatest challenges, even as it's ripping out your heart. You are the farthest thing from a disappointment." His father tugged him into an embrace. "I couldn't be more proud of you."

"We all are," Robert said, as he and his mom joined the family hug.

Clancy sagged in their arms, getting his first taste of relief in days. One battle won. The toughest was still to come.

Chapter Eleven

Clancy parked in the sandy lot and double-checked the location on his GPS against the address in Miller's text. This was definitely the place. The big lots were surely filled to capacity in season, but on New Year's Day, downtown Southport was a virtual ghost town, just his rental and a couple other cars in the lot. A handful of people, locals probably, had been milling around the town square and the pier up the street, but all the dock-side restaurants appeared closed.

Except one.

Smoke puffed from a rooftop vent of the small green building with the huge Provision Company sign out front. The door beneath it was open, a view clear through the screen to the dock out back, and on the patio to the left, through the clear vinyl screens, Clancy spied a group of people gathered around a table.

He unfolded from the car, inhaling the salty sea breeze tinged with grill smoke. His stomach gave a grumble of interest, until his brain reminded him why he was there and his appetite withered. He beeped the car locks and half a dozen heads turned his way. Clancy only had eyes for the one with the chestnut beard and blue eyes.

It had been four days since he'd last seen Miller. Four long days since he'd awoken on the couch in his father's office to a voicemail from Sloan, informing him she was taking Miller back to the Bay Area. There'd been a text from Miller that minimally cushioned the blow.

Give me time, it'd said, along with the date, time, and address for this place.

Clancy had been torn, frantic for information yet trying to respect Miller's wishes. He'd asked his oncologist for an update, but she wasn't legally allowed to give it to him. He wasn't technically a doctor at the Cancer Center anymore, and Sloan and her medical POA were no longer effective there. He'd begged Miranda to contact her new bestie, and all that had gotten him was a ticket for a Sunday night red-eye to North Carolina.

Add a four-hour drive and that brought him to here, to Miller's hometown. And to now, with his missing half pushing open the screen door. By the haggard look on Miller's face, Clancy had no idea if he'd won the battle or not. This was supposed to be the last stop on their tour. Miller's last supper. Was that why Miller was here with his family? Why he needed Clancy with him? If that's what Miller needed, Clancy would give it to him, would lend his support, but he hoped like hell they were here for a different reason.

"Hey, Doc."

Clancy didn't think. He ran, barreling into Miller. He considered, belatedly, that the collision of bodies may have been too hard, that Miller could still be sore from last week, and he began to pull back. Miller's big arms wrapped around him, holding him close, and a chuffed breath ruffled his hair. Clancy inhaled and sank deeper into Miller's embrace. "I missed you."

"I missed you too." Miller kissed the crown of his head, and Clancy figured he was forgiven for the enthusiastic greeting. "Didn't miss this shirt, though." Miller plucked the blue Dodgers shirt, visible under Clancy's unzipped hoodie.

"I wore it just for you."

"I'd hoped you'd burned it with Gingy."

"You're a monster!"

Miller's laugh rumbled under Clancy's ear. Wanting to see it, Clancy leaned back and reached a hand up, tracing the laugh lines he loved so much. Miller lifted a hand, covering and holding Clancy's, their fingers tangling. He lowered their joined hands and tugged Clancy forward. "Come on, I want to introduce you to some people."

Following Miller inside, Clancy was surprised at the super tight quarters. He shouldn't have been, given the outdoor dimensions of the building, but how this place functioned during summer crush was a mystery. No bigger than a college dorm room, there was a service counter to the left, and behind it, two deep fryers, a flattop grill, oven, cabinet fridges, and a small prep area. Smaller even than some of the food trucks he regularly visited. To the right, there was an alcove with empty drink fridges, two darkened soda fountains, and a condiment stand. And that was it before you hit the back door to the patio.

Miller put a hand to the screen, about to push outside, when Clancy ground to a halt. "This was the last place on the tour, wasn't it?"

"That's right." Miller glanced around the compact space—fondly. There was no other word to describe the soft, adoring look on his face. "It's my favorite spot, hands down."

Before their tour, Clancy would have called him a liar. A Michelin-starred chef, who'd staged at the top restaurants in New York and the Bay Area, who'd had a fine dining establishment of his own, did not favor a dockside dive above all others. Clancy knew better now. Miller was a man of many tastes, and each tour stop had meant something to him. He'd saved his favorite for last.

"Why's this one special?"

Miller smiled. "Besides the fact it's the best shrimp you'll ever eat, it was one of the few places, growing up, that my family could afford. My sisters and I all bussed tables here at one point or the other, and my mom worked the register in the summers when she wasn't teaching. We got the employee discount, and my parents would save up all winter long, so that every Monday night in season, we'd be here. They only missed one summer."

"The summer you and Sloan left," Clancy pieced together. "That's the money they cobbled together so you two could get married and leave." Miller's hand clenched around his; it was all the confirmation Clancy needed. "No wonder it's your favorite."

Miller cleared his throat and gestured to the cooking area. "Owner opened it up for us today. I was planning to cook for you."

Clancy wiggled his nose, happy for the smile it drew from Miller. "Smells like you already did."

"You were right on time. Let's go, I just served it up."

Even if Clancy hadn't taken a slew of genetics classes, he would have recognized Miller's family, all standing around the two tables pushed together on the patio. Miller shared his blue eyes with his youngest sister, inherited from their mother, and his chestnut hair matched the long wavy locks on his other two sisters' heads, and on his bald father's chin, the older man's goatee flecked with gray. He was a giant of a man like Miller.

"Everyone," Miller said. "This is Clancy. Clancy, this is my family."

His mom, a surprising five foot nothing, dressed in jeans and a cable-knit sweater, with her hair pulled back in a short ponytail, approached first. "I'm Michelle, and I'm a hugger, if that's okay with you?"

"More than okay." Clancy stepped into her embrace, bending to hug her back. "It's a pleasure to meet you, Michelle."

The introductions and hugs continued from there, Miller's sisters—Lisa, Allison, and Erin—and then his father, Sam.

"It really is nice to meet you all," Clancy said, as he lowered himself into the open chair to Miller's right.

"Eat, Clancy," Michelle said from Miller's other side.

"You look like you need it." Clancy didn't take offense. His own mother had been saying the same all weekend.

Clancy lifted the paper plate off the place setting in front of him, revealing a crispy crab cake and a dozen or so shrimp, still steaming hot. He managed a few bites of the crab cake, Miller's beloved blue crab, and was peeling his third shrimp—coated in Old Bay seasoning, steamed, and tossed on the flattop just before serving, Miller explained—when he dropped the shrimp and lowered his shaking hands. Everything tasted amazing, but his stomach was still a wreck. As it had been since he'd gotten that text from Miller. Longer even, since he'd found Miller on the bathroom floor of the Ritz, sick and weakened to the point of passing out.

"You don't like?" Miller asked.

"I do like, it's delicious, I'm just..." He snatched a napkin from the middle of the table, avoiding everyone's stares and taking entirely too long to clean his hands.

Miller closed one over his. "I was waiting for you to get here to tell them."

"Tell us what?" Erin asked. "Your faces don't say happy news."

Oh God, this was going to be harder than Clancy imagined, whichever way Miller decided. After meeting Miller's family, after spending only fifteen minutes with them, listening to their laughter and chatter, after learning what they'd done for Miller and Sloan, Clancy knew they'd feel Miller's pain as if it were their own. That's the kind of family they were, same as Clancy's. Understanding that now, he couldn't blame Miller for wanting to shield them from it. He could appreciate the decision Miller had made, to not put his family through the brutal, no-guarantees slog of cancer treatment. He'd had patients who'd made the same call. But had Miller's decision changed? Because even understanding the family dynamics better now, Clancy still wanted Miller to choose life, and he was sure his family would too.

Either way, he'd promised to be there for Miller. Sucking up his courage, he tossed the shredded napkin on the table and took Miller's hand in both of his, resting their joined grip on the table. "I'm with you, every step of the way."

Miller kissed his cheek with a whispered "thank you," then, after a deep breath, glanced around the table at each family member. "I want you to listen and let me finish before you ask questions. Can you do that, please?"

Five pale faces nodded.

"I'm sick. Cancer." Gasps echoed around the table, and a choked cry came from behind Michelle's hand over her mouth. Miller took her other hand. "You all knew about the culinary tour, that I'd planned for it to end here. It was a tour of my last meals, all my favorites, because I'd chosen to die. You deserved to enjoy your retirement," he said to his parents. "And your families and success," he said to his sisters. "I didn't want to put any of you through the ups and downs of treatment. Treatment that will risk my sense of taste. I didn't know who I'd be if I couldn't taste, if I wasn't a chef. So I planned this trip, and this stop at the end, because it's the place that means the most to me. I wanted to be with my family, at the end."

"Sweetie." Michelle's knuckles were white where they curled around Miller's.

"Let me finish, please."

On her other side, Sam scooted his chair closer and put an arm around Michelle, while Miller's sisters huddled up around the other end of the table.

"I'd made that decision," Miller said. "But then my family expanded."

Clancy's heart jolted at Miller's "but." Was that hope? Miller looked over at him, smiling wide, and Clancy's heart leapt the rest of the way into his throat.

"I met someone." Miller's eyes stayed locked with Clancy's. "He convinced me I'm more than just my taste buds, and this last stop became something else."

"Miller, what are you saying?" Clancy asked, cautious but hope swelling.

"This isn't the end. It's the beginning. I'm going to get treatment."

Allison's "Oh thank god," was a mirror image of Clancy's thoughts.

"You changed your mind?" he asked.

"*You* changed my mind."

Clancy curled over their joined hands, resting his forehead atop them, his world spinning. The good way. There were other sounds around him—Lisa shushing Erin, Michelle sniffling, Sam yanking napkins out of the dispenser—but Miller's voice at his ear claimed all of Clancy's attention.

"You showed me a future, Doc. One I'm not ready to give up on yet, if you're willing to fight alongside me for it."

Clancy lifted his head, not giving a damn about the tears on his cheeks. "Every step."

Miller kissed him, hard, and for the first time, hope flowed both ways between them.

Dishtowel wrapped around his fist, Miller dried the evening's cookware while his mom wiped down the granite countertops and sink.

"Thanks for helping," she said, voice quiet, as everyone else had gone to bed. They'd always been the night owls of the family, even though she was the first to rise in the mornings.

"I am the one who asked for it." Miller nodded at the tinfoil-covered pie pan on the kitchen island. After dinner, which Miller had cooked, they'd finished off the pecan pie Michelle had made for him yesterday. But this pie, his absolute favorite, he'd ask her to make special. And he only wanted to share it with one person.

She tossed a wad of paper towels in the trash, wiped her hands off on her jeans, and retrieved her coffee mug from the dining bar where she'd left it. "The pie's for him?"

Miller tossed his dishrag the length of the kitchen, right into the washer in the adjacent utility room.

She clicked her tongue against her teeth. "All that talent and height wasted."

He rested against the counter beside her, bumping her shoulder. "What can I say? I liked home-ec better."

"And I like him," she replied, not letting her earlier question go.

"I knew you would. Clancy's hard to dislike."

"I love him, though, for what he's done for you." She set her mug aside and wrapped her arms around his middle. "And for us. He's given us a chance at more time with you."

Miller returned the embrace, his mom's hugs always the best. "It may not work, Ma. You need to prepare yourself."

"I know that," she said with a sniffle. "But we may not have had a chance at all otherwise." She pulled back, sniffled once more, and patted his cheek. "It's a new year. I'm going to think positive on this first day of it."

He smiled down at the tiny, indomitable woman who'd held their family together through thick and thin, who'd always given him what he needed, including a future he couldn't wait to tell Clancy about. "I love you, Ma."

"Love you too, sweetie. Now..." She turned, opened the silverware drawer, fished out two forks, and laid them atop the pie pan. "Go give that boy a taste of the South, in all the ways that count." She shimmied on her way to the stairs, throwing an exaggerated wink over her shoulder. Miller buried his face in his shoulder, stifling a half groan, half laugh. Good to know, at forty, that he could still be embarrassed by his mother.

He turned toward the downstairs primary suite where Clancy had passed out after dinner, the jet lag finally catching up to him, but then Miller paused, set the pie back down on the island, and opened the built-in wine fridge. He contemplated for a moment, needing something bright and acidic to balance out the sweetness of the pie. He spied the top row of tall, slender bottles with the swirl logo on the foil, his mother's favorite dessert wine from a small vineyard he'd discovered in Ramona. He hoped she wouldn't mind him filching one. He tucked it under his arm, grabbed a couple glasses from the cabinet, pocketed a corkscrew, and picked the pie back up, careful not to let the forks slide off. Balancing his bounty, he headed again for the primary suite and pushed the cracked door open with his toe.

Clancy was awake, wrapped in a blanket and sitting curled up on the far end of the parlor couch. The shades were raised on all the floor-to-ceiling windows and Clancy had opened the two corner ones closest to where he huddled, letting in the sounds and smells of the ocean. A single lamp dimly lit the room, casting much of it in shadow, but there was enough light to see the soft, contented smile on Clancy's face.

Miller pushed the door closed with his heel, making his presence known. "Didn't realize you were up."

Clancy increased the wattage on his smile to full stunning, and Miller barely felt the chill from the open windows. "Was giving you and Michelle some time."

"How about I give you some dessert?" Miller flicked his gaze down to the pie dish as he stepped toward the couch.

Clancy uncurled a leg, halfway to bounding up. "Oh, sorry, let me help!"

Miller shook his head. "No, here, just take these." He

handed Clancy the glasses, then shifted sideways so Clancy could slide the wine bottle out from under his arm. He lowered himself onto the edge of the couch next to Clancy, set the pie pan on Clancy's knees, and fished the corkscrew out of his pocket. Retrieving the bottle, he got to work cutting through the foil and twisting into the cork. "You like it here?"

"It's mesmerizing." Clancy's gaze drifted back out the windows to the sea beyond the dunes. "Especially with the water and sound all around."

Miller couldn't agree more. Located on Oak Island's southernmost point, just across the inlet from Sheep Island and Holden Beach, the vacation home was surrounded on three sides by dunes and water. Knowing he'd spend a good part of his early career moving, Miller, when he'd saved enough to buy real estate, had bought this place. While his parents still lived in Southport, they'd down-sized to a condo as soon as his youngest sister had fled the nest. But he and his sisters still regularly visited, and Miller had wanted to provide the place his amazing family had always deserved. "This is the one asset I haven't liquidated yet," he said, as he filled their wineglasses. "I bought it as a place for my family to gather."

"It's gorgeous."

"I'm going to sell it."

"What?" Clancy twisted around so fast that Miller had to speed juggle, shoving the bottle between his knees and creating a barrier with the glasses, slowing the pie's careening trajectory off Clancy's lap.

"Save the pie!" Miller exclaimed, laughing as he

remembered Clancy's "save the chowder" at Oscar's. The timing of the memory couldn't be more perfect.

Clancy rescued the tin pan from the edge, wrapping the full length of his forearms around it. "Okay, the pie's safe," he said, once it was firmly back in his lap. "But I'm having trouble following the thread."

Miller handed him a glass, moved the bottle to the floor, and picked up the fallen silverware. He wiped it off on his pant leg, handed Clancy a fork, and peeled off the tinfoil. Buttery aromas, from the pie filling and the home-made crust, filled the air. Clancy inhaled deep, eyelids fluttering.

"Try the pie first," Miller said. "Please."

"I have no idea what's going on, except pie." He took a sip of the wine, then dug into the pie. His lips had barely closed around the tines when his face lit up. It was the same look of wonder and discovery that Miller had been falling in love with on each stop of their tour. He was thinking it was his favorite Clancy expression, until he remembered his lover's blissed-out post-orgasm face in Laguna. Food-blissed-out was a close second.

"What is this?" Clancy asked around his next bite.

"The pie I promised you." He extended his right arm. "Chess pie, my mother's recipe."

Clancy traced again the ingredients Miller had spelled out for him in New York.

"Like I said then, it's rather simple."

"Simple but delicious," Clancy replied.

"Which is what I should have been cooking all along. You helped me see that." He took Clancy's glass, set it on the floor with his, and moved the pie pan there next. Righting himself, he took both of Clancy's hands in his. "If I make it through this treatment, if I can taste, or hell, if you can taste test and tell me if it's good, I want to open a new restaurant and that pie will be the centerpiece."

Clancy's face filled with bright, beaming hope. "That sounds wonderful, but you don't have to sell this place to finance it. I'm sure we can find backers—"

Miller put a finger over Clancy's lips. "I already talked it over with my family. They're more than happy to vacation with us on Martha's Vineyard."

"Us? Martha's Vineyard?" His brow furrowed, trying to figure out the problem.

No, *this* was Miller's favorite Clancy expression. He reached out, nudging Clancy's glasses down enough so he could smooth his thumb over the crease between his brows.

The tension gave way under his thumb. Clancy's revelation came the next second. "Wait, are you going to—"

Miller nodded. "I'm going to sell this place and buy Oscar's building in Edgartown, if you think you can get a job in Boston and wouldn't mind the commute." He wanted Clancy with him in the future he'd made Miller see—them together, in Oscar's big open space, a lively restaurant with a view of the water and a home for them upstairs, maybe eventually children too.

"Do you know how many hospitals there are in Boston?" Clancy said.

"A lot, I hope."

Clancy's smile was massive. "A lot a lot. And there's

even one on Martha's Vineyard. I may have already looked."

"Is that a yes?"

Clancy moved as if to stand, and for a split second, Miller panicked. Had Clancy changed his mind? Had Miller asked too much? But rather than stand, Clancy rose on his knees and threw one over Miller's lap. Straddling him, he glided his hands up Miller's chest and around his neck. "As long as there's a piece of that pie waiting for me at the end of every day, I'll be there."

Miller wrapped his fingers around Clancy's wrists, feeling the wild, hopeful beat of his pulse, and feeling his own race to match it. "I hope I'm there at the end of every day with you."

"Are you willing to fight for it? For us and that future?"

Now that he'd found who and what he wanted, there was no turning away from it. "Yes."

"Then I'll fight with you, every step of the way." Clancy leaned forward, resting his forehead against Miller's. "We'll make it happen."

Miller brought their lips together in a slow, deep kiss, full of hope and the flavor of life.

Chapter Twelve

MARTHA'S VINEYARD

Three Years Later

Light bloomed behind Clancy's eyelids and he shoved his head under the pillow, groaning.

The bed dipped behind him and warmth blanketed his left side, a heavy arm draped over his back. "Who's the sleepyhead this morning?"

"Late night," Clancy mumbled to the human space heater dotting wet kisses and beard tickles over his shoulder blades. "Hmm, that feels good."

So good he had no desire whatsoever to move, especially as it'd been after ten last night before he'd left the hospital, and after one by the time he'd crawled into bed. A bed he loved so much more than the one in their Boston brownstone. Not that that one wasn't comfortable, but his city nights were often spent alone, catching sleep between hospital shifts. Here, in the place he considered home, the bed was always warm and never lonely. He couldn't wait until he was done with his residency and could move more days of his week to the hospital here on the island.

Kisses trailed down his spine and a big, rough hand crept beneath the sheet tangled around his waist. "I see you finished off the pie when you got home."

"Not enough." There was never enough pie as far as Clancy was concerned.

The hand slapped his ass. Not too hard, just enough to sting and make his morning wood take notice.

"There was half a pie left."

Clancy tried to shift onto his side, and the warm weight countered, settling fully atop him. Exactly like Clancy had wanted.

"You can't sleep away the day, Doc."

The pillow over Clancy's head disappeared and brightness shattered his dark cocoon. But the heat remained, a big body pressing his into the mattress and warm, wet kisses teasing the nape of his neck.

"It's our big day."

Clancy eked open one eye, let it adjust to the light, then opened the other. He still couldn't see much without his glasses, but the arm next to his was unmistakably inked. Scrolling, elaborate designs that Clancy would recognize even half blind. And assuming his nose wasn't lying, he smelled the very sauce the recipe for which was woven into the tattoo. Among other decadent aromas drifting up from the floor below.

"How long have you been awake?" Clancy asked.

"Long enough there's fresh bread and chicory coffee in

it for you," Miller said. "If you get your sexy ass out of bed."

Clancy tilted his hips up. "Something else in mind for my sexy ass."

Judging by Miller's naked body stretched out over his, and by the erection nestled against his ass, Miller had the same thing in mind, despite his leave-the-bed suggestion to the contrary.

Clancy glided a hand down the inked length of Miller's arm, fingers tangling on the pillow, the morning light catching their matching gold bands. They'd gone for simple, so Miller could have his resized as needed. Back to his pretreatment weight, the band fit snug on his ring finger, just like his body was currently fit snug to Clancy's, in all the right places. Well, except for one.

"Tell me what you have in mind," his husband said, rutting against him.

"I shouldn't have to at this point."

Miller laughed, not a gray streak in it, the storm clouds well and truly gone. As much as Clancy had loved Miller's laugh before, he adored it even more now. A whole new sound that lit up his world every time he heard it. Including this morning, the puffs of laughter trailing down his spine made sweeter by the kisses, nips, and swipes of Miller's tongue. His husband's weight shifted off his back, his fingers untangled from his, and Miller's hand with the sun-warmed band pushed out his thigh, spreading him open.

"This what you were thinking, Doc?"

"Not ex—"

His words died as Miller licked a trail from taint to hole.

"Yes," Clancy moaned. That's exactly what he'd been thinking.

Stretching both arms over his head, Clancy clutched at the sheets and hung his head, face buried in his pillow, fighting the urge to drive his cock against the mattress. He didn't dare move, not wanting to lose the exquisite torture of Miller's tongue teasing his rim, firing all his sensitive nerve endings. Flicking and kissing, around and finally in, spearing him with heat. Tingles of pleasure coursed through Clancy, then a lightning bolt struck, searing his blood, as Miller inserted a finger alongside his tongue, his touch aimed expertly at Clancy's prostate.

Straining, Clancy fought but ultimately lost the battle with his instincts, lowering his hips, cock aching for friction. Miller levered up, settling his weight atop Clancy again, pressing him down and bringing his release that much closer. "That's it, baby," he said, thrusting his fingers in time with Clancy's rolling hips. "Let me see how much you need it."

"Need you," Clancy keened, riding back on Miller's hand. "Please."

Miller's fingers disappeared, the very opposite of what Clancy wanted, and he cursed a protest, but then Miller slid an arm under him, around his belly, and flipped him onto his back. The sheer power of the move, something that a year ago would have been impossible, brought Clancy out of the pleasure clouds. It had not been an easy road to here, to this place and time where Miller could work for hours in the kitchen, then manhandle him in bed. A year ago he couldn't walk up the stairs.

"Hey, Doc, where'd you go?" Miller tossed the lube he'd fetched from the bedside drawer onto the mattress and planted a hand next to Clancy's head. "You still with me?"

"Yeah, I'm here." Clancy swallowed down the knot in his throat. "Just a bit overwhelmed. I can't believe we're here, finally."

Miller smiled, those lines around his eyes that Clancy loved so much deepening. "Don't tell me you're getting opening day jitters."

That hadn't been where Clancy's mind had drifted, but now that Miller had mentioned it. "Are you nervous?"

"Not in the slightest." No hesitation, no worries about living up to expectations this time. Hell, just being here, alive, he'd exceeded them. "I've never been more sure about anything."

And God, Miller was sexy as hell when he was cocky. Clancy rolled his hips, bringing their dicks back into contact. "Never?"

Miller countered, grinding. "Are you fishing for a compliment?"

"Me, never."

Miller lowered to his elbow, and with him closer, Clancy could see the emotion swirling in his bright blue eyes, the gold shining in the morning light. Despite the teasing, he hadn't missed where Clancy's thoughts had drifted. "That day in Southport, I wasn't sure. I had no idea what was ahead of us, but I did know I wanted to live and that I wanted a life with you."

Clancy ran a hand over Miller's jaw and up over his prickly buzz cut. His chestnut beard and hair had started growing back after treatment, even before his taste buds had returned, but Miller had never had the patience to get past the Chia-Pet stage, ranting and raving that it looked ridiculous on a fortysomething man. Which it totally had. And the buzz cut was easier to maintain for a full-time chef. Tie a bandana on, always plaid, and call it a day. It was also fitting for a fighter.

"You wanted to fight," Clancy said, letting every bit of love and admiration he had for his husband shine through his voice.

"I had no idea how hard it would be."

Hard was putting it mildly. *Hell* was more accurate, and that was from Clancy's perspective, not as the patient but as the spouse who knew a truckload too much about what his loved one was going through. For as awful as the actual treatment had been, it'd been the look of abject fear and despair in Miller's eyes every day afterward that he couldn't taste that had been the worst. Clancy had been there for him, as the promised taster, and Greg too, helping Miller use his sense memories as they'd developed concepts for the restaurant, but it'd only been this past Christmas, fittingly at Eli O's, that Miller had tasted the salt on his fingers after preparing a margarita glass for Sloan.

His favorite flavor had been the first to return.

That day had been the best of Clancy's life, until

today. "You are the bravest person I've ever met, Miller Sykes."

"I couldn't have done it alone." He lowered his lips to Clancy's, the kiss slow and deep, like it'd been that night in Southport, like Miller was tasting every nook and cranny of his mouth, wallowing in the flavors, before he came up for air again. "I didn't know then, but today, I know. I know down to my soul that I'm where I'm supposed to be, cooking the food in the place where I'm supposed to, and sharing my life with the person I'm supposed to be with."

Clancy was one hundred percent sure of the same. Of committing himself to a career in oncology, to this man, and to their life together here. Lifting up, he captured Miller's lips, the both of them smiling. "Then make love to your husband, and let's get on with our second big day."

He brandished his wedding band under Miller's nose, briefly remembering Valentine's Day three years ago in the Ritz Carlton's gazebo, with the ocean behind them and friends and family around them, all who'd accompanied Miller to the hospital the next day for his first treatment.

Miller halted the train of his thoughts, bringing Clancy back to the here and now with the *snick* of the lube bottle. He poured a generous amount in his palm, then took them both in hand, pumping them together and ramping their need back up. With his other hand, he tangled their fingers, their clasped fist pressed into the pillow above Clancy's head.

With each up and down of Miller's fist, Clancy's world narrowed, from their room, to their bed, to the big body on top of him, the heart beating against his, and the need rocketing up his spine and making his belly clench. Miller was feeling it too, his cock rock hard against Clancy's, his breath ragged at his ear, the speed of his motion—hand and hips—ratcheting up.

Clancy threw back his head and arched his back. "Now, now, now," he begged, shamelessly spreading his thighs and lifting his hips, making clear what he wanted. He was fine with being the top in their bed most of the time, but this morning he wanted Miller all around and in him.

"I've got you, baby." Miller slipped his cock free of his grip and nudged Clancy's rim.

"Yes," Clancy hissed, anticipating the divine. Miller pushed in, and Clancy tightened his fingers around Miller's, their clasped hands slipping higher, into a sun-warmed spot on the pillow.

Warm and bright.

Together, in sickness and in health, for richer or poorer, until death do they part, decades from now Clancy hoped, with every fiber of his being. Decades of life and love with this man who'd shattered both their expectations.

He lifted his legs and circled Miller's hips, hauling him the rest of the way in, all the way to the root, and tumbling Miller down, fully on top of him. Miller drew back as far as Clancy's locked ankles would allow, then drove back in, driving a deep moan out of Clancy.

Miller nuzzled the center of his chest, lips soft, beard prickly, while his dick continued to pound inside him. "That's what you like, huh?"

"What I love." Clancy arched up, directing Miller's

dick right at his prostate. Jolt after jolt, perfect, building, and once his hand fisted Clancy's cock again, on the verge of explosion. A foreshock rumbled through Clancy.

Miller skated his lips from chest to neck, along Clancy's jaw to the spot behind his ear. "Love you too, Doc."

Hands still clasped, their lives and hearts as one, they came.

Together.

"Uncle Miller! Uncle Clancy!"

Miller braced for impact, two small bodies colliding with his and latching on to his legs. He ruffled the hair on their heads, the toddler's ginger and the kindergartner's blond. "Looks like we've got some early arrivers." He smiled over his shoulder at Clancy, who was locking the door to their upstairs residence.

"Or maybe they're burglars." Clancy advanced on Greg and Tony's adopted son, Amos, catching him from behind and tickling his sides.

The towheaded boy slipped away, giggling. "We're not burglars! We're staff!" He jumped and spun at the same time, nearly losing his balance, the kid all awkward limbs, but he recovered and pointed to his back, where the word STAFF was emblazoned across the back of his T-shirt.

Molly, Sloan and Tyler's adorable ginger cannoli, detached herself from Miller's leg and ran to stand beside her best friend. She took her thumb out of her mouth long enough to jut it at her back. "Me too!"

They looked the part, in miniature form, dressed in the restaurant's official uniform of jeans and a T-shirt, except these tees were a certain someone's favorite lavender plaid. Not the standard black-and-white ones like Miller had on under his chef's coat. "Did you have something to do with this?" he asked Clancy.

Clancy held up his hands. "For once, this is not on me. Well, not the initial idea, at least. I did, however, pick the plaid."

"No sh—"

Clancy slapped a hand over his mouth. "Children," he playfully chided. "You have to go a year without a curse word in front of them before we put in an adoption application. That was the deal." He withdrew his hand, putting both on his hips with a huff. "And I'm tired of waiting."

More good things in his future to look forward to, growing the family they already had with children of their own. Granted, he'd only been in remission for eighteen months but neither he nor Clancy wanted to put their family on hold any longer. Miller wasn't a spring chicken, cancer or not, and they wanted their kids to grow up with Greg's and Sloan's as playmates, whenever they were all in the same place. Clancy knew the risks better than anyone —that he could wind up a single parent like Julie's husband, who Miller had met at the benefit that spring, and seen every spring since, Clancy now an organizer of the annual event—but Clancy still wanted to make the leap. Miller was ready to make it with him. He bet he could get Clancy down to six months on that whole no cursing test.

"Carry!" came a demand from on low, together with a thirty-pound weight on his toes. Molly raised her arms for a lift, and Miller swung her up, his heart warming at her squeals of delight. He gave her a couple tosses, then settled her on his hip and followed Clancy and Amos into the main dining room.

"So, if it wasn't you behind the shirts," Miller said, "my second guess is..." He let the direction of his gaze—to the redhead behind the new bar they'd added, hand-carved by Clancy, complete with dire wolf heads for corners—make his suspicion known.

Sloan feigned ignorance. "Who me?" Snickering, she returned her attention to the pitcher of Negroni she was funneling into a bar top aging barrel.

"You have no idea what we went through for these shirts." Greg stepped out from the kitchen where he was helping out for opening week. He removed his own stained chef's coat, revealing the same plaid tee, the back of his reading, GUEST CHEF. He picked a wad of plaid up off the end of the hearth and tossed it to Miller. Snatching it out of the air one-handed, Miller shook it out and held it up with Molly's help.

"Chef!" Molly proclaimed proudly, like she'd been diligently practicing the single syllable word.

Miller hoped his laugh didn't sound too watery. "Yeah, baby girl, I am."

A long, slim arm circled his waist from the other side. "Congrats, Chef," Clancy said softly.

Miller's heart stuttered. He loved hearing his husband call him that now, knowing he'd fallen in love with Miller not as a chef first, but as a person, one he'd seen through hell. Now that they were on the other side of it, Miller was able to give Clancy the chef part of himself too, one hundred percent. Hearing that recognized, appreciated, and loved, every time Clancy called him "Chef" felt like another gift he'd been given.

As did the T-shirt Clancy wore today. The hoodie he'd previously worn gone, Clancy's tee was the same purple plaid as the others. Miller looked over his shoulder at the back and laughed out loud at the CHIEF TASTER title.

He put Molly down and gave her a little push, sending her racing across the black-and-white checkered floor toward the farm table. Brought out from Napa, from that barely visited room in his first restaurant, it now sat in the center of the space here, surrounded by family and staff, all of them in the same purple plaid shirts. He pulled Clancy closer and buried his face in his mop of brown hair. "Thank you, for everything, especially the plaid."

Clancy tilted up his face. "I loved that about our trip. We couldn't start this new adventure without an homage to our first one."

Fuck, what had Miller done to get so lucky? To find this man who filled every day with sun, this unabashed foodie who'd come into Miller's life when he'd thought his world was destined for black. When he'd thought there'd be no stopping the crash landing that would ultimately drown him. Clancy had been the parachute that saved him, beyond golden, helping him stay afloat in rough waters until he was ready to fly again, higher than ever.

Doing what he loved most with the person he loved most at his side.

Fuck Icarus.

Clancy clamped a hand over his mouth again. Oops, had he said that out loud? "Yes, you did," Clancy answered the unspoken question, trying to appear stern despite the twitching corners of his mouth.

"You better worry less about his cursing," Sam said from his spot by the front window, "and more about how to get all these people in here." He shifted Sloan's other ginger munchkin from one hip to the other. "The line stretches around the block."

Miranda approached, holding out the binder of menus from their trip three years ago. "Probably because of the write-up. Flip toward the back."

Miller turned through the binder pages full of their tour menus, memories he would cherish forever. After the last one, a photo of the Provision Company's chalkboard menu that Clancy had snapped, he flipped the page and stared down at today's front page of the *Boston Globe*'s Food & Dining section. He looked from Miranda to Sam to Clancy. "We're in the *Globe*?" They'd had a soft opening last week for critics and reviewers, as was customary, but no industry birdies had told him there was a *Globe* reviewer among the guests.

But there was the review, under a headline of "Checkmate" with a byline by the paper's most well-known food critic. It was the article on the adjacent page, however, that made Miller's vision wobble. There was a picture of him and Clancy on their wedding day, in the gazebo at the Ritz, the Pacific Ocean behind them, under a byline by Dr. Clancy Rhodes, with the headline, "The Experience of a Lifetime."

Without taking his eye off the page, Miller held out a hand and Clancy's fingers laced through his. He skimmed the article, scary words like *cancer, near-death*, and *lost his taste buds for over a year* jumping out at him, but those terror-inducing words, and the memories that tumbled back with them, were outnumbered by the other words —*fight, love, survivor, shattered expectations*—and the vision of a future they carried with them. The vision they were living right this second. By the time he reached the end, Miller could hardly read for the water pooling in his eyes.

"Turn the page," Clancy said softly.

Miller did, to today's opening menu for Chess, their dream come true. He blinked back the tears and ran his finger down the menu, full of all his favorite dishes. Simple, approachable comfort food. Home for everyone, Miller most of all. "I didn't know you were going to do this."

With his free hand, Clancy closed the binder and handed it off to his mom. "Because it was a surprise."

"You were the surprise." He drew his husband into his arms, holding him tight. "You saved my life. I wouldn't be here, this dream, this future wouldn't have been possible, without you."

"I just wanted to hang out with a famous chef and eat and talk food for two weeks." Clancy tugged at the lapels of Miller's chef's coat. "Turns out I found a pretty spectacular human being and husband beneath this thing too."

"No, baby, you're the stunning one." Miller hauled him in for a kiss that was not at all chaste or safe for children, and he couldn't care less. He wanted to capture the taste of this moment, of his husband in his arms, of life on the brink of everything he wanted and everything he never thought he'd have. Judging by the cheers and applause that went up around them, no one else cared about their PDA either. The more love the better.

They came up for air, the both of them grinning, and Miller stepped back, holding out a hand to his husband. With the other, he gestured toward the farm table where their family had gathered, all of them wearing equally big smiles. "Care to dine with me again, in our restaurant?"

Clancy pushed his black-rimmed glasses up his nose. "As long as there's pie."

"You see what I named the restaurant, right?" He gestured at the Chess name and logo hand-stitched on the pocket of his chef's coat.

"Is that a promise?"

"It's a promise." He rubbed his thumb over Clancy's wedding ring. "As sure as this band on your finger."

Clancy smiled, brighter than the summer sun reflecting off the Nantucket Sound outside. "Then yes, Chef, I'd love to dine with you, every day for the rest of our lives."

The future was here, now, and it'd never tasted sweeter. "Let me show you to our table."

Reviews are an invaluable tool when it comes to spreading the word about great reads. Please consider leaving an honest review for *Dine With Me* on your favorite review site.

Thank you for reading!

Acknowledgments

I am a foodie, I make no secret of this. From my grandmother's table to Michelin-starred restaurants, I have eaten and loved it all. This book is my love letter—to the family recipes that I carry into my own home kitchen, and to the countless chefs, kitchens, and servers who have opened their doors and put their own stories, in the form of amazing dishes and dining experiences, onto the table in front me. And to the chefs like Grant Achatz, Sean Brock, and so many other who battle through adversity to bring us their talent, you are an inspiration and heroes. It'd be impossible to thank everyone who has inspired my love of food and this book, but to Larry, Lauren, Moira, Michael, Melody, Peter, David, Violaine, and my husband, I owe a special thanks. I would not be where I am, this book would not be possible, without you.

Second Edition: It's been a long road, but we're finally here. *Dine With Me* gets its Miller-in-plaid cover and all is right with the world. The minute I saw this Jase Dean photo years ago, I knew it had to go on the DWM cover one day, and that day has arrived. Thanks to Wander, Jase, Molly, and Kate for helping to make it all happen. And thank you, readers, for keeping Miller and Clancy in your hearts and minds for so long. S'mores for everyone!

Angel's Share

Fog City:

Prince of Killers

King Slayer

A New Empire

Queen's Ransom

Silent Knight

What We May Be

Perfect Play:

Dead Draw

Bad Bishop

King Hunt

Best Play

Soul to Find:

Icarus and the Devil

Jason and the Storm

Paris and the Reaper

Atlas and the Traitor

About the Author

Layla Reyne is the author of *What We May Be* and the *Agents Irish and Whiskey, Changing Lanes,* and *Table for Two* series. She writes sexy, intense LGBTQIA+ romance featuring competent adults in kitchens, sports arenas, car chases, and other high-stakes situations. Whether it's adrenaline-fueled suspense, rival athletes, vampires and shifters in alt-realms, or love mixed with mouth-watering foodie goodness, queer folks finding happily-ever-afters is guaranteed.

You can find Layla at laylareyne.com, in her reader group on Facebook—Layla's Lushes, and at the following sites:

facebook.com/laylareyne

instagram.com/laylareyne

bookbub.com/authors/layla-reyne

tiktok.com/@laylareyne